ACCLAIM FOR ROBIN LEE HATCHER

"Tender and heartwarming, Robin Lee Hatcher's *Who I Am with You* is a faith-filled story about the power of forgiveness, second chances, and unconditional love. A true delight for lovers of romantic inspirational fiction, this story will not only make you swoon, it will remind you of God's goodness and grace."

—COURTNEY WALSH, NEW YORK TIMES AND USA TODAY BESTSELLING AUTHOR

"Whenever I want to fall in love again, I pick up a Robin Lee Hatcher novel."

—FRANCINE RIVERS, NEW YORK TIMES BESTSELLING AUTHOR

"Hatcher's richly layered novels pull me in like a warm embrace, and I never want to leave. I own and love every one of this master storyteller's novels. Highly recommended!"

—COLLEEN COBLE, USA TODAY BESTSELLING AUTHOR

"Engaging and humorous, Hatcher's storytelling will warm readers' hearts . . . A wonderfully delightful read."

—RT BOOK REVIEWS, 4 STARS, ON YOU'RE GONNA LOVE ME

"Hatcher has written a contemporary romance novel that is a heartwarming story about love, faith, regret, and second chances."

—CBA MARKET ON YOU'RE GONNA LOVE ME

"Hatcher (*Another Chance To Love You*) creates a joyous, faith-infused tale of recovery and reconciliation."

—PUBLISHERS WEEKLY ON YOU'RE GONNA LOVE ME

"*You're Gonna Love Me* is a gentle romance that offers hope for second chances. Author Robin Lee Hatcher has a gift for welcoming readers into fictional close-knit communities fortified with love and trust. With each turn of the page, I relaxed into the quiet rhythm of Hatcher's storytelling, where she deftly examines the heart's desires of her characters set against the richly-detailed Idaho setting."

—BETH K. VOGT, CHRISTY AWARD-WINNING AUTHOR

"*You're Gonna Love Me* nourished my spirit as I read about a hero and heroine with realistic struggles, human responses, and honest growth. Robin Lee Hatcher makes me truly want to drive to Idaho and mingle with the locals."

—HANNAH ALEXANDER, AUTHOR OF *THE WEDDING KISS*

"I didn't think *You'll Think of Me*, the first book in Robin Lee Hatcher's Thunder Creek, Idaho series, could be beat. But she did it again . . . This second chance story will melt your heart and serve as a parable for finding redemption through life's lessons and God's grace. Thunder Creek will always hold a special place in my heart."

—LENORA WORTH, AUTHOR OF *HER LAKESIDE FAMILY*, ON *YOU'RE GONNA LOVE ME*

"With two strong, genuine characters that readers will feel compassion for and a heartwarming modern-day plot that inspires, Hatcher's romance is a wonderfully satisfying read."

—RT BOOK REVIEWS, 4 STARS, ON *YOU'LL THINK OF ME*

"A heart-warming story of love, acceptance, and challenge. Highly recommended."

—CBA MARKET ON *YOU'LL THINK OF ME*

"*You'll Think of Me* is like a vacation to small town Idaho where the present collides with the past and it's not clear which will win. The shadows of the past threaten to trap Brooklyn in the past. Can she break free into the freedom to love and find love? The story kept me coming back for just one more page. A perfect read for those who love a romance that is much more as it explores important themes."

—CARA PUTMAN, AWARD-WINNING AUTHOR *SHADOWED BY GRACE* AND *BEYOND JUSTICE*

"Hatcher is able to unravel emotions within her characters so brilliantly that we sense the transformation taking place within ourselves . . . readers will relish the warmth of . . . the ranchland."

—RT Book Reviews on Keeper of the Stars

"Hatcher fans will be left smiling and eagerly awaiting her next novel."

—CBA Retailers + Resources on Keeper of the Stars

"True to the contemporary romance genre, Robin Lee Hatcher's Keeper of the Stars will satisfy romance fans and give them a joy ride as they travel the road of pain and forgiveness to reach the happily-ever-after."

—BookTalk at Fiction 411

"Robin Lee Hatcher weaves a romance with heart that grabs readers and won't let go. Whenever You Come Around pulled me in from the get-go. Charity Anderson, a beautiful, successful author with a deadline and a painful secret, runs into Buck Malone, a handsome, confirmed-bachelor cowboy from her past, and he needs her help. I was captivated, and I guarantee you'll be rooting for them too."

—Sunni Jeffers, award-winning author of Heaven's Strain

"A heartwarming and engaging romance, Whenever You Come Around is a splendid read from start to finish!"

—Tamera Alexander, USA TODAY bestselling author of To Whisper Her Name and From a Distance

"A handsome cowboy, horses, and a hurting heroine make for a winning combination in this newest poignant story by Robin Lee Hatcher. A gently paced but delightful ride, Whenever You Come Around will take readers on a journey of healing right along with the characters. Readers will feel at home in Kings Meadow and won't want to leave."

—Jody Hedlund, bestselling author of Love Unexpected

"First loves find sweet second chances in Kings Meadow. Heartwarming, romantic, and filled with hope and faith, this is Hatcher at her best!"

—LISA WINGATE, *NEW YORK TIMES* BESTSELLING
AUTHOR OF *BEFORE WE WERE YOURS*

"In *Whenever You Come Around* Hatcher takes a look at the pain of secrets that kill the heart. But love indeed conquers all. Robin Lee Hatcher is the go-to classic romance author."

—RACHEL HAUCK, AWARD-WINNING, *NEW YORK TIMES*
BESTSELLING AUTHOR OF *THE WEDDING DRESS*

"Robin Lee Hatcher has created an emotionally engaging romance, a story of healing and self-forgiveness wrapped up in a package about small-town life and a cowboy who lives a life honoring God. I want to live in Kings Meadow."

—SHARON DUNN, AUTHOR OF *COLD CASE JUSTICE* AND
WILDERNESS TARGET, ON *WHENEVER YOU COME AROUND*

"*Whenever You Come Around* draws you into the beauty and history of the horse country of Kings Meadow, Idaho. With every turn of the page, Robin Lee Hatcher woos readers with a love story of a modern-day cowboy and a city girl. Buck and Charity rescue each other from the lives they had planned—lives limited by fear. Instead, they discover their unexpected God-ordained happily ever after. A discerning writer, Hatcher handles Charity's past heartbreak with sensitivity and grace."

—BETH K. VOGT, AUTHOR OF *SOMEBODY LIKE YOU*, ONE
OF *PUBLISHERS WEEKLY*'S BEST BOOKS OF 2014

"*Whenever You Come Around* is one of Robin Lee Hatcher's pure-romance best, with a heroine waiting for total redemption and a strong hero of great worth. I find myself still smiling long after the final page has been read."

—HANNAH ALEXANDER, AUTHOR OF THE *HALLOWED HALLS* SERIES

"*Whenever You Come Around* is a slow dance of letting go of the past and its very real pain to step into the light of love. It's a story that will wrap around your soul with the hope that no past is so dark and haunted that it can't be forgiven and overcome. It's a love story filled with sweetness, tension, and slow fireworks. Bottom line, it was a romance I couldn't—and didn't want to—put down."

—CARA PUTMAN, AWARD-WINNING AUTHOR OF *SHADOWED BY GRACE* AND *WHERE TREETOPS GLISTEN*

"In *Love Without End*, Robin Lee Hatcher once again takes us to Kings Meadow, Idaho, in a sweeping love story that captures the heart and soul of romance between two people who have every reason not to fall in love. With an interesting backstory interspersed among the contemporary chapters, and well-drawn, relatable secondary characters, Hatcher hits the mark with her warm and inviting love story."

—MARTHA ROGERS, AUTHOR OF THE SERIES *WINDS ACROSS THE PRAIRIE* AND *THE HOMEWARD JOURNEY*

"*Love Without End*, the first book in the new Kings Meadow Romance series, again intertwines two beautiful and heartfelt romances. One in the past and one in the future together make this a special read. I'm so glad Robin wrote a love story for Chet who suffered so much in *A Promise Kept* (January 2014). Kimberly, so wrong for him, becomes so right. Not your run-of-the-mill cowboy romance—enriched with deft writing and deep emotion."

—LYN COTE, AUTHOR OF *HONOR*, QUAKER BRIDES, BOOK ONE

"No one writes about the joys and challenges of family life better than Robin Lee Hatcher, and she's at the top of her game with *Love Without End*. This beautiful and deeply moving story will capture your heart as it captured mine."

—MARGARET BROWNLEY, *NEW YORK TIMES* BESTSELLING AUTHOR

"*Love Without End*, Book One in Robin Lee Hatcher's new Kings Meadow series, is a delight from start to finish. The author's skill at depicting the love and challenges of family has never been more evident as she deftly combines two love stories—past and present—to capture readers' hearts and lift their spirits."

—MARTA PERRY, AUTHOR OF *THE FORGIVEN*,
KEEPERS OF THE PROMISE, BOOK ONE

"I always expect excellence when I open a Robin Lee Hatcher novel. She never disappoints. The story here reminds me of a circle without end as Robin takes us through a modern-day romance while looping one character through a WWII tale of love and loss and the resurrection of hope and purpose. *Love Without End* touched my heart and guided me to some wonderful truths of how God's love is a gift and a treasure."

—DONITA K. PAUL, BESTSELLING AUTHOR

"A beautiful, heart-touching story of God's amazing grace, and how He can restore and make new that which was lost."

—FRANCINE RIVERS, *NEW YORK TIMES*
BESTSELLING AUTHOR, ON *A PROMISE KEPT*

Who I Am with You

ALSO BY ROBIN LEE HATCHER

Who I Am with You

A LEGACY OF FAITH NOVEL

ROBIN LEE HATCHER

THOMAS NELSON
Since 1798

Who I Am with You

Published in Nashville, Tennessee, by Thomas Nelson. Thomas Nelson is a registered trademark of HarperCollins Christian Publishing, Inc.

Thomas Nelson titles may be purchased in bulk for educational, business, fundraising, or sales promotional use. For information, please e-mail SpecialMarkets@ ThomasNelson.com.

Library of Congress Cataloging-in-Publication Data

Names: Hatcher, Robin Lee, author.
Title: Who I am with you / Robin Lee Hatcher.
Description: Nashville, Tennessee : Thomas Nelson, [2018] | Series: A Legacy of faith novel ; 1
Identifiers: LCCN 2018031310 | ISBN 9780785219262 (paperback)
Subjects: | GSAFD: Christian fiction. | Love stories.
Classification: LCC PS3558.A73574 W49 2018 | DDC 813/.54--dc23 LC record available at https://lccn.loc.gov/2018031310

*In memory of my beloved mother, who gave me a
Living Bible that God then used to bring me to Jesus.
What a legacy of faith she left behind her.*

Prologue

BOISE, IDAHO

"Jessica?" Her mother's voice seemed to come from a great distance. "Darling, what are you doing up here?"

Jessica Mason blinked as she pulled her thoughts from the funeral. Not her grandmother's—the one she'd attended that very morning—but the one that had happened on an icy December afternoon five months earlier. Joe . . . Angela . . . A large casket beside a much smaller one.

She swallowed the threatening tears, the pain hot in her chest.

The mattress gave as her mother sat beside her on the bed. Then an arm went around her shoulders. "It's hard."

Jessica nodded, knowing her mom truly understood. Understood that it wasn't her grandmother she'd been remembering, although it should have been. Knew but didn't judge. "I loved Grandma Frani so much."

"Of course you did."

"But I wish I'd gone home after . . . after the service. I didn't expect the memories to come flooding back the way they have."

She took a long, slow breath and released it, afterward whispering, "Mom, why does it still hurt so much?"

"Why do you think it shouldn't? You lost a husband and a daughter. And five months is not very long ago." Her mother's arm tightened, and then silence filled the room.

At long last Jessica said, "I'm sorry."

"No need to be sorry, dear. We can't shut off our feelings whenever we want. They are what they are."

"Oh, Mom."

Again her mother's arm tightened. "There's something your grandmother left for you. Wait here while I get it."

Alone again, Jessica grabbed a tissue and pressed it against her eyes. A few deep breaths helped her feel as if she might gain control of her careening emotions.

Five months. She cupped a hand over her rounded belly, remembering the angry words she and Joe had exchanged the morning he and Angela died. Words she hadn't shared with another soul. Not even her mom. Pain sliced through her, along with guilt. Guilt because if she and Joe hadn't fought, perhaps her husband and daughter would still be alive. Pain because if her husband had lived, he still wouldn't be with her today.

"Here we are." Her mom reentered the room. She sat on the bed beside Jessica, running a hand over the worn cover of the large Bible that now rested on her lap. "Grandma Frani left this for you."

A chill passed through Jessica's heart. A feeling of loneliness, of being set adrift.

"The night before she died, your grandma told me to give this to you after her funeral." Her mom's voice was soft, almost reverent, as she spoke. "This Bible belonged to her father, Andrew Henning. He said it was Mom's until the day God told her to give it to someone

2

else in the family, and then that person was to have it until the day God said to pass it along again. And so on and so on." She slid the Bible from her lap to Jessica's. "My Grandpa Andrew didn't have a lot of money or material possessions to leave as a legacy to his descendants. But he had his faith to share, even with those who would come long after he was gone." She patted the cover of the Bible. "Because it's in here."

"Mom—"

"Let what you find inside bless you, honey. Let it comfort and teach you."

Bitterness burned Jessica's tongue, but she swallowed it because she had to. Because she didn't want her mom to know how far she'd wandered. From God. From His Word. From believing or even from hoping.

"Okay, Mom," she whispered at long last. "Okay."

KUNA, IDAHO
Thursday, October 24, 1929

Late afternoon sunlight filtered through the windows of the small Methodist church, casting a golden glow over the bride and groom as well as the family and friends who had gathered to witness the exchange of vows between Andrew Henning and Helen Greyson.

Andrew had fallen in love with Helen almost the instant they'd met in late autumn of 1924. She'd been sixteen at the time. Too young for him, he'd told himself, and life too complicated. He'd been nearly twenty and preparing to leave for his first semester of college up in Moscow. He'd had no time for romance. He'd needed to stay focused on one thing—obtaining his degree.

And yet romance had blossomed between them, despite the distance and long absences. Over the next four and a half years, they'd written countless letters to each other. He'd studied and held down a part-time job and dreamed of the day she would become his bride.

Today was that day. Five long years after first meeting her.

As he looked at Helen now, he knew there had never been a more beautiful bride. Her dark hair was mostly hidden by the white of her veil, but nothing concealed the rosy blush in her cheeks as she promised to love, honor, and obey him.

How was I lucky enough to win her heart? How did I ever convince her to wait for me?

It amazed him every time he thought about it. He was twenty-four years old, a university graduate—the first in his family to earn a college degree—and recently employed by a bank in Boise. His income was good, and his future seemed bright. Still, Helen could have had her pick of much more successful men, had she wanted. But she hadn't wanted. She'd chosen him. She loved him.

He wouldn't ever let her regret that choice. Not ever. When he'd proposed, he'd promised her a good life, full of all kinds of modern conveniences and luxuries, and he meant to keep those promises. Nothing would keep him from it.

Chapter 1

HOPE SPRINGS, IDAHO

The drive through Hope Springs took Ridley Chesterfield all of about a minute or so, even at only fifteen miles per hour. Downtown consisted of a few small retail shops, including a grocery store and a large local government building that appeared to house the post office, the mayor's office, and the police station. Off the main drag, he caught sight of a couple of school buildings as well as a town park. No traffic lights. No parking meters. A slice of Mayberry RFD.

His mom had told him the town had charm. He would have to trust her on that.

After arriving at the log house a short while later, he unlocked the front door and stepped inside. The air was cool, the room cloaked in shadows. Rather than reaching for the light switch, he stepped over to the nearest window and opened the blinds, letting daylight spill into the sparsely furnished room.

His mom and stepfather—they currently lived and worked in Arizona—had purchased this property a couple of months before. Located in a remote mountain valley north of Boise, it was to be their vacation home until they retired from their respective jobs a decade or so from now. Then they planned to live in Hope Springs year round.

Ironic, wasn't it? A man without hope taking refuge in a town with that name. A laugh devoid of humor escaped his throat.

His mom had told him the two-story house had a charm similar to the town's, and he supposed she was right about that. But it also needed work, both inside and out, and for that he was thankful. The more things he had to do to keep himself busy, the better. And the more physical the labor, the better. Anything to keep him from dwelling on the circumstances that had brought him there. The less he thought about that, also the better.

"'Whatever is true,'" he reminded himself aloud, "'whatever is honorable, whatever is right . . . dwell on these things.'"

Easier said than done. For the past few weeks, he'd waffled between regret and rage, between the need to justify himself and the desire to beat himself up for his own stupidity and blind trust. Dwelling on what was true, honorable, right, and whatever else that verse in Philippians said was a whole lot harder than he'd imagined.

Clenching his jaw, he did his best to shut off his thoughts altogether. Instead, he concentrated on a tour of the house.

The lower level had a large great room with vaulted ceilings and a stone fireplace, a spacious kitchen and dining area, a bathroom with a soaking tub, and a master bedroom. Upstairs he found an open area set up as a small library with bookshelves and two comfortable chairs. A window provided a spectacular view of the northern end of the valley. On either side of the library was a bedroom. And finally, there was another bathroom, this one with a shower but no tub.

"Use the master bedroom," his mom had told him. "We don't have our vacation planned until the end of August."

Now that he was inside the house, he knew he wouldn't follow her instructions. It wouldn't feel right. No, he would take one of the upstairs rooms. That way, if he was still in residence come the end of August—

Ridley closed his eyes and drew in a slow breath. Better not to put a timetable on anything. Next month. Next year. Who knew how long it would be before he was left alone to find new employment? Surely the newsmongers and internet trolls would turn their attention elsewhere before too long; he was a small fish in a big pond, although that didn't mean his troubles with the campaign wouldn't follow him around when it came to finding a job.

With a grunt, he headed down the stairs and went outside to retrieve his things from the car. Suitcases and duffel bags had been packed in a hurry. He hadn't cared about organization once he'd made his decision to leave Boise. Hopefully, he would manage to find his toothbrush before bedtime.

Lucky for him, his mom and stepfather had furnished the house shortly after buying it, complete with sheets and blankets for the beds and all the necessary dishes, utensils, and appliances for the kitchen. All Ridley needed to do was make a quick trip into Hope Springs for some grocery items to stock the fridge and pantry, and he would be set.

"Might as well get that over with." He dropped the last duffel bag on the floor of his new bedroom and headed back outside, car keys in hand and a baseball cap pulled low on his forehead.

⌒❦⌒

Jessica Mason had fallen in love with Hope Springs the moment she'd seen it a decade ago. She and Joe had moved to the small mountain town a few weeks after their wedding, happily settling into their fixer-upper on several acres of land. In no time at all they had become a part of the community. Jessica hadn't even minded those times when Joe traveled for work. She'd been busy with making their house a home as well as becoming involved in their church and the local community. She'd made friends with a number of young wives. Her days had been full—and even more so after the birth of Angela. Her life had been everything she'd dreamed it should be.

But Joe hadn't been as happy as Jessica. When that had changed, she didn't know for certain. She felt she should be able to pinpoint the moment he'd stopped loving her, but she couldn't.

Shoving away the painful memories, Jessica entered the grocery store on the eastern edge of Hope Springs, her shopping list in hand. She never took her time or browsed as she once had. She shopped quickly and went straight home. After the accident, it had been instinctive. She hadn't been able to bear the words of condolence she'd heard over and over again. Now it was habit.

Her mom had told her more than once that it wasn't healthy to isolate herself. Maybe not, but Jessica preferred it that way. It was less painful. Besides, when she was with people, she had to pretend too much. She had to lie too often. It was better to spend her days creating in her studio, working at her computer, and running her online shop where she sold her crafts and paintings. Better to be alone than to be reminded of all she'd lost.

In the produce department she was looking at the tomatoes when another cart bumped into hers.

"Oh. Sorry."

She glanced up. The stranger was tall and broad shouldered, well-developed biceps straining the sleeves of his T-shirt, but his baseball cap and dark glasses hid his eyes. "It's all right," she said, thankful it wasn't someone she knew.

He gave her a quick nod before moving on.

Jessica reached for another tomato, then looked over her shoulder in time to see the man fill a plastic bag with plums. He didn't check for soft spots or to see if they were too green or too ripe. He simply loaded the bag, not seeming to care about quality.

Men. She returned her attention to the tomatoes.

It took her about fifteen minutes to finish her shopping, pay for her groceries, and get her few bags into the back of her SUV. Once upon a time, she'd loved to discover new recipes and shop for the ingredients. She used to spend hours in the kitchen, cooking to please her husband. These days she cared little about what she ate. For the baby's sake, she tried to eat healthy, but she preferred whatever was quick and simple. She had no one to please, no one to impress.

Once home and everything put away, she tried to immerse herself in her latest art project, but she couldn't seem to concentrate on it. Giving up, she went outside to weed her flowerbeds.

She was nearly finished when a familiar but unexpected sound reached her ears. She straightened, resting on her heels, and looked toward the neighboring property. The log house—about an acre away from her own—had stood empty for almost two years. Then, in early April, the *For Sale* sign had come down. She'd wondered who bought it, but the house had continued to stand empty. Until now. A man, wearing Levi's and a white T-shirt, wielded an ax with expertise, chopping the logs that had long ago been stacked near the shed and covered with a tarp.

A good neighbor would have crossed the acre that separated them to say hello and introduce herself. A good neighbor might have taken over a plate of fresh-baked chocolate-chip cookies. But Jessica had forgotten how to be a good neighbor.

She stood, at the same time removing her gardening gloves, and went back inside.

BOISE, IDAHO
Monday, November 11, 1929

Andrew stood outside the bank's entrance, a cold wind blowing through his coat and another through his soul. When he'd kissed Helen goodbye that morning, he'd been employed. Now he wasn't. They'd used most of his savings for their honeymoon to the Oregon coast. It hadn't seemed extravagant at the time. Now he wished they'd been more prudent.

He pulled his coat collar up around his neck as he turned and began to follow the sidewalk in the direction of his automobile.

"I'll find another job," he whispered as he walked.

How difficult could it be? Certainly what had happened in the stock market a few weeks earlier had shaken financial institutions throughout the country, but it wouldn't last. And besides, he didn't *have* to work for a bank. His degree qualified him for many positions in industry or even in local or state government. He had the promise of good recommendations even if his work experience was limited. He would find another job soon enough.

Although his thoughts were meant to bolster his self-confidence, he dreaded telling his wife of less than three weeks that he was now unexpectedly unemployed.

He frowned and his footsteps slowed. As a bank employee, he'd been aware of the recession hitting the country earlier in the year, but he hadn't thought it would last. He hadn't thought it would worsen. He hadn't expected a crash or that men would throw themselves out of tall buildings over it. Certainly he hadn't expected that any of it would affect him personally. How wrong he'd been.

Another blast of cold air struck him, and he hurried on.

The drive home didn't take long. Andrew parked his Model T Ford in a space off the alley and walked to the rear of the large home, then went down the ten steps to the basement apartment he'd rented shortly before his wedding day. Since returning from their honeymoon, Helen had been happily making their little place as attractive as possible. There was the living room with its cold, tiled floor; an eating nook; a kitchen one could barely turn around in; a bathroom just large enough for the sink, toilet, and shower stall; plus one bedroom. Helen moved furniture on an almost daily basis, fussing over this and that while making lists of things she wanted to purchase when possible. In fact, she was pushing the sofa to a new location when he opened the door and stepped inside.

"Helen."

She gasped and whirled around. Her hand went to her throat as she let out a breath. "Andrew. For heaven's sake. You startled me. What are you doing home at this hour?"

He removed his hat and hung it on the rack near the door. His coat followed it.

"Andrew?"

He met her gaze again. "I'm afraid I have some bad news."

"Bad news?"

"Helen, I've lost my position at the bank."

Her face paled. "But why?"

As he walked across the room, he wondered if his bride ever

looked at the newspaper. Then again, he always read the newspaper, and he'd still been caught off guard.

"Andrew?"

He took hold of her shoulders. "The bank must take cost-savings measures because of what happened in the stock market. Cutting back on employees is where they started. I was among those they let go today." He drew her close. "Don't worry. They've promised me an excellent recommendation. I'll find another position soon."

God, don't let that be a lie.

Chapter 2

Ridley awakened the next morning while daylight was only a promise. To his surprise, he'd slept hard throughout the night. A good eight hours straight. He'd begun to think he would never sleep soundly again, and he was pleased to have been proved wrong.

Mountain air, no doubt. Mountain air plus a long stretch of chopping wood yesterday. Not that he had need of wood to burn. But attacking that woodpile had helped him rid himself of some of his frustration.

His cell phone rang, and he knew without looking at the screen that it would be his mom. She'd always been an early riser.

"Hey, Mom."

"Hi, honey. How are you?"

"Good." He pushed himself up until his back rested against the headboard. "I like your place."

"Then you got there all right."

"Not like it was hard to find. Drive through town and keep going east for three miles, then head south for another four, and turn right at the stone pillar. Like I said. Not hard to find."

"No. Of course not."

He heard the concern in her voice, heard all of her unspoken questions. He pretended he didn't. "I should have come up to see it before now. Maybe I'd've moved in sooner."

She didn't reply, and he knew his attempt at humor had fallen flat.

After a few moments of silence, he said, "I'm grateful I could come up here, Mom. I needed to get away from it all. This is the perfect place to be alone, get my head together, figure out what I want to do next."

"And you're all right?"

"I will be. At least I can say I'm at peace with God. Finding peace with people will take me a little longer."

"I'll keep praying for you, dear."

He smiled wryly. "I know you will."

"Honey?"

"Yeah."

"I know you want to escape what's happened, but don't shut everyone out. You need other people. Whether you think you do or not."

He wished he could give his mom a hug. "I know."

"Go to church."

"I will."

He heard her laugh softly. "I'm through lecturing."

"I love you, Mom."

"I love you too."

They exchanged a few more words before saying goodbye and ending the call.

Knowing there was no going back to sleep, Ridley got up and headed for the shower. When he was done and dressed, he went downstairs to fix himself a breakfast of eggs, bacon, and toast.

There was no television in the house so he couldn't watch the morning news as was his habit. In fact, the lack of both television and internet had been a great deal of this location's appeal. He'd come to Hope Springs to escape the news. Better to be ignorant of state and national affairs, lest he see his own face plastered on the screen again. He'd had enough of that for ten lifetimes.

After eating breakfast, he washed and dried the frying pan and other dishes before heading outside. At the bottom of the back porch, he stopped to survey the property again. A detached three-car garage was off to his left. The woodpile, where he'd spent a good deal of yesterday afternoon, was on the right side of the yard beside a small shed. The three acres of partially fenced land that went with the house was spotted with a few clusters of aspens and lodgepole pines and carpeted with wild grass. At the far end trickled a creek and a small pond, a few ducks bobbing for bugs, tail feathers stuck in the air. The property lay at the end of a dirt road, and it felt remote—more so than it actually was. Something else he liked about it.

The silence of the morning was broken by the barking of a dog. Ridley caught sight of the long-coated canine as it raced across the land toward the pond. Several ducks took flight. A few others waited to see if the dog would plunge into the water after them. It didn't. Instead, it raced around the pond, continuing to bark.

Using his hands, Ridley vaulted over the white board fence and strode toward the pond. When he got closer, he said, "Hey, there. Settle down."

The dog ignored him.

"Come on. Settle down. Those ducks couldn't care less about you."

The raucous noise continued.

Deepening his voice, Ridley said, "No!"

At last he had the dog's attention.

"Sit," he commanded.

To his surprise, the dog did so.

He took a few steps closer. The dog—a sheltie, judging by its smaller size and its sable and white coat—was desperately in need of a bath. It wore no collar. "Can I touch you?" He reached out slowly. "You look a little thin beneath all that hair and dirt. When did you eat last?"

The dog whimpered.

He patted its head. "How about I get you something? Come with me."

Again the sheltie obeyed the command.

"Anybody missing you?" Doubt rose to answer the question. No collar and underweight. Either the dog had been neglected or had been lost a long time.

They walked to the house, the sheltie on his left side.

"I don't have any dog food, but I'll bet you like scrambled eggs."

After the dog was fed, Ridley decided, he would check with the neighbor. Maybe someone knew where the canine belonged.

⚬⚬⚬

The sound of the doorbell startled Jessica. It was too early for Carol Donaldson to bring one of her deliveries. But who else could it be? She never had visitors anymore. She left her computer and walked to the front door as the bell sounded a second time.

"I'm coming," she muttered before pulling the door open. Any additional words died in her throat when she saw the man standing on her front porch. It was the stranger from the grocery store. She recognized him at once. Same hat. Same dark glasses.

If he recognized her in turn, his sunglasses hid it from her. "Hey." A brief smile tugged at the corners of his mouth before he glanced down at his side. "I found this dog and wondered if you might know who she belongs to."

She followed his gaze, then looked up again. "No. Sorry. I've never seen her before. Where did you find her?"

He jerked his head toward the house next door. "Out by the pond."

Not just the stranger from the grocery store. The man she'd seen chopping wood yesterday. He must be one and the same.

"You're my new neighbor?" she inquired softly.

He shrugged. "For now."

She arched her eyebrows, not sure what to make of his answer.

"The house belongs to my parents. I'm staying for . . . for the summer." He paused again, this time longer, then added, "I'll be making repairs around the place." He turned his head, his fingertips now shoved into his pockets. "My name's Ridley." He removed his sunglasses and met her gaze.

"Jessica." She forced herself to offer a hand. "Jessica Mason."

He shook it but didn't respond with his own last name. She would have to make do with Ridley. Not that it mattered to her, one way or the other.

"Have they got an animal shelter in town?" he asked.

"No. But the Hope Springs police handle animal control. You should call them."

"I'll do that." He took a step back. The dog did too.

She started to close the door, then paused. "Good luck."

"Thanks." He gave her another of his brief half grins before slipping his dark glasses back into place.

This time she pushed the door all the way closed.

Moments later, back at her computer, she found it difficult to focus on her accounting program. Ridley No-Last-Name had taken over her thoughts. Wasn't it strange that a man his age—she guessed him to be in his midthirties—was living in his parents' house? He'd said it was for the summer. Didn't he have a job? Didn't he have a family, other than his parents?

"None of my business."

She swiveled the chair away from the computer and stared out the windows of her spacious studio. After a while, her gaze lowered to the nearby bookcase. Resting on top of it was her great-grandfather's Bible. She hadn't looked at it since placing it there the day of her grandma's funeral. Hadn't so much as opened the cover. Guilt tugged at her chest, but it didn't change anything. She'd learned to ignore feelings of guilt. If she didn't, they would drive her insane.

"Let what you find inside bless you, honey."

"No thanks, Mom." She got up and left her office for the second time.

❧

Staring at the sheltie through the closed screen door, Ridley thanked the officer for her help and ended the call. No dog meeting this one's description had been reported missing in the area in the past year. Ridley had been given a couple of options: keep the dog until the owner could be found, if possible, or surrender it to someone who would take it to the shelter down in Boise. He didn't think much of the second option. He'd read somewhere that over two and a half-million pets were euthanized every year in the United States because there wasn't enough space in shelters nor enough people ready to adopt them. He might not be in the market for a dog, but he wasn't about to risk this sheltie's life either.

"I guess I'd better go into town again." He pushed open the screen. "You need food, shampoo, and a brush."

The dog wagged her tail, then trotted into the house as if she'd expected to be let in all along.

Chuckling, Ridley added, "Not to mention a name for me to call you."

A name. His conscience twinged at the word. At the start of the call, he'd told the police officer that his name was Ridley and he was staying for the summer in the home of his parents, Roger and Grace Jenkins. Later, the officer had called him Mr. Jenkins. He hadn't bothered to correct her. It wasn't as if he'd lied. She'd made an assumption.

"Mankind is adept at self-justification," his dad's voice seemed to whisper in his ear.

He winced, convicted by the memory. He preferred to think of himself as like his dad, an honest man, a man who never shied away from the truth, even when it was uncomfortable. Was that still true of himself?

He leaned over to ruffle the dog's ears before walking to the window in the great room. All he'd wanted was to get out of Boise, to escape the whirlwind, to somehow rid himself of the sense of despair that had enveloped him from the moment the news story broke. Was it so awful that he didn't want anybody in Hope Springs to know his identity? At least not yet. Was it too much to want at least a short period of anonymity?

He knew the answers to the silent questions.

KUNA, IDAHO

Tuesday, December 24, 1929

Candles flickered at the ends of the pews, and the pine-scented air inside the church felt hushed and reverent in the moments before the start of the Christmas Eve service.

Seated between his wife and Frank Greyson, his father-in-law, Andrew closed his eyes and tried to force away the worry that was ever present after nearly six weeks of unemployment. How could he enter into the celebration of the season when he had yet to find a new position? With things as they were, he hadn't even been able to buy his bride a Christmas present. She'd said she understood, but still he felt awful about it.

I'm failing her, God. Not even married two months, and I'm already failing her. It wasn't supposed to be like this. I promised so much and—

Helen took his hand in hers and squeezed. The fabric of her gloves felt warm against his skin. He opened his eyes to look at her. She smiled gently, and it was a look devoid of condemnation or blame. He returned the squeeze, trying to let thankfulness chase away worry, at least for tonight.

Organ music filled the once quiet sanctuary, and from the back the choir sang the first words of "Joy to the World" before beginning their procession down the center aisle. The congregation rose, hymnals in hand.

Andrew wasn't an imaginative man, but in that moment he seemed to feel his Savior's hand alight upon his shoulder, and the touch quieted his spirit. Worry slid away. Perhaps it would return in the morning, but for now it was gone and he could rejoice.

Chapter 3

That afternoon, Jessica met the delivery truck out by the road.

Carol Donaldson, the driver, grinned. "I hear you've got a new neighbor at last. Have you met him?"

Jessica nodded.

"I hear he's good-looking. Is he single?"

"I haven't a clue."

Carol looked toward the log house. "The place belongs to his parents, I guess. Jenkins is the name. His name's . . ."

"Ridley."

Her friend grinned. "Yeah, that's it. Ridley. I've always liked that name. It's masculine sounding. Don't you think?"

Jessica ignored the question. Carol was a friend—the only one Jessica saw these days—but she was forever trying to drag Jessica "back to the world of the living," as she put it. Carol was a constant reminder that Jessica used to be involved with so many others in the valley, that her life had been full to overflowing, that she'd once been loved and happy. The reminder caused hurt on one hand and at the same time stirred a longing within.

"The monthly fellowship tea is this Saturday." Carol put the delivery truck in gear. "Why don't you come with me? It'd be good for you."

"I've got work to do."

"You always have work to do. But a couple hours on occasion won't hurt your bottom line." Carol glanced at Jessica's rounded belly. "And before long you're gonna be even busier."

Jessica pressed the box Carol had given her against her body like a shield. "Sorry. Not this time." She turned away before her friend could say anything more.

Back inside the house, she carried the box of new art supplies to her studio. She used a pair of scissors to cut the tape that sealed it closed, then opened the lid to view the contents. Acrylic paints in her most used colors. Jars of both clear and white gesso. Some new brushes. A large selection of paper products. An X-Acto knife to replace the one she'd misplaced. Canvas in various sizes.

She smiled as she settled onto a stool, thinking how much she appreciated the convenience of online shopping. Even living far from a big craft store, she seldom had to wait longer than two days to get something she needed for her business. Online shopping and a good internet connection were her best friends. Fortunately for her, her customers liked the convenience of online shopping as much as she did. She was grateful, since that's what allowed her to make a living.

She swiveled the stool to face her latest project. The background painting was about half finished. Then would come the calligraphy of Jeremiah 29:11. One of her most requested Bible verses. *"For I know the plans that I have for you," declares the* Lord, *"plans for welfare and not for calamity to give you a future and a hope."*

"But what about me, God?" she whispered. "Do You have good plans for me?"

It didn't seem so. She'd felt abandoned by God long before she'd abandoned Him.

The joy of the new art supplies evaporated from the room. Jessica made a noise of disgust as she walked down the hall and out the back door. She stopped in the sunshine, tipped her head back, and closed her eyes, enjoying the warmth on her face. Unfortunately, with the warmth came a flood of memories. She used to come outside with Angela to enjoy the sunny, pleasant days of June. Even now, she seemed to hear her daughter's laughter as she ran around the yard and slid down the slide and swung in the swing. Only in sleep had Angela liked to be still. From the moment she'd learned to crawl, Jessica's daughter had been an active child.

Jessica moved to one of the patio chairs and sank onto it, allowing the bittersweet memories to continue.

She recalled the day she'd purchased the pregnancy test. She and Joe had been married for three years at the time, and Jessica had been so ready to have a baby. Joe had paced the hallway while he waited for the results. Later, they'd celebrated with sparkling cider, a big bowl of buttered popcorn, and a favorite movie on DVD.

She remembered the night of Angela's birth and the excitement in their combined families in the days that followed. It hadn't been long before Jessica was eager to give Angela a little brother or a little sister. But another pregnancy hadn't happened. Not until it was already too late. Not until—

She closed her eyes, the breath catching in her chest. Anger, confusion, regret, grief. It was all a jumble inside of her.

A shout from across the field caused her eyes to open. In the backyard of the neighboring house, she saw Ridley holding a hose in one hand and gripping the stray dog with the other. The dog was in a large metal tub. Jessica had to assume that was for the purposes of a bath. But the sheltie wasn't cooperating. She fought to get out of the tub and away from the water. If Jessica were a gambler, she'd put money on the dog to win this particular battle.

As if to prove her right, the canine tore away from Ridley's grasp, leaped out of the tub, and raced across the field in Jessica's direction, soapsuds flying in the air behind her. Jessica laughed until she realized the dog wasn't just headed for her yard. The dog was headed for Jessica. Directly for her. And she wasn't slowing down.

Jessica jumped up from the chair, but not in time to avoid the wet dog as she hurled herself into Jessica's arms. The weight knocked her backward, and they went down together. She was stunned for a moment, thankful she'd avoided hitting her head on the concrete. Then she began to feel the places that *had* landed hard. Her shoulders. Her elbows. Her tailbone.

"Get off me." She pushed the dog away.

"Hey, are you all right?"

"I think so." She inhaled, waiting to see if anything twinged. Nothing did. "Yes. I'm fine." She looked up to find Ridley standing over her.

"You sure? You went down hard." He held out a hand. "Let me help you up."

She hesitated at first but finally took hold of it. A shiver passed through her as he drew her to her feet with ease. Her pulse hammered, making it hard to focus. Maybe she'd hit her head after all.

"I don't think she likes water much." Ridley released Jessica's hand and reached for the dog's collar.

She quieted her rapid pulse. "You think?"

Ridley laughed—a bold, male sound that burst around her, filling the air. It felt unexpected and out of place, and Jessica took a small step back, as if to escape it.

"Hey, really. I am sorry." His expression sobering, Ridley straightened as much as possible while still holding onto the dog's collar. "She's obedient most of the time, but she has a definite aversion to water. I think I need at least four hands to manage giving her a bath."

"I guess I could help." Jessica's own words surprised her. Whatever had possessed her to say that? But it was too late to take back the offer.

"That'd be great. Are you sure you don't mind?"

"I'm already wet," she replied, more to explain her reasons to herself than to him.

⁂

Ridley didn't know why he accepted Jessica's offer to help bathe the dog. After all, he'd wanted to stay under the radar as much as possible during his stay in Hope Springs. The last thing he needed was to get involved with the locals, especially one who lived right next door. Involvement would only lead to questions about who he was and why he was in Hope Springs. But it was his own fault. He was the one who'd said he needed four hands. He couldn't tell her to go home without sounding ungrateful.

They were halfway across the field that separated their two homes when a breeze caught Jessica's oversized cotton shirt. His eyes widened as he realized what he'd missed earlier. She was pregnant. A shiver of alarm shot through him. What if the blasted dog had hurt her or the baby? It would be his fault. Wouldn't the reporters have a field day with that?

He winced at the selfishness of his thoughts.

"You don't have to do this if you don't want to," he said as they drew near to the tub.

"No. I'm here. I'll help."

Should he point out the fact that she was pregnant and had taken a fall? Or was it better to stay silent about that? He wasn't sure. "Well . . . okay. This shouldn't take long." He grabbed for the dog's leash and fastened it to the collar he'd bought in town. Then he lifted the sheltie in his arms and set her in the center of the tub.

"You didn't find her owner, I take it." Jessica knelt on the grass, picked up the large plastic cup that floated on the surface of the water, and began wetting down the dog's thick coat.

"Nope. No one's reported her missing."

Jessica applied soap—the dog having blown away the first application during her escape attempt—and worked up a nice lather while Ridley kept a tight hold on the leash. The rinsing went even faster, and before long, the dog was free from her leash, had shaken away as much water as possible, and was racing around the yard in wild abandon.

"A new meaning for the term *blow dry*," Jessica said.

Ridley laughed again. He couldn't help it. He liked her wry sense of humor.

"New collar. New leash. A bath." She stood. "Looks like you plan to keep her."

He shrugged. "For now, anyway. Didn't want to risk her being put to sleep just because her owner can't be found."

"And her name?"

"Still haven't decided. Any ideas?"

A look of concentration pinched Jessica's brows as she watched the dog. After a lengthy pause, she said, "She likes to run. Name her after a famous athlete. What about Kristin Armstrong? She's an Idaho Olympian."

"That's kind of a mouthful."

"Kris for short."

He looked away from Jessica. "Kris." The dog stopped running, as if in answer to the name. "Kris," he said, louder this time. The sheltie looked at him. "Come here, Kris." The dog obeyed. Apparently Ridley had been forgiven for the bath. Either that or he'd chanced to discover the sheltie's actual name. Highly unlikely it was the latter.

"I guess Kris it is. Thanks, Jessica."

She patted the dog's head. "Glad I could help." She motioned her head toward her house. "I'd better go. I've got work awaiting me."

"What is it you do?" He regretted the question the instant the words left his mouth. After all, it would give her the right to ask the same of him.

"I sell paintings and other crafts on the internet."

"Wow. Really? You must be talented if you make your living at it." More regret. He needed to shut up. "I'd better not keep you from it. Thanks again for helping with the bath. And with a name for the dog."

"You're welcome," she answered softly before walking away.

As he watched her go, another thought flitted through Ridley's mind. She didn't wear a wedding ring. Was there a Mr. Mason that went with her pregnancy?

Whoa! His neighbor—his *temporary* neighbor—might make him laugh, but he wanted distance from everybody right now. And especially from anybody who was attractive and female.

"Come on, Kris." He clipped the leash to the collar. "I've got stuff to do too." Although at the moment he couldn't think what that stuff was.

BOISE, IDAHO
Monday, March 10, 1930

Your faith is being tested, a voice whispered in Andrew's heart as he stood on the sidewalk outside a diner on the east side of Boise. *Mine along with many thousands of others*, he added, although the truth of it didn't make him feel any better.

The book of James said believers should consider the testing that happened in life, the trials that came their way, a joy. He'd even underlined the words in his Bible when he'd read them recently. But how was he supposed to make that joy happen? For a couple of months, he'd thought he had a handle on it. For a couple of months, the worry had stayed at bay. But now?

Now the worry had returned with a fury. He was still unemployed, and his bride of less than six months was expecting a baby.

A baby!

Andrew wanted children with Helen. He'd imagined the two of them with a houseful of kids. But not yet, and not when he couldn't provide for them. Not when they were within a few weeks of having to move out of their rental and in with Helen's parents. The latter option wasn't appealing, no matter his fondness for them.

Discouragement rolled over him. He couldn't even get a job in a diner. He'd been willing to bus tables and wash dishes, but it seemed he was overqualified for that position. Funny considering he'd held a similar job while going through school. However, the owner of this diner wouldn't even consider him.

"You have a college degree," the man had said a few minutes ago. "You wouldn't stay. I need someone who will stay."

But the man was wrong. In the midst of a depression, Andrew would have stayed. Any income was better than none. He was smart enough to know that. But too smart for this guy, it seemed.

Now what?

He thought of his in-laws, Frank and Madge Greyson. Salt-of-the-earth people whose company he enjoyed. He loved them as much as he loved his own parents. But to live with them in their farmhouse near Kuna? His ego felt bruised at the thought of it. And how could he afford the extra gasoline he would need in order to drive into Boise to look for work? He didn't drive his Ford now as it was. He hadn't the money. He walked everywhere. The soles of his shoes were proof of that. Even now there was newspaper in the bottom of his right shoe, covering a hole.

His head began to swim, and he moved to a nearby bench and sank onto it. His stomach growled, reminding him how long it had been since he'd eaten his meager breakfast—a slice of toast with strawberry jam and a glass of milk. The previous night's dinner hadn't been much more substantial.

He closed his eyes and drew in a slow, deep breath, waiting for the dizziness to pass. It did soon enough. Still, his situation hadn't changed when he opened his eyes. He remained in serious financial trouble.

Taking another deep breath, he rose from the bench and turned toward home. Home. But it wouldn't be home for long. A few weeks more. Unless something changed.

"God," he whispered, "is there no end to this?"

He strained to hear the answer that all would be well, longed to feel some sort of confirmation in his heart. Anything to give him hope and encouragement. But there was only silence.

When he reached the corner, he looked down the street to his right. Two blocks down, a line had formed outside a church. Hungry men and women waiting for a lunch of soup and bread. Andrew's stomach growled at the thought, but he wouldn't go eat without Helen, and pride made it hard for him to take her to wait outside a soup kitchen for a meal. He'd never imagined he might need to accept charity from strangers.

The Henning family had never had a lot in the way of money, but they'd never been afraid of hard work either. They'd been farmers, for the most part, usually working someone else's land as tenants. But when Andrew was a toddler, his father and mother had been able to buy their own acreage. After that, his parents had scrimped and saved in order to pay for a higher education for their only son.

A bad investment, it now seemed to Andrew.

He trudged on, leaning into the March wind while holding the collar of his coat closed at his throat. As he walked, he tried to pray, tried to choose joy over despair. He wasn't sure he would be any more successful with that than he'd been at finding employment.

Chapter 4

On Thursday, Ridley decided to tackle the kitchen cabinets. His mom wanted the room, including cabinets, painted a buttery shade of yellow. She wanted new hardware, too, and had emailed him examples of her preferences.

Ridley made an early morning trip to the hardware store in Hope Springs. Fortunately, he was able to get everything his mom wanted. If not, he'd have had to wait for the store to order in whatever was missing. No way was he driving down to Boise this soon after his hasty departure.

He'd just pried the lid off a can of paint when the doorbell rang. Kris barked, then watched to see what Ridley would do. He considered ignoring it. He didn't know anybody in the area, with the exception of his neighbor. Who else could it be?

The bell rang again.

"Coming." He wiped his hands on a rag as he walked into the living room, Kris beside him, and pulled open the door expecting to see Jessica Mason. Instead, he found a tall, thin man with a broad smile and graying hair at the temples.

"Mr. Jenkins, I'm Michael Phelps, the pastor at Hope Springs Community Church." A twinkle lit his eyes. "And no, I'm not the swimmer." He chuckled, as if pleased with his own punch line. One he'd doubtlessly used many times.

"And I'm Ridley." He almost left it there, but finally added, "The last name's Chesterfield. Not Jenkins."

"Chesterfield? I must have misunderstood Evie."

Evie, he assumed, was the police officer he'd spoken to on the phone yesterday. "Jenkins is my stepdad's last name. He and my mom own the place."

"Ah. I see. Well, no matter. It was you I came to see."

Ridley sighed internally before widening the door. "Would you like to come in, Pastor Phelps?"

"Thanks. And call me Mick. Everyone does." The pastor moved into the living room. "I won't intrude on your time for long. I simply wanted to welcome you to Hope Springs."

"Thank you. I appreciate it." It was partially true. It was nice to be welcomed, even if he wanted privacy for the time being. On the other hand, Mick hadn't connected the dots when he'd heard Ridley's last name. Perhaps others wouldn't either. Maybe none of them read the *Idaho Statesman* or watched the network channels located in the Boise area or surfed the internet for news. Or maybe folks up here didn't take much interest in Boise area politics. It was possible his fifteen minutes of fame—or notoriety—were over already. He could hope that was true.

Mick looked around the living room. "It's nice to have this place lived in again. It sat empty for too long."

"It isn't what I'd call 'lived in' exactly. I'm a temporary resident, and my mom and stepdad don't plan to move here until after they retire, which is still years away. Until then, it'll be their vacation home." He motioned to the sofa.

The pastor nodded as he sat. "Must say, that's disappointing.

That no one will be here year round, I mean. How long do you mean to stay?"

Settling onto a chair, Ridley shrugged. "A few months. Maybe into fall. Just depends."

Depends on what? Mick's eyes seemed to ask. Then his gaze shifted to Kris. The dog lay on the floor next to Ridley's chair. "Evie mentioned you'd found a stray."

"Yeah."

"Appears that she's moved in."

He shrugged again. "I haven't owned a dog since high school. I kinda like having her around."

"Pets make a home." Mick smiled, his eyes still on the dog. "At least that's true for my family. We have three dogs and two cats at our house." He put his hands on his knees, prepared to rise. Then he stilled. *Chesterfield*, he mouthed.

And Ridley knew the man had connected the dots.

But Mick Phelps, to his credit, schooled his expression. "I promised I wouldn't keep you long. However, I would like to extend an invitation for you to join us for worship on Sundays. It's a great way to meet your neighbors. Even if your stay is temporary." He stood. "Think about it. Service begins at ten."

Ridley stood. "Thanks. I'll think about it." He wondered if the man believed him. He wasn't sure he believed himself.

⚬⚬⚬

Jessica hit Send on the email and leaned back in her desk chair with a sigh of satisfaction. Her in-box was empty. It wouldn't last, which was good news for her business. But it was nice to see it like that for a short while.

She closed the program and stood. A twinge in her lower back told her she'd sat without moving for much too long. "I need to take a walk." She grabbed her sweater off the back of her desk chair, knowing the morning air would still be brisk, at least at the start of her walk.

When she pulled open her front door, she nearly collided with a man standing on her stoop. She gasped as she stumbled back.

"Sorry, Jessica."

Her heart pounded in her ears. "Pastor Mick?"

"Didn't mean to startle you."

"It's okay. Was there something you needed?"

"Not really." Disappointment flickered in his eyes. "I was out this way and thought I would stop by to check on you. It's been a long time since I saw you."

"Yes. It has been a while." Not unexpected, guilt sluiced through her. She detested the feeling.

"We all miss you, Jessica," the pastor said softly.

"I know." She looked down the road. Anywhere but at him. "I've been . . . busy."

She heard Mick take a long, slow breath. After what seemed an eternity, his hand alighted on her shoulder. "I'll keep praying for you."

"Thanks." She swallowed the unwelcome lump in her throat as she lowered her gaze to the toes of her shoes.

"Call me anytime."

"Okay."

She stayed where she was until the crunch of tires on gravel told her that he'd driven away. After a slow, deep breath, she closed the door and began her walk, setting a brisk pace. Unfortunately, she couldn't outwalk thoughts about her pastor.

My pastor.

Was that even true anymore? If she didn't attend church, if she rarely saw Mick Phelps, even in passing at the grocery store, could she still consider him *her* pastor?

There'd been a time when Hope Springs Community had been her second home. She'd been deeply involved in the women's ministries. She'd helped others cook countless meals in the church's kitchen off the fellowship hall, and she'd served in the children's department on many a Sunday. But after the funeral, she'd found it easier to stay at home than to go out. For many weeks, she'd worn her pajamas all day, every day. What had it mattered what she wore or how often she showered and fixed her hair? Her work—when she'd been able to work—was done in the home and on the computer. Her clients never saw her.

Oh, she'd had callers in those first weeks, but she hadn't cared what her friends thought, seeing her hair disheveled and her eyes puffy from crying. They'd known she was mourning her loss, although they hadn't known the depth of her despair. But their lives had gone on, and eventually they'd stopped dropping by. She lived far enough out of town that it wasn't convenient for them, especially when she was less than welcoming when they did make the effort. In time, when she never returned their phone calls, most had stopped calling too. And she couldn't complain. It was what she'd wanted.

Jessica held her head a little higher and inhaled the crisp, clean air. "At least I'm not still in my pj's."

No, but you're not living either.

She wanted to argue with herself, to deny the truth in her own thoughts. She'd done so often enough in the past. But she couldn't argue today. It was true. She wasn't living. Not really.

"Mom's right," she whispered. "It isn't healthy."

Yet even as she said it, she couldn't imagine changing the pattern of her solitary life. She didn't know how to break free. This *was* her life. It was comfortable, uncomplicated. At least for now. And to enter that church again when her heart remained riddled with anger and doubt and questions? That would make her even more of a hypocrite, wouldn't it?

She stopped walking. "Hypocrite." It wasn't what she wanted to be. It wasn't what she'd set out to be. And maybe it wasn't completely true. It wasn't that she didn't believe in God. It wasn't that she didn't remember the day she'd said yes to Jesus. But she couldn't seem to stop wondering why God had punished her in this way. If He loved her, why had He taken her marriage and her precious daughter from her? Why had He left her so alone?

She knew what Grandma Frani would have said to that. *"Look at His word. He'll tell you what you need to know. You aren't alone. You're never alone."*

"It doesn't feel that way, Grandma," she whispered. "But I'll try."

She sighed and turned around, looking down the curved dirt road toward her home. She would change. She couldn't change everything at once, but she could change one thing at a time.

Motion caught her attention, and a second later she recognized her neighbor's dog flying down the road in her direction. At least soapsuds weren't trailing behind the canine the way they had yesterday.

"No, Kris! No!" She braced herself, expecting to be plowed into a second time, but to her surprise, the dog slowed and then sat a few feet away from her. Jessica grinned. "Good girl." She stepped forward and stroked the dog's head.

"Kris!"

Jessica looked up to see Ridley jogging down the road toward them, a leash and empty collar held in one hand.

"Sorry," he said as he drew near. "She slipped right out of her collar and took off the minute she saw you on the road. She likes you."

"The collar must be too loose."

"Obviously." He unfastened the buckle, leaned down, and secured the collar around the sheltie's neck.

"Use the two-finger test."

He looked up, a question in his eyes.

"They say you should be able to put two fingers under the collar. That'll keep it from being too tight or too loose."

"Thanks." He slid his whole hand beneath the collar. "I see your point." He adjusted it. "I guess I was fooled by all that hair." He straightened and met Jessica's gaze again. After a moment, he smiled.

Warmth whirled in her chest.

Ridley motioned toward the road behind her. "I was going to take Kris for a walk. Care to join us?"

Yes. The silent desire to be with him caught her unawares.

"Come on. It won't be a long walk. I've got to get back to the painting."

"Painting?"

"I'm starting in the kitchen."

Somehow she fell into step beside him, once more walking away from her house. It surprised her, how natural it felt to do so. Especially after trying to convince herself she didn't mind being alone because it was uncomplicated.

"I admit," he said, "I don't like house painting, but I do like helping my mom." He shrugged. "So it balances out."

"What color are you painting it? The kitchen, I mean." Again she was surprised by the ease of talking to him. Perhaps because he was a stranger. She didn't have to pretend with him as she had to with those who knew her well.

"Yellow. Mom loves her yellow kitchens. No matter where we lived when I was a kid, the kitchen was always the same color."

"Did you move a lot?"

"It felt like a lot."

"Military brat?"

"No, but Dad's work transferred him every two or three years." He was silent awhile, then asked, "What about you?"

"Me?"

"Did you move around much when you were growing up?"

She shook her head. "No. I grew up in Boise. Lived there my whole life. Until I . . . until I married Joe. Then we moved to Hope Springs." She hadn't meant to mention Joe. She rarely said his name aloud. Who would she say it to?

"I didn't know if you were married or not." He hesitated. "I didn't see a ring."

She took a slow breath. "I'm not married. Anymore. I'm a widow." She took another breath before adding, "My husband and our daughter, Angela, died in a car accident last winter." Her heart squeezed as she pictured her daughter's bright smile on that last morning, and it surprised her that she was able to continue in a soft but steady voice. "She was only six years old."

It was his turn to be silent. Finally, he said, "I'm sorry, Jessica. Really sorry."

She stopped walking and looked at him. "Thank you."

"When—" He paused, as if reconsidering what he was about to say, then continued, "When's your baby due?"

"End of August or early September." Tears stung her eyes, and her hand went protectively to her stomach. She rarely had cause to talk to anyone about her baby either.

Ridley seemed to understand. "Want to keep walking?" Then he jerked his head, indicating the other direction. "Or would you like to go home?"

"Let's walk," she answered, unwilling to be alone with her own thoughts just yet.

KUNA, IDAHO
Monday, May 10, 1930

At the sound of Helen's sigh, Andrew turned in the doorway. His wife stood near the bedroom window, looking over the fields of her parents' farm. Still wearing her nightgown, her long dark hair disheveled, she stood with her hands folded over the gentle swell of her belly. There was a sadness in her expression that caused his gut to tighten and his heart to ache.

They'd argued again last night, and later each had lain on their side in the bed, back to the other. He didn't know if Helen had slept, but he knew for certain he had not. This morning, although he'd done his best to get her to look at him, to give him a chance to say he was sorry, she'd stood at that blasted window, her back stiff, her gaze averted.

Stubborn woman. She was the one in the wrong.

He turned on his heel and left the bedroom. Rather than risk running into either or both of his in-laws in the kitchen, he went out the front door and circled round to the barn. There he began to milk the first of the three dairy cows. When that chore was done, he entered the chicken coop to gather the eggs.

Despite the depression that gripped the country, no one living on the Greyson farm would starve. Andrew's father-in-law was a prudent man, never spending carelessly, never allowing others in his family to do so either. Nor was he a man with great trust in banks, so when those institutions had begun to fail, he hadn't had to worry about losing everything.

By that time, Andrew hadn't had to worry about banks closing either. He'd had nothing left to lose.

A curse rose in his throat, but he couldn't speak it. His upbringing wouldn't let him, nor would his faith.

My faith?

He felt like a fraud, applying the word to himself. Part of him trusted God to see them through, but another part felt abandoned and betrayed. The rain fell on the just and the unjust, so he was told. Rain? This was more than rain. He was drowning. He was being washed away in a torrential downpour. Not to mention he was overwhelmed by self-pity. A disgusting habit of late.

He set the bucket of eggs on the ground and walked to the corral that held four plow horses. Morning sunlight gilded their sorrel coats. One of them snorted at him.

"All right. You're next." He tossed hay into the feed boxes. Then he leaned his forearms on the top rail and watched them eat.

His thoughts returned to his wife. Why wouldn't she see things from his point of view? He couldn't go on living on this farm, depending on the generosity of his in-laws. He needed to find employment that utilized his education and skills. Sure, he could milk cows and collect eggs, but that wasn't what he wanted to do to support his wife and child. He'd gone to college so he could leave the farm behind.

But whenever he suggested that he should stay with his cousin in the Portland area while hunting for work, Helen burst into tears. She wouldn't leave her mother, she said, and she couldn't bear the thought of him going without her.

"Be patient with her, son," his father had told him. "Expectant women are emotional at times."

Emotional Andrew could handle, but Helen was being unreasonable.

"Andrew." His wife's soft voice drew him around.

He felt that tightness in his gut again. He'd promised to make her happy. She wasn't.

"I don't want us to fight." She took a few more steps toward him, drawing a robe tight about herself against the early morning chill.

"I don't want that either."

"I know it hasn't been easy for you, these past few months."

"Or for you."

She offered the smallest of smiles. "Can't you wait a few more months before you look for work elsewhere? Father appreciates your help here on the farm, and the baby is due at the end of summer. Please. Just give it until the end of summer. Until after the baby comes. Then, if that's still what you want to do, we'll go to Portland. All three of us."

If she'd continued to argue with him, he would have stuck to his guns. He would have insisted he widen his job search to bigger cities. But how could he resist her gentle plea? He couldn't.

"All right, Helen. We'll stay put for the summer."

Chapter 5

Ridley could have stayed at the house on Sunday. He was able to worship on his own. He could put a CD in the player in his mom's kitchen and open his Bible and have church right where he was. And yet he found himself driving into Hope Springs, looking for the community church pastored by Michael Phelps, no relation to the Olympic swimmer. He chuckled at the memory. He hoped the pastor included the same kind of dry humor in his sermons. Ridley had come to Hope Springs to hide out, to get away from the press and the gossip, and now he was risking his much desired privacy for an hour or two with other believers. But he needed that hour or two. He knew he needed it.

He managed to slip into the back pew of the sanctuary without making eye contact with anyone, but his luck didn't last long. A man approached and introduced himself, shaking Ridley's hand. More welcomes followed, but everyone he met seemed satisfied when he gave only his first name.

The quaint church, circa 1930s if he was any judge of architecture, still had an organ, and a plump woman in a lilac-print dress began to play it, causing members of the congregation to scatter to their pews. Soon they were all standing, hymnals in hand, and singing one of his great-grandmother's favorite hymns, "Morning Has Broken."

He grinned to himself, remembering the elderly woman seated in her recliner, eyes closed, palms up, greeting the day as she sang the hymn in her reedy voice. As a kid, he'd loved to spend a weekend with GeeGee Gwen. She'd been ancient—in her nineties—but sharp as a tack. She'd kept her wit right to the end of her life.

He wondered what GeeGee Gwen would think of the predicament he'd landed himself in. What advice would she have for him if she were alive today? Maybe she would have told him to develop a thicker skin. He knew he was innocent of leaking information to the opposition campaign, and his actual integrity had to matter more to him than the lies of others. He knew he hadn't betrayed Tammy Treehorn by exposing what she'd hoped to keep hidden. He couldn't even blame her for wanting to keep it a secret, although anybody involved in politics had to know it was almost impossible to keep anything secret nowadays.

With a small shake of his head, he shoved away the thoughts and concentrated on the words of the hymn. Eventually he would let himself analyze and decipher all that had happened in recent months. This was not the day or the hour.

After the congregation took their seats again, Ridley let his gaze roam the sanctuary while someone shared announcements. He recognized no one but the pastor, of course. How could he? Then he realized he'd hoped to catch sight of his neighbor. Not a good impulse. But not surprising either. She'd stayed on his mind after their walk the other day. He supposed it was sympathy for her loss. He'd have to be heartless not to feel sorry for her.

The offering basket came down his pew, pulling him from his wandering thoughts. After dropping in some cash, he focused his attention on the pulpit. It was easy to do since Mick Phelps preached a sermon that held Ridley's interest through to the end. When the congregation rose to sing a closing hymn, Ridley sent up a silent thanks to God for drawing him into town. He'd needed this worship service even more than he'd believed.

As he left the sanctuary, he shook a few more hands and acknowledged a few more words of welcome with smiles and nods of his own. He was already outside the church when he heard his name called, and turned.

"Ridley," Mick repeated as he hurried down the few steps toward him, grinning widely. "Glad to see you here."

"Glad I came."

"Listen, would you like to join my wife and me for Sunday dinner? It'll be a quiet one. Just the three of us. Our daughters are visiting their grandparents in California."

Should he accept? As if to rescue him from making a wrong decision, his mobile phone vibrated in his shirt pocket. Only a few people had this new number. He held up the index finger of his left hand while reaching for his phone with his right. He felt a jolt in his chest when he saw who was calling: Selena Wright. Out of habit, he considered answering it. Then good sense took over and he hit Decline. His gaze darted back to the pastor and good sense triumphed a second time. "I'll have to pass today. But thanks anyway."

"Sure thing." There seemed to be real regret in Mick's eyes.

The pastor could probably become a good friend, given the right circumstances. Only these weren't the right circumstances. Ridley wasn't in the market for new friends. He'd been let down by people he'd thought were friends. Better not to take chances.

Moments later, as he slid onto the driver's seat of his Subaru, his phone vibrated again. He glanced at the screen. Selena again. She wouldn't give up. "Hello."

"Ridley, it's me. Selena."

"I know." He almost asked how she'd discovered his new number. But then he remembered. He'd given it to her, about thirty minutes before she told him she never wanted to see him again. Why hadn't he seen that coming?

"Listen, I left my sweater at your house the last time . . . the last time I was with you. But my key to your front door won't work." She drew a breath, then demanded, "Where are you anyway?"

"Out of town."

"Where?"

He wanted to tell her it was none of her business where he was, but he swallowed the retort, along with the anger that rose with it.

After a few seconds of silence, she must have realized he wasn't going to answer. "So how I do I get in?"

"You don't get in, Selena. You'll have to wait until I'm back in town. I'll make sure your sweater is returned as soon as possible."

She called him a name, and the phone went silent.

Ridley dropped the offending object onto the passenger seat, then raked the fingers of both hands through his hair, pushing down his anger a second time. He could at least be glad he'd changed the locks on his house before leaving town. Not that he believed Selena had left her sweater there. Whatever her reasons for wanting inside, it had nothing to do with an article of clothing.

He turned the key to start the engine, then drove toward home, thoughts churning once again.

He'd first met Selena Wright at a party about seven months ago. A good friend of his next-door neighbor, Selena was pretty with a quick wit and a bright laugh. She and Ridley had hit it off at once.

They both liked basketball, mountain biking, and technology, to name a few things they had in common. Ridley had assumed they would go on discovering similarities. Instead, differences had begun to crop up. He'd known, long before the disaster with the Treehorn campaign surfaced, that he and Selena weren't going to be together for the long term. He'd known it was time to end their relationship. Still, he hadn't expected her quick wit to transform into a razor-sharp tongue, cutting him to ribbons when he was down.

☙

Jessica left the kitchen, carrying a mug of hot cocoa in her right hand. Movement beyond the large living-room window drew her gaze in time to see a red Subaru pass by. Dust swirled down the road in its wake. Her neighbor, returning from town. She hadn't seen Ridley since the day they'd walked together. It seemed they both preferred to keep to themselves when possible.

"And in a statement from her campaign headquarters, Ms. Treehorn, after a lengthy silence, promised to hold a press conference later this week."

Sipping her cocoa, she looked toward the television in the corner of the room.

"Our reporter asked if staff member Ridley Chesterfield, who has been accused of leaking the files regarding the pro-life candidate's abortion, would be present at the press conference. The representative stated that Mr. Chesterfield no longer works for the Treehorn campaign and refused any further comment."

Jessica nearly choked on her cocoa when her neighbor—handsome, smiling—flashed onto the screen, standing beside the candidate. What on earth?

Since the news clip was over, she turned and walked to her studio, where she sat in front of her computer and opened a browser. She typed in his name. Links to articles, blog posts, and news sites filled the computer screen. She clicked the first one and began to read.

Half an hour later, she twirled her chair away from the computer.

No wonder her neighbor had preferred not to give his last name. She didn't know the full story of what had happened inside the political candidate's campaign—even she could spot the many holes in the reporting—and she wasn't completely sure what Ridley's role had been. But she knew the internet wolves were out in force, tearing to shreds whatever and whoever they could.

KUNA, IDAHO
Sunday, July 20, 1930

Andrew was pulled from a dreamless sleep by a sound he couldn't immediately identify. As he sat up, he heard it again. A groan, long and low. Predawn light filtered through the curtain, enough for him to see his wife, curled on her side, her face grimaced in pain.

"Helen?"

"Get . . . Mother."

He jumped out of bed, his heart racing. "Do you—"

"Hurry."

Barefoot and wearing only pajamas, he dashed across the hall. "Mother Greyson." He knocked on the door. "Helen needs you."

His mother-in-law answered within moments, clad in her nightgown, her graying hair disheveled. He'd never seen her wearing anything but a dress and sensible shoes, with every strand of hair in place. Her appearance seemed to add to the fear he felt.

"Helen sent me for you. I think . . . I think she's in pain."

Andrew saw alarm in Madge Greyson's eyes before she brushed

past him. He followed right behind but had barely reached the room he shared with Helen before Madge said, "Tell Frank to call the doctor."

He looked over his shoulder and saw his father-in-law hurrying toward the living room, pulling on his robe as he went. He turned to tell Mother Greyson so, but the words caught in his throat. The sheet beneath Helen, now exposed, was stained red with her blood. Panic clawed at his chest.

"What can I do?" He hurried to the opposite side of the bed.

"Pray," Madge answered softly.

He knelt on the floor and reached for his wife's hand. "I'm here, Helen. Don't be afraid. It'll be okay."

She met his gaze. Her dark eyes were filled with fear.

"It'll be okay," he repeated.

She groaned again, a primal sound, coming from somewhere deep inside of her. Andrew hadn't thought he could be more frightened. He'd been wrong. Her hand squeezed his, and it seemed she had the strength to snap his fingers in two.

Frank Greyson appeared in the bedroom doorway. "The doctor's on his way. What can I do?"

"Put water on the stove to boil. The doctor might need it. And bring me some old bedding. There's some in a box inside the shed to the right of the door."

Frank disappeared without a word.

Andrew wished he'd been the one sent to boil water and fetch old bedding. Action would have been easier than kneeling here, helpless to ease his wife's pain.

The minutes passed like agonizing hours, but finally Dr. Russell entered the bedroom. Edmond Russell was a physician whose mere appearance demanded trust. A man in his late fifties, he had a full head of stone-gray hair. His beard was closely trimmed. Even in the middle of the night, he wore suit coat, vest, and trousers. His black shoes shone, as if he hadn't walked across the dusty driveway to enter the Greyson house.

The doctor took Mother Greyson's place beside the bed. "What have we here?" He leaned over Helen.

Her response was another long groan.

"Can you do something to help her, Dr. Russell?" Andrew asked.

The doctor looked at him. "I think it would be good if you joined Frank. Husbands are generally in the way at a time like this."

"It's too soon for the baby to come. She's not due for another two months."

"I know, son. I know. You go on now and let me see to your wife."

Reluctant to leave, yet reluctant to stay at the same time, Andrew joined his father-in-law in the living room. Frank's expression mirrored the tumultuous feelings roiling inside Andrew. He sat on the sofa, neither man speaking. Andrew wanted to pray but didn't seem to know how.

"For we know not what we should pray for as we ought." The whisper in his heart caused him to still. *"But the Spirit itself maketh intercession for us with groanings which cannot be uttered."*

His fears didn't vanish—he could still hear the sounds of Helen in pain through the bedroom door—but the Bible verse did bring him comfort. It helped to know that the Holy Spirit was praying for Helen and their baby when he couldn't find the words to do so himself.

Just as it had been as they waited for the doctor to arrive, so now the minutes dragged as they waited for whatever news the doctor would bring them. Waited for it. Dreaded it.

Daylight filled the living room by the time Dr. Russell appeared in the doorway. His expression was grim as he dried his hands on a towel. Both Andrew and Frank rose to their feet.

"I'm sorry," the doctor said at last.

Frank's hand alighted on Andrew's shoulder.

"There was nothing I could do."

"The baby?" Andrew whispered.

The doctor nodded. "Stillborn. He was too small to survive outside the womb, I'm afraid."

"*He.*" A son. Andrew swallowed. "And Helen?"

"She'll be fine, given a little time. She's weak from blood loss, but she is young and healthy. She'll make a full recovery."

"May I . . . May I see her?"

"Madge is attending to her right now. Give her a little more time, and then you may go in." He shook his head slowly. "I'm very sorry, my boy."

Andrew sank back onto the sofa, a crushing weight pressing on his chest as he remembered his first reaction to the news that Helen was pregnant. He hadn't been happy about it. He'd thought it a bad time for them to start a family. He'd hated the idea of moving in with his in-laws and being dependent upon them for the care of his family. And now . . . Now there wouldn't be a baby.

Guilt and regret washed over him, and he wept.

Chapter 6

Ridley watched dawn creep across the ceiling of the bedroom, as awake now as he'd been when he retired around midnight. He blamed Selena's phone call for the sleepless night. For a few days, since his arrival in Hope Springs, he'd avoided dwelling on all that had happened in Boise. His former girlfriend's call had opened the floodgates again.

He'd taken a cut in pay to go to work as the IT specialist for the Tammy Treehorn campaign. It had been worth it because he believed in the woman. He'd been hired to make certain the campaign's network was secure, that opponents or troublemakers of any ilk couldn't hack into the Treehorn computers and devices. He'd done his job and done it well. His downfall had been blind trust. He'd assumed everyone was who they appeared to be and everyone meant what they said.

"I'm an idiot."

Although disappointed by Tammy's silence to the press—especially that she hadn't spoken out in his defense—he sincerely hoped she would survive the tumult, that she would be able to rise above the disclosures about her past. If not this year and this campaign, then in the future. He hoped less positive things for Tammy's aide, Rachelle Ford. His gut told him she had more to do with this mess than it seemed on the surface. In fact, he should have paid heed to his gut when she'd given him that laptop with instructions to recover the data from the hard drive. It hadn't been an unusual request. He'd done the very same thing many times over the course of his career. But there had been something in her manner that seemed . . . off. If he'd questioned it . . .

He groaned as he shoved aside the sheet and sat on the side of the bed. He needed to stop going over it again and again and again. It didn't matter that there were pieces that didn't make sense, even to him. He needed to lie low and wait out the storm. Then he could have a life again. But what would that life look like? With his integrity in question, who would want to hire him to manage their confidential data? He might as well face it. He was finished both in politics and in any sort of internet security work. So what was next for him? It seemed to him he would be starting from scratch. If true, he'd best discover something he could be passionate about.

"Give it time," his stepdad had told him.

Time. His life had been circling the bowl, and the advice he got was to wait it out. Be patient. Give it time.

"Stop it," he muttered. Then he stood and headed for the shower, hoping hot water would wash away the persistent thoughts.

Half an hour later, hair still damp and feet bare, he went downstairs. He opened the door to the utility room and let Kris into the kitchen. She went straight to her food and water bowls and sat down, watching him with expectation in her eyes. Her tail slapped against the floor as he opened the pantry door to remove the bag of kibble. Amazing how quickly they'd established this routine.

When he'd found the stray, he hadn't expected to be glad to have her for a companion. He hadn't owned a pet since leaving for college and hadn't thought he missed having one around. Just proved a person didn't always know what he was missing until he found it.

Kris gave a clipped bark.

"Yeah, yeah. It's coming."

He scooped a cup of kibble into her bowl. The dog buried her nose in the food and crunching sounds filled the kitchen. He suspected she feared more food wouldn't be forthcoming.

"That's okay, Kris. We'll have you fattened up in no time."

While the dog finished scarfing down her kibble, Ridley scrambled himself a couple of eggs. He ate them standing up, hip leaned against the counter, his gaze moving around the room, checking his work. His mom had her yellow kitchen. She'd be pleased.

As he stood there, he became aware of the ticking of the clock on the wall. Then the refrigerator began to hum. The two soft sounds made him aware of the overall silence now that he and the dog were finished eating. He'd come to the mountains for solitude, and now that he had it, he didn't much care for it. Maybe he should have gone to Arizona to see his mom rather than coming to Hope Springs. Maybe isolation wasn't the answer. He hadn't seen a newspaper or watched the news on TV or surfed the internet in days. What was happening now? Did anyone care that he'd left Boise? Had the attention turned elsewhere?

He didn't expect his notoriety to last, of course. His name would soon fade from the memory of most people. It was the lingering thread on the internet that concerned him. All that had been said, all the accusations, proven and unproven, would be there, in any internet search by a possible employer, forever. And there wasn't anything he could personally do to get the facts of the case listed first. That's what stung the most.

He turned toward the sink, nipping the temptation to go buy a paper. He needed to follow the advice to give it time. Give it all time. Like somebody had once said, never explain. Your friends didn't need it and your enemies wouldn't believe you anyway.

He looked at the dog. "I could look up who said that if I had an internet connection or something beyond 1X service on my phone. Good thing I don't. Slippery slope, as Mom would say."

Kris cocked her head to one side, as if trying to figure him out.

Ridley chuckled, but it was a sound without humor.

"Come on, girl. Let's get some work done."

⟨◦⟩

Jessica stepped back from the easel and eyed the canvas. Satisfaction warmed her chest, and the feeling surprised her. It had been absent from her work for such a long, long time. As if noticing the difference, the baby moved inside her. She covered the spot with her hands.

"Hello, there, pumpkin," she whispered, a smile tugging at the corners of her mouth. "What do you think? Do you like it?"

Some days she was so afraid of the future, of raising this baby alone. Some days she wondered if she would look at her child and only remember the sadness that had been present at the time of its conception. But on other days, she let joy of this new life blossom. Today was one of those days.

She stroked her rounded belly, wondering if the baby was a boy or a girl. She'd told her doctor she didn't want to know the gender of her child. Perhaps that had been the shock talking—shock over the deaths of husband and daughter, shock over discovering she was pregnant—but she'd stuck with the decision through all of the weeks since her ultrasound. Joe had called her stubborn. In fact, those had been almost his last words—angry words—to her the morning he died.

The joy she'd felt moments before evaporated. Tears pooled as she sank onto her work stool.

Other fights flickered through her memory—furious words tossed across rooms, slamming doors, buckets of shed tears, screeching tires as Joe drove away. To others, they'd appeared a happy couple. How well they'd lived that public lie.

She reached for a tissue and dried her eyes.

What if she'd become pregnant weeks or months earlier? What if Joe had known she carried his child? Would it have changed anything? A sound—half sob, half laugh—escaped her throat as another question formed: Would she have wanted to become pregnant if she'd known Joe was cheating on her? That he meant to leave her?

"O God," she whispered.

The words felt like a prayer, and that prayer drew her gaze across the room to the bookshelf. Sunlight spilled onto her great-grandfather's Bible. She rose and went to it, brushing her fingertips across the worn cover before picking it up and carrying it out to the living room. As she settled onto the sofa, she would have sworn she heard her grandma whisper, *"At last."*

Jessica almost feared lifting the cover. Would the binding fall apart when she did? But after a lengthy wait, she took hold of the leather edge and opened it. The delicate Bible pages were slightly curled, the first page torn at the bottom. She turned it carefully, then paused to stare at the title page.

To our beloved son,
Andrew Michael Henning,
on the occasion of his graduation
from the university.
Follow God and you will never lose your way.
Papa and Mama
Kuna, Idaho
May 1929

Jessica's heart fluttered as she read the words. She'd never known her great-grandfather, and yet she felt the strangest connection to Andrew Henning as she ran a fingertip over the inscription. The writing seemed slightly unsteady. Had the words been written by Andrew's father or mother? His father, she decided. It seemed more of a masculine hand.

She imagined a man, wearing a work shirt and overalls and sporting a neatly trimmed beard, seated at a desk, lamplight spilling onto the open book as he wrote in it. Perhaps he held a fountain pen between his calloused fingers. Perhaps his wife stood behind him, one hand on the back of the chair as she looked over his shoulder, smiling.

First generation Idahoans, her great-great-grandparents had been farmers. Simple people, according to her grandma. What had they sacrificed in order to send their son to college? It must have been significant. And when Andrew graduated from the university, this had been their gift to him—a Bible and the advice to follow God. What's more, he'd treasured it enough to keep it through the years and then want to pass it along, first to his daughter and now to his great-granddaughter.

Jessica slid a finger deeper into the pages and opened the Bible to Psalms. There she found passages underlined, both in pencil and in ink. A few notes had been written in the narrow margin. For some reason, the tiny, faded script made her smile. Andrew Henning hadn't just kept the Bible. He'd used it.

"I wish I'd known you," she whispered.

The sound of a small engine penetrated her musings. A break in the normal silence. She slid the old Bible off her lap and walked to the back door. A few moments later she saw Ridley on a riding lawnmower, cutting the wild grasses in the field behind his house. Kris bounded around him, running ahead, circling back behind, barking happily. The sight made her laugh aloud.

Suddenly, almost as if the dog had heard Jessica's mirth, Kris tore away and raced across the land that separated the two properties. Jessica moved to one of the chairs on the patio to await the dog's arrival. Before that happened, the mower went silent. Jessica lifted her gaze in time to see Ridley hop off the seat and stare in her direction. She waved at him. What else could she do? In answer, he strode in her direction.

Kris arrived, tail wagging, tongue lolling. But despite her obvious pleasure, she didn't jump on Jessica. Instead, like the day on the road, the dog sat and waited for a command.

"Hello, girl." Jessica ruffled the dog's ears, but her eyes returned to Ridley. Remembering what she'd heard and read the previous evening, she couldn't help wondering how much of it was true. Empathy welled in her chest, even without knowing if he was guilty of what had been accused. She knew something about wanting to hide from the world, and she was thankful her own painful secrets were still that—secrets.

Stopping a few feet behind the dog, Ridley said, "I can't seem to keep Kris away from you."

"It's all right. I like her, too, now that she isn't throwing herself on me."

His expression turned serious. "She'd better not ever do that to you again." His gaze flicked to Jessica's abdomen and back again. "You could get hurt."

"I'm tougher than I look."

One of his eyebrows rose slightly. His mouth hinted at a grin. "You know what? I believe you."

She smiled, realizing she believed it too. She *was* tougher than she looked. "Thanks."

"Come on, Kris." He took hold of the dog's collar. "I've got to finish the mowing."

Jessica nodded her farewell. Then, without giving herself time to consider what she was about to do, she said, "Ridley, I'm fixing fried chicken for dinner. I'm in the mood for comfort food. The kind I usually avoid. Would you like to join me?"

That same eyebrow cocked.

"I'll have too many leftovers if you don't. Six o'clock?"

"Okay. I'll be there. What can I bring?"

"Just yourself." Her smile returned. "And Kris, of course. She's welcome too."

PORTLAND, OREGON
Thanksgiving Day, 1930

Andrew stood at the window in the attic bedroom, staring out at the rainy day. The gray skies befit his mood. Today was Thanksgiving. He would go to church with his cousin Mark and Mark's family, then share the Thanksgiving meal at their table. But all he wanted was to be back home with Helen.

He'd found a job in Portland at the end of August. He was

employed in a bank again, but this time as a teller. He didn't need his college degree for the work he did, but it was better than gathering eggs in a chicken coop. Or would be if his wife had been willing to join him there. She wasn't. *Not yet* was what she wrote in her letters.

"Not yet," he whispered, his gaze lowering to the stationery on the table he used as a writing desk.

Maybe it had been a mistake to leave her so soon after the loss of their baby boy. Ralph, they had named him, after a favorite uncle of Helen's. It was the name chiseled into the small tombstone in the Kuna cemetery.

Shaking off the memory, he lifted Helen's letter and read it again. He almost had it memorized. No matter how hard he tried, he couldn't hear tenderness in her words. They were cool and distant, as if he were a mere acquaintance and not her husband.

I hope you are well, she'd written before signing her name. No words of love. And that wasn't like her. At least not like the woman he'd married. Helen had always been demonstrative and vocal in her affection. But these past months . . .

He placed the letter back onto the table as he turned from the window. He'd better hurry or he wouldn't be ready in time.

Two hours later, Andrew sat beside Mark Henning in the center pew of the church as the Thanksgiving service drew to a close. On Mark's other side were his wife, Nancy, and their two young boys, Jefferson and Abraham.

Remind me of all I have to be thankful for, Andrew silently begged God. *I know it is much.*

He had employment when so many others were unemployed.

He had food to eat when so many others remained hungry. He had a roof over his head when so many others were homeless. He had a loving family when so many others were all alone.

A family who loves me.

Instead of bringing him comfort, the words had the opposite effect. He felt alone. He needed to see Helen. He needed to hold her in his arms. He needed to feel the sweet warmth of her lips against his. He needed to lie in bed and hear the soft rhythm of her breathing as she slept.

I need to be at home.

It shamed him, how tempted he was to throw away the job that had taken him many months to find. Wasn't it enough that he earned money and helped to support his wife, even if they had to be apart so he could do it? He'd felt like a failure when he was jobless. Why wasn't he satisfied now that he was employed again?

If it wasn't for her silence . . .

The service over, the Henning family, including Andrew, walked toward their home five blocks to the east. A few automobiles chugged by them, but mostly the streets were devoid of traffic. Halfway home, Mark patted Andrew's shoulder. "Maybe you should call home. Might lift your spirits to talk to Helen rather than wait for a letter."

"Sorry." He forced an apologetic smile. "Didn't mean to look so down in the mouth."

"Hey. It's understandable. I'd feel mighty blue if I was away from Nancy for months at a time."

"Long distance isn't cheap. Last I checked, a few minutes would cost about twenty dollars. I can't afford that." *Especially if Helen doesn't want to talk to me*, he added silently.

"Well, then, what about a trip home for Christmas? Round trip on the train is about sixteen dollars."

"No time. I'll only have Christmas Day off."

"Then have Helen come here. She'll be more than welcome."

His gaze flicked ahead on the sidewalk to Nancy. How would she feel about having another person invade her household? Things were crowded as it was. Andrew tried to stay out of the way, but still—

"Nancy and I talked about it this morning," Mark said, apparently anticipating Andrew's concern. "In fact, it was her idea to ask Helen to come to see you."

Andrew rubbed the back of his neck. "I suppose I could manage it. It would mean a longer visit. A lot better than just a couple of minutes on the phone."

"Sure you could manage it. And we could kick in a little money, too, if you need it."

"It would be good to see her." A smile tugged at the corners of his mouth, and for the first time that day, he felt a lightness in his spirit. "I'll write to her today."

"Good." Mark patted his shoulder a second time. "Glad that's settled."

"Yeah. Glad that's settled."

He let the smile spread. A few weeks and he would see Helen. Just a few weeks.

Chapter 7

"What was I *thinking?*"

It wasn't only that Jessica rarely allowed herself to eat fried foods. It was that she hadn't cooked a full dinner in over six months. There was no pleasure in preparing meals for one. She had to force herself to get all of the daily nutrients required by her pregnancy. But now she had extended the invitation to Ridley Chesterfield, and a decent meal was required.

"What *was* I thinking?"

She made a quick run into town to buy the ingredients for her planned menu. In addition to the fried chicken—prepared the way her grandma had made it—she would have deviled eggs, corn bread, and fresh green beans sautéed with mushrooms. There was decaf iced tea in the refrigerator. If Ridley didn't care for that beverage, he could have water to drink. For dessert, she would make a root-beer cake.

In the grocery store, she moved quickly up and down the aisles, tossing items into her cart, then checking them off the list. She was down to the last few purchases when she turned around an endcap and almost bumped carts with Billie Fisher.

"Jessica."

"Hi, Billie." Billie Fisher was a longtime friend, one of the few whose phone calls had persisted over the past months despite Jessica's resistance. Billie had also been Angela's first-grade teacher at the time of the accident.

Billie's smile was both sad and filled with understanding. "How are you?"

"I'm good."

"I never see you anymore."

Jessica chose to nod and say nothing.

"How much longer until the baby comes?"

"The end of August. Maybe early September. I was nearly three weeks late with Angela." Saying that, remembering it, was bittersweet, and she felt her heart catch. The flight instinct kicked in, and she wished for escape.

"Could we meet for lunch sometime?" Billie asked. "I'm off for summer break."

She resisted the urge to run away, reminding herself that she was determined to get out more, to start living. "Sure. I'd like that." Her answer probably surprised Billie, as she'd issued other invitations that Jessica had always declined.

"Good. I'll call you. Soon." With a little wave, Billie moved on.

First inviting her neighbor to dinner and now promising to go to lunch with an old friend. Her mother would be pleased when Jessica told her what she'd done. She supposed she was pleased with herself. They might be small steps, baby steps, but at least she was moving forward and not staying stuck in a rut.

She hurried through the remainder of her shopping and was checked out and on her way in under twenty minutes. At home, she emptied her shopping bags, then decided to do a quick straightening of the living room and her studio before she baked the root-beer cake and corn bread. She didn't want Ridley to think her a complete slob.

Shortly before six o'clock, the house was in order, the dinner prepared, and Jessica was showered and dressed with her hair blown dry. She'd even remembered to apply a little mascara, something she hadn't done since the day of her grandma's funeral. At least tonight she wasn't likely to cry it off, leaving black circles under her eyes.

The ringing of the doorbell, although expected, made her heart jump. It felt strange to have a guest, invited or otherwise. Brushing back hair from her face, she went to answer it.

Ridley smiled when their gazes met. From behind his back, he whisked out a bouquet of wildflowers. "Not much," he said with a shrug, "but I didn't want to come empty-handed."

"I like wildflowers." She took them from him, then took a step back.

"I thought you might."

"Where's Kris?"

"I decided to leave her at home." He stepped inside, his gaze moving slowly around the room. "This is nice. Nothing like my folks' place, though, is it?"

"No."

"Down in the city, you get used to house plans being more cookie cutter in some neighborhoods."

She offered her own small smile. "Can you call two houses on a dead-end road out in the middle of nowhere a neighborhood?"

"I guess we can if we want to."

It felt good, having him in her home, and that surprised her too. It hadn't felt normal to have anyone there—not even her parents—in many months. Even before Joe died, it hadn't felt right to have guests. There'd been too many emotions to hide from others. Out in public, away from the house, it had been easier to pretend. But right here, within these walls . . .

She drew a quick breath and forced an even brighter smile. "I'll put these flowers in water, and then we can eat. Dinner is ready."

⌒∽⌒

Ridley followed Jessica as far as the doorway to the kitchen. He stopped there, leaning his shoulder against the archway, and watched as she put the wildflowers into a large mason jar and filled it with tap water. Delicious odors filled the air. He hoped she didn't hear his stomach when it growled in response.

The table in the adjacent dining room was set for two. Early evening sunlight spilled through the slats of the mini blinds, pooling on the floor behind the closest chair.

"Can I help with anything?" he asked, looking in Jessica's direction again.

"You could take those to the table." She tipped her head toward two serving dishes on the raised counter.

"Sure." He took a plate with squares of corn bread in one hand and a bowl of green beans in the other and carried them into the dining room.

Jessica followed behind him with a platter of fried chicken. After setting it in the center of the table, she motioned to a chair. "Please. Sit."

Instead of doing so immediately, he stepped to her place and pulled out the chair. She glanced up at him, her surprise evident, then dropped her gaze and settled onto the seat. For some reason, the look in her eyes made his heart pinch. A woman like her shouldn't have to look surprised over an act of simple courtesy.

Softly clearing his throat, he moved to his place and sat down. "This is real nice of you. To ask me over. As pesky as Kris has been, I should've been the one to ask you to dinner. I owe you." Funny, he'd been determined to remain anonymous when he came to Hope Springs, determined not to get involved with anybody, and here he was, barely a week later, sitting down to a home-cooked meal with his attractive—and very pregnant—neighbor.

Like Mom would say, I need my head examined.

Jessica slid the platter of chicken toward him. "Help yourself."

In the living room, he'd noticed a couple of plaques on the wall, each with words from a familiar Bible verse. Assuming they meant something to his hostess, he said, "Would you mind if I said grace?"

Again he saw surprise in her eyes. Surprise but not displeasure. "I'd like that," she answered before bowing her head.

"For food in a world where many walk in hunger, for faith in a world where many walk in fear, for friends in a world where many walk alone, we give You thanks, O Lord. Amen."

"Amen," she whispered, then looked at him. "Thanks, Ridley. That's a nice blessing."

"It's one my mom taught me when I was a kid."

Silence settled over the dining room, as if Jessica didn't know where to take the conversation from there. Then for the second time, she nudged the platter in his direction. "Better dish up. The food's growing cold."

Ridley helped himself, realizing he didn't know where to take the conversation either. If this had been a first date, he'd have had a better idea. After all, he'd been on lots of first dates in the past couple of decades, beginning when he was fifteen and ending with Selena. He'd had more first dates than he cared to count, come to think of it, because, despite appearances to the contrary, he wasn't a confirmed bachelor. He would like to meet someone special with whom he could have a long-term relationship. He'd like to fall in love, marry, have a family. Not right now, of course. Right now he didn't want any emotional entanglements. Hadn't the energy for them.

"Ridley?"

The sound of Jessica's voice drew him from his thoughts, and he looked at her.

"I should tell you something."

He cocked an eyebrow, waiting.

"I saw a photo of you on the news the other night. It was about the Treehorn campaign."

Hunger became a stone in his belly.

"All I want to add is that I'm sorry this is happening to you."

Politeness kept her from asking, but he saw the questions in her eyes nonetheless. "I'm not sure what it said, but just for the record, it isn't true that I was the one who leaked the information about Ms. Treehorn. I believed in her and wouldn't have done anything to damage her run for office."

With a nod, she lifted the butter dish and held it toward him. "For your corn bread?"

Relieved that she didn't press for more details, he offered a fleeting smile. "Thanks." He took the dish, and their fingers brushed in passing. For some reason, the touch drained the last of the tension from him.

"You told me you moved around a lot because of your dad's job." She put a drumstick on her plate. "Where all did you live?"

"California. Texas. Florida. Pennsylvania. Ohio. Colorado. Oregon. Idaho. We were living in Meridian for my senior year in high school. I liked it there, so I came back after I graduated from college."

Her eyes had widened. "You really did move around a lot."

"Yeah."

"I've lived in one state and only two towns in my whole life. In fact, I've lived in two houses in my whole life. I feel a little . . . What's the word? Provincial?"

The self-deprecating look she tossed across the table made him chuckle. He didn't know if she was provincial, but he did believe she was sweet. Considering her tragic losses of the past winter, she had plenty of reason not to be.

He took a bite of the fried chicken. As soon as he could, he said, "Wow. That's good."

"Thanks." Her smile blossomed. "It's my grandma's recipe. She taught me how to make fried chicken like this when I was a girl." She closed her eyes for a moment, still smiling. "I loved going to her house on weekends when I was little. She always taught me something new in the kitchen. I never became a great cook, but anything I do well is because of Grandma. Even my mom says that."

He could almost see the memories written on her face as they floated through her mind.

She opened her eyes again. "I loved Grandma so much."

"She's passed away?"

"Last month."

So recent. And right on top of two other deaths. Ridley wondered how Jessica could bear it. Made his own troubles—ruined reputation, job loss, betrayals—seem less important.

"She was eighty-six years old and a very special woman." Her voice softened. "I hope I live and die as well as she did."

Ridley decided it was time to take the conversation in another direction, so he asked a question about Hope Springs. That's where they remained for the rest of the meal.

PORTLAND, OREGON

Tuesday, December 23, 1930

Excitement welled in Andrew's chest as he watched the train roll into the station. His anticipation was not unlike that of his cousin's boys, waiting for Christmas morning. Any moment now, Helen would step out of one of those passenger cars. His heart seemed to pound in his ears as he looked for her.

"Daddy!" a young girl in a red dress with frilly white petticoats shouted before tearing away from her mother and racing into the arms of a man just off the train.

Envy gripped Andrew's chest as he watched the grinning father lift the girl into the air. It surprised him, how often that profound sense of loss swept over him. Loss . . . and guilt. Guilt because he'd been less than excited about the timing of Helen's pregnancy. If he hadn't been so worried about providing for a family, if he hadn't fought with Helen so often . . . Even months later it felt like the stillbirth had been his fault. In his head, he knew that wasn't true. If only he could convince his heart.

He forced his gaze away from the joyous father-daughter reunion in time to see Helen step from a car farther down the station ramp. She looked nervous, even a little anxious.

"Helen!" He lifted his arm high above his head. "Helen!"

She found him with her eyes at last, and a small smile lifted the corners of her mouth.

He felt another catch in his chest as he moved toward her. "Helen." He embraced her, breathing in the scent of her favorite cologne. After several heartbeats, he drew back enough to kiss her. "You look wonderful."

She laughed softly as she patted the curls that showed beneath her hat. "I doubt that. I'm exhausted."

"The train was late. They said it was due to weather."

"It snowed from Boise all the way through the Blue Mountains. I didn't think we would make it up one of the mountains, the snow was coming so hard."

The words seemed stilted, as if they were two strangers having a chance conversation.

He took her suitcase with one hand, then hooked her elbow with the other. "Let's get out of here. Mark and Nancy can't wait to meet you. The boys too."

"I hope my coming isn't too much of an imposition."

"It's not. They've been looking forward to your visit." He squeezed her arm against his side. "Come on. Mark loaned me his Ford so I could pick you up."

"That was nice of him."

"He's a good guy. He and Nancy have been very generous and kind to me."

She was silent awhile, then said, "So were my parents."

"Yes," he answered without hesitation. "They were. They still are. I love your folks. You know that."

Helen stopped walking, causing Andrew to do the same. She stared up at him for a long while, and in her eyes he saw that he hadn't been forgiven for taking the job in Portland. Not yet. What would it take for that to happen? Was time enough, or was something else required of him? His absence certainly hadn't made her heart grow fonder. Not that he could tell, anyway.

He released her arm. "Come on. Nancy's planned a special welcome dinner for you." He turned and moved toward the automobile. The click of her heels told him she followed.

Frustration replaced excitement. Their reunion was not turning out as he'd hoped it would. He'd expected her to be happy to see him. He'd expected her to have missed him. It seemed neither was true.

How do I fix it? How do I make it better?

He didn't know if that was a prayer or simply trying to work things out in his own head. And he didn't like that he couldn't tell the difference.

Chapter 8

Jessica stepped into the room ahead of Ridley, flipping on the overhead lights as she moved through the doorway. "And this is where I work."

Her workroom wasn't merely a bedroom that had been converted into an artist studio. Ridley could tell that right off. This room had been designed for her use. Counters lined three walls, much of it cluttered with what he supposed were art supplies. Large windows let in natural light, but there was plenty of electrical lighting as well. Two easels were set up, their backs to him, each with a canvas on it. He resisted the urge to peek at whatever was on them. In the corner off to his right he could see an iMac with an extra-large display, while in the center of the room sat an island. The top of the island was splashed with various paint colors and mediums. A couple of cloths lay wadded up near one corner, and a large toolbox sat in the center. There was a sink to his left. It, too, was stained with colors—bright red, olive green, teal, sky blue, sunshine yellow.

"Impressive," he said at last. "What do you paint?"

"Wall decor mostly, but I'm a crafter too. I enjoy working with leather. I make bracelets."

His gaze returned to the computer. The screen was black. If he touched a key, would it awaken? Would he see a browser window? Would he be able to find the local news in a few clicks of the keyboard? Not that he needed to see it.

"Would you like to see one of my creations?" Jessica asked.

Grateful for a reason to turn away from the temptation, he answered, "Sure."

She opened a drawer, lifted something from within, and placed it on the center island.

He stepped closer to examine it. A bracelet, made of narrow strips of leather, rope, and wooden beads. From the center hung a sterling silver ichthus. "It's beautiful, Jessica." He glanced up. "Your husband must've been proud of what you do."

The change in her expression was infinitesimal and yet it struck him powerfully. Did he hear her suck in a breath before she turned away? He couldn't be sure. But one thing he knew: he'd hurt her by mentioning her husband. The last thing he'd meant to do.

"That's all there is to see." She dropped the bracelet back into the drawer, her voice brisker than before.

"Thanks for showing all of this to me. And thanks for dinner too." He moved out of the studio, on his way to the front door, then stopped and turned again. "And listen. Thanks for not asking a bunch of questions about the Treehorn thing. You're the first person who's discovered my identity and hasn't tried to interrogate me about what happened. Well, except for Pastor Phelps. He knows who I am."

"I didn't know you'd met him."

"Yeah, we met. And I went to hear him preach yesterday." He waited for her to say something, perhaps admit that Hope Springs Community was her church home. She said nothing. "Well, thanks again. It was a nice evening."

⌒∾⌒

After closing the door, Jessica leaned her forehead against it and let the hurt wash over her.

"Your husband must've been proud of what you do."

Had Joe ever been proud of her? She couldn't remember. Maybe once, early in their marriage. He'd built her the studio then, before she got pregnant with Angela. Neither of them had suspected she would one day sell her creations. The studio had been to help keep her occupied and less lonely during his frequent travels. But somewhere along the way, Joe had stopped caring what she did with her art or anything else. He'd barely noticed her toward the end.

She turned, now leaning her back against the door.

"I don't want to live like this anymore." Joe's voice was low but full of anger. "I want out. I want a divorce."

She twirled away from the closed bedroom door, sucking in a gasp. "A divorce?"

"Yes. I'm miserable. You're miserable."

"We can't divorce, Joe. We can't break up our family."

"Jessica, we're already broken. Can't you see that?"

She moved to the bed. Silent tears streaked her cheeks as she sank onto the edge of the mattress. He'd made love to her in this bed last night, and this morning he wanted a divorce. How could that be? If he didn't love her, how could he—

"I love someone else, Jess."

She gasped aloud this time.

"You must've known."

He might as well have called her stupid. And yes, deep down in her heart, she supposed she had known he was seeing another woman, that he'd been cheating on her for a long time. Even when he was home, he was absent. But last night . . .

"We'll get through Christmas. Then I'll move out and we can tell our families."

She went cold. "You want to live here with me and pretend everything's all right?"

"Why not? It's just more of the same."

She wanted to hit him. She wanted to throw up. Either. Both.

"We'll keep it together through Christmas for Angela's sake."

"Joe." She held out a hand toward him. "Don't do this. We can get counseling. We can save our marriage. We can be happy again. It isn't right to throw it all away. God wouldn't want us to give up."

He walked to the bedroom door. "Angela's waiting for me. We've got Christmas shopping to do." The anger was gone from his voice, leaving only frustration in its wake.

"Don't go yet. We haven't settled anything."

Over his shoulder, he tossed her an irritated look. "It's already settled, Jess. You'vre just too stubborn to admit it." He opened the door and left the room.

That was the last time she'd seen Joe—or Angela—alive.

"And I'm still pretending that we were happy at the end," she whispered, tears blurring her eyes. "All these months later, I'm still pretending. I still care what others think, even when I'm hiding away here by myself."

Honesty required her to admit she did have a bit of a stubborn streak, that she'd clung to Joe and their marriage, in the end more out of desperation than love. And because of Angela.

In her mind, she once again saw her daughter, sitting in the back seat of Joe's car, so excited about a day of Christmas shopping with her dad. She'd worn a bright red knit cap with a fluffy ball sewn to the top and her new red winter coat.

"I'm gonna get you a surprise, Mama. I'm gonna get you a surprise for Christmas."

Why had she allowed Angela to go with Joe that morning? Why hadn't she realized how angry he still was? If she'd faced the truth then—

A groan tore at her throat, and she bent over at the waist. Her tears splattered the floor. "God, why? Why my precious girl?"

There was no answer from above. She'd asked the question so many times over the months, and there'd never been an answer. Only pain.

Talk about it.

She straightened slowly, her breath catching. For a moment, she almost wondered if God was answering her at last. But why would He? She'd shut Him out as surely as she'd shut out the rest of the world. Still, she pushed away from the door and walked to the phone, pulled there by a need that couldn't be ignored. She pressed the speed-dial button and waited for someone to answer.

"Hello?"

Tears threatened again. "Mom, it's me. I need to talk. Could we meet tomorrow?"

"What is it, dear? Is it the baby?"

"No. The baby's fine. I just need to talk. But not over the phone."

"Of course. Come for lunch. We'll have the house to ourselves."

"Okay. See you then." She drew a quick breath. "I love you, Mom."

"I love you, too, sweetheart. Drive carefully."

"I will. 'Bye."

PORTLAND, OREGON
Christmas Day, 1930

The attic bedroom got plenty cold at night, despite rising heat from the woodstove in the room below. It was cold enough to cause Helen to draw close to Andrew beneath the sheet and blankets. It was the first time since her arrival that she'd touched him voluntarily, but he wasn't sure it counted since she'd done it in her sleep. Still, he took her hand in his and pressed both against the shirt of his pajamas.

There had to be a way for him to close the gap that had been widening between them ever since he'd lost his job at the bank in Boise a year ago. But how? He didn't even know the real cause. It had to be more than his unemployment that had dragged on for months. It had to be more than having to move in with her parents. He thought it was even more than losing the baby. But what? What had caused the change between them?

Maybe if he had some wise counsel . . . But he couldn't talk about his marriage with Mark. His cousin wasn't much older than Andrew himself, although Mark had been married longer. Still, he didn't seem the right person to confide in. If Andrew were at home, he could talk to his father. Or he could talk to his longtime pastor. But he wasn't at home, and there was no one like his father or pastor here in Portland. No one he trusted, at any rate.

Helen murmured something. A few moments later, she pulled her hand from his and moved a few inches away. Cool air seemed to flow between them under the blankets.

"Good morning," he said softly as he rolled onto his left side.

"Morning."

"Merry Christmas." The room was dark, but he pretended he could see her smiling at him.

"You too."

No, maybe he couldn't imagine her smiling. "I don't think anyone else in the house is awake yet. It's too quiet."

"It's cold too."

"Come over here. I'll keep you warm."

The wait seemed to last forever, but finally she slid close to him again. His left arm was under her head, and he held her close with his right. "I'm glad you're here, Helen. It's been lonely without you."

"Mmm."

"Maybe it's time I looked for a place of my own so you can join me. My boss at the bank seems to like me. I think I'll get to stay on."

"No." The word came swiftly, passionately.

It felt like a knife in his chest.

He heard her draw a breath before she continued, her voice gentle now, almost pleading. "It's too soon for me to leave Idaho, Andrew. We need to save money. As long as Mark and Nancy will have you, you should stay with them. I'm all right with Mother and Dad."

A little over a year ago, Helen hadn't been able to bear being parted from Andrew for more than a day. Now she didn't seem to care if they were separated for months, even years.

Her fingers played with the button on his pajamas. "I know you hate being in Portland without me, but you need to understand. The doctor wants me to continue to rest. He . . . he feels that my constitution was compromised when I . . . when I lost the baby."

"Why haven't you told me this before?" He pressed his chin against the top of her head, his eyes staring into the darkness.

"I . . . didn't want to worry you."

He didn't believe her. The realization stunned him. He'd known and accepted that there was a distance between them, but he hadn't expected her to lie.

The creak of a door cut into the growing silence.

"Sounds like the house is stirring," he said, glad for an excuse to pull his arm from beneath his wife's head. He sat on the side of the bed and reached for his robe, putting it on while sliding his feet into his slippers. "I'll go build up the fire. Give it a little while, and the room will warm up."

He hurried down the narrow staircase and into the kitchen. There, he fed the stove with wood. Before he was done, Nancy entered the room, already dressed for the day.

"Merry Christmas, Andrew." She took hold of his shoulders, rose on tiptoes, and kissed his cheek. "Is Helen awake?"

"Yes. She'll be down soon. I promised her some warmth before she had to get up and dress."

"It has been especially cold. The humidity gets into my bones when the temperature dips." She hugged herself and shivered, then turned toward the refrigerator.

Andrew watched as she made preparations for breakfast. It reminded him of the first months of his marriage to Helen. He'd loved watching her as she moved around the kitchen. Just seeing her crack an egg over a hot skillet had brought him pleasure. "What makes a woman fall out of love with her husband?"

Nancy stopped what she was doing and turned to look at him, her eyes wide. "What did you say?"

It wasn't until then that he realized he'd asked the question aloud.

"Andrew?"

"Nothing. Sorry. I was talking to myself. Nothing important."

The look in her eyes told him she'd heard every word.

"I'd better get dressed. I imagine the boys will be up soon and eager to get to the presents under the tree."

"Yes."

Maybe Nancy hadn't needed him to say anything. Maybe Helen's feelings had been obvious from the moment the two women met. But Andrew hadn't realized the fullness of the problem until he'd given voice to the question.

Helen's fallen out of love with me.

And now the question was, how could he win her love back again?

Chapter 9

Ignorance, Ridley discovered, wasn't bliss. Since hiding out in Hope Springs, he'd learned he missed checking his favorite blogs and news sites whenever he wanted. He missed not having his finger on the pulse of the world or at least of his local community. It was harder than he'd imagined to go cold turkey from social media. No emails. No texts. No television. It made for a lot of silence and solitude. That's what he'd wanted, but maybe it wasn't what he'd needed.

He'd enjoyed his evening with Jessica Mason much more than expected. While the food had been good, it was the company that had satisfied him most. Sure, there had been awkward moments. Neither of them seemed to want to share too much about their lives. But there'd been good moments too. Jessica was a nice person, and she hadn't treated him like a creature about to be dissected beneath a magnifying glass.

It was midmorning and Ridley was working on fence repairs when he saw her back her SUV out of the garage and drive away. He waved but doubted she was looking his way. If she'd seen him, if she'd stopped, he would have gone over and thanked her again for the previous night. Maybe he could have made up for upsetting her by mentioning her husband. But she hadn't looked, hadn't seen him.

He went back to work on the fence and had been at it for at least half an hour when he heard a car on the road. He looked up, expecting to see Jessica returning from town. But it wasn't her vehicle. It was a blue truck. One he knew well.

He removed the tool belt from around his waist and walked toward the front of the house, arriving about the same time as the truck came to a halt. Dust swirled into a cloud, coming from the rear wheels forward. Ridley closed his eyes while it rolled past him. When he opened them, his friend was out of the truck.

"Chad."

"Ridley."

"How'd you find me?"

"Your mom."

"I should have known."

Chad Evers walked toward him. "I got worried when you never answered your phone. I went by your house a couple of times, but no answer there either."

"I needed to get out of Dodge for a while." He motioned with his head toward the house. "Come in and I'll get you something to drink."

"Thanks."

Chad and Ridley had been good friends since their senior year in high school. Ridley trusted him like a brother. It was Chad who'd introduced Ridley to Tammy Treehorn. Not that he could have foreseen what would happen all those months down the road.

A short while later, cold cans of soda in hand, the two men sat down in the living room.

Chad was the one who broke the silence. "I'm really sorry about the press."

Ridley shrugged.

"I know the stuff they said and implied isn't true."

Anger churned in his stomach. He almost asked what had been written about him lately, but he managed to swallow the question. It wouldn't help to know. It wouldn't change anything.

As if reading his mind, Chad added, "It's dying down already, if that's any help."

"A little."

"I tried to talk to Tammy. No luck."

"Yeah, her handlers set up quite a hedge around her the minute the information leaked."

"You shouldn't have quit. You should've stuck around."

"Maybe, but at the time quitting seemed the right thing to do."

Chad shook his head. "There are two stories. There's the news about Tammy herself, and there's the news of how the information got out. Right now it's playing like you wanted to take her down."

"I'm sure Rachelle Ford knows the truth." He felt the anger rising inside of him again. "She could clear things up, at least as far as I'm concerned. But I suppose she's too busy protecting herself."

"Then let the press know that. Let them go after her."

Ridley straightened, his friend's suggestion affecting him in a strange way. Would he want anyone else to be subjected to the press or, even worse, the internet trolls the way he'd been? Even if Rachelle knew more than she was letting on, did he want her to have to deal with lies and innuendos? "No," he answered after a lengthy silence. "No, it isn't worth that."

"Don't you want the truth to come out?"

"Sure. But not if it inadvertently harms somebody who's

innocent. And I don't know for sure who is and who isn't innocent. Better to leave it alone."

"But—"

"Look, Chad, I appreciate you trying to encourage me this way. I really do. But for now, I want to lay low. I think I need to pray more about the right thing to do. When I think about what's being said about me and all that's happened, I get angry. And making decisions when I'm angry isn't wise. At least that's been my experience."

"Yeah. I suppose you're right about that. So what are you going to do next? Hide up here for the rest of your life?"

Ridley grunted. "No. This is temporary while I get my head together. I'm going to have to figure out what I want to do next. It definitely won't have to do with politics. I learned pretty fast that I don't have the stomach for it." He drew in a deep breath. "Besides, it wasn't just my work life that was out of whack. Things weren't so good in my personal life either."

"Speaking of which, Selena called me."

"Selena called you?"

"Yeah. She wanted to know where you are."

"I don't get it. She's the one who broke things off. She called me, too, but all she said was she wanted a sweater she left at my house."

"You ask me, she's upset because you didn't beg her to come back. She wanted you to crawl."

Ridley knew his friend had never cared for Selena and so might be slightly prejudiced against her. But in this instance, he suspected Chad might be right about his former girlfriend's motivation. He'd witnessed her vengeful streak before, although it hadn't been directed at him. He'd excused away her negative personality traits as they popped up because he'd wanted things to work out. "You didn't tell her where I am, did you?"

"No. I'm not stupid." Chad released a short laugh.

Ridley nodded grimly. He had begun to wonder if he was a poor judge of character when it came to women. He didn't like to think it, but Selena Wright was evidence to prove the case against him.

❦

From the age of sixteen, Jessica had been a sensible driver. She drove defensively, the way her father had taught her. But after the accident that killed her husband and child, fear had hovered nearby whenever she was behind the wheel. On short trips from home to town and back, she kept that fear at bay, but away from her cozy community it seemed to sit in the back seat, whispering how dangerous it was, reminding her how quickly she could lose control of her vehicle. She told herself that one day she would get over it. For the present, she had to grit her teeth and ignore the feeling.

Shortly before eleven forty-five on Tuesday morning, Jessica arrived at her parents' home. Tension knotted the muscles across her shoulders and upper back, and after turning off the engine, she sat for a while and did some deep breathing, trying to relax. She didn't have time to succeed. Her mom appeared on the front stoop, waving a dish towel in Jessica's direction.

She pasted on a smile before opening the door. "Hi, Mom." She headed up the walk.

"Oh, honey. It's so good to see you." Her mom made it sound as if it had been ages since they'd seen each other. In fact, it had been less than two weeks. "How was the drive?"

"Not bad. Traffic was light."

"That's good." She kissed Jessica's cheek. "Come on in. I'm putting the last touches on our lunch." She took her by the crook of the arm and drew her inside. "This is a treat to see you in the middle of the week."

"Yeah." While she followed her mom to the kitchen, Jessica breathed in the memories that hid in every nook and cranny of this house.

"I'm making BLTs and tomato soup," her mom said.

"Two of my favorites."

"I know."

Jessica plucked a small bit of bacon off a plate and popped it into her mouth.

Her mom laughed as she laid lettuce leaves on top of strips of bacon, sliced tomatoes, and bread, then covered both sandwiches with second slices of bread. "Go ahead and sit at the table, honey, and I'll dish up the soup."

"Okay."

The breakfast nook held a small, round oak table for four and an old, scarred buffet that had once belonged to Jessica's grandmother. More memories welled as she sat in the same chair she'd sat in since before she could remember. Her older sister, Deidra, had sat directly across from her. Mom had used the chair closest to the kitchen, Dad the one by the window.

A lump formed in her throat, and she had to breathe deeply to keep tears from forming. She'd been so blessed in her childhood. So many happy memories. She'd wanted Angela to experience the same kind of family, the same kind of love. That couldn't happen now. And the baby she had yet to meet? There would be plenty of love, of course, but it still wouldn't be the same.

"Deidra called yesterday." Her mom set the sandwich plates on the table. "Trish is starring in a community theater's production of *Peter Pan*."

"Wow." Jessica swallowed, sniffed, and once more forced a smile. "That's great. When's the production?"

"In about six weeks. I told your dad I thought we should fly down for it, but he's not sure he can take the time off work. You know how it is for him in the summer." She returned with the bowls of soup, setting one before Jessica. "I wish you could go with me."

"It would be fun, but you know I can't. I'll be eight months pregnant by then. I don't want to fly when I'm that far along. Besides, I need to work hard now because once the baby comes, it's going to be difficult to squeeze in much time in my studio."

"I know." Her mom sighed, then held out a hand for Jessica to take. "Let's thank God for the food before the soup gets cold."

After the blessing, they ate in silence for a short while. But Jessica could feel her mom's questioning gaze and knew she wondered what had prompted this visit.

Unable to wait any longer, she set down her sandwich. "Mom. I need to tell you something. About Joe. About Joe and me."

Her mother's expression was tender and patient.

"Before he . . . before he and . . . and Angela died, he told me he was in love with another woman and wanted a divorce."

"No!" Disbelief erased the patience. "But—"

"I knew, deep down, that he wasn't happy. But I thought . . . I hoped . . ." The words faded away, and she shook her head. This confession was more difficult than she'd expected. Perhaps pretending had been the better way. But the truth, like the proverbial cat, was out of the bag now. There was no going back. "I pretended I didn't know he was being unfaithful because I didn't want others to know the truth. As long as he didn't tell me, I could go on pretending we would be all right. That our marriage could be saved." Her voice fell to a whisper. "But then he did tell me."

"Jessica." Her mother reached out and touched the back of her hand.

"We fought that morning." She didn't have to explain what morning she meant. "He was so angry at first. We said awful things to each other. Then, by the time he drove away, he just seemed cold and . . . and frustrated." She drew a slow, deep breath and released it. "He'd told me he would stay through Christmas, for Angela's sake, but then he was going to move out." A sharp laugh—devoid of humor—tore from her throat. "I got pregnant the night before he told me he was leaving me. Isn't that ironic or . . . or something?" Now the tears came, streaking her cheeks. "I was such a fool. I was so stupid."

"Oh, Jessica." Her mom rose from the chair and came to embrace her, rubbing the top of her head with her cheek. "I'm so sorry."

She hated that Joe—even in his absence—could still make her cry sometimes. She hated it bitterly. Pulling back from her mom, she reached for a napkin on the table and dried her eyes. "I'm okay," she whispered. A lie if ever she'd spoken one.

"Why didn't you tell us when you two first started having trouble?" Her mom settled back onto her chair. "Perhaps your father and I could have helped in some way."

"Joe said it's because I'm stubborn. Too stubborn to admit when something is over." Jessica stared down at her hands that were folded in her lap. She'd removed her wedding ring several months ago, and now she rubbed the place it had once been.

"Maybe you weren't being stubborn. Maybe you were just hopeful."

She loved her mom so much in that moment.

"Jessica, have you been blaming yourself all these months for the accident?"

She lowered her eyes to her half-eaten sandwich. "A little." *Or maybe a lot.*

"You mustn't. No matter what you quarreled about, no matter how angry he was, the accident was not your fault. The police were very clear about that. It was the road conditions that caused it. It was the black ice."

"But if he'd been paying better attention, if he hadn't been driving too fast—"

"Jessica, listen to me." Her mom took hold of Jessica's right hand. "You cannot live with what-ifs. Trying to do so will drive you crazy. It isn't what God wants for you."

Pain pressed against her chest. "If God cares, why did He take Angela? She was innocent. She didn't deserve to die."

"And Joe did?"

Jessica sucked in a breath as she looked up. "I didn't mean it that way."

Her mom said nothing.

Maybe I did mean it that way. Maybe I did mean Joe deserved to die.

"Sweetheart, there is a great deal I don't understand in this life. But this much I know: there isn't a single one of us who leaves this earthly life one moment sooner or one moment later than God allotted. I don't know why Angela was only given six years. But look at the joy she gave us in those years. Look at what a blessing she was to others. She touched so many lives in that brief time." She stopped to brush away tears of her own. "We will always miss her, and I don't pretend that it will ever be easy not having her with us. But we can take comfort in knowing we'll see her again one day. She isn't lost to us forever."

"Oh, Mom. I want to take comfort in that. I do. But I'm not comforted. It hurts. It just hurts."

Her mother rose and came to her again, pressing Jessica's head to her stomach and holding her tight. "I know, darling. I know."

NAMPA, IDAHO
Saturday, February 28, 1931

"Andrew." His mother released him from her tight embrace. "You look so thin." She touched the side of his face with the flat of her hand. "It's good to have you home, my son."

"I'm glad to be home, Mama." He shook his father's hand, then looked down the length of the station platform. "Helen's not here?"

"No. She's waiting for you at her parents' house."

"How is Mr. Greyson, Papa?"

"Not good. He's not expected to recover."

"Helen must be devastated. Mother Greyson as well."

"They are. Both of them. But they'll be glad you're here to help see them through." His father took a valise from Andrew. "The automobile is over this way."

Andrew took up his other two suitcases. They held everything he'd taken with him last August. After all, there was no job for him to go back to in Portland. He'd had to resign his position with the bank before coming home. Someone had to see to the affairs of his father-in-law while he was incapacitated, and that task had fallen to Andrew.

But it wasn't Frank Greyson who concerned him at the moment. Instead, he wondered what sort of welcome he would receive from Helen. When she'd left Portland the day after Christmas, her kiss had been brief and cool. She'd written him only three letters in the two months since her departure, and none of them had done anything to help the worry he felt in his heart. It was as if she'd written to an old school acquaintance rather than to her husband. As if they'd never been married. As if they'd never created a child together.

In his own, more frequent, letters home, he hadn't known what to write to her except to continue to express his love in as many ways as he could think of. After all, what else could he do from over four hundred miles away? But now he was home again. Now he could work on mending whatever had come between them.

"I'll ride in back," his mother said when they reached the Ford sedan. "You'll want time with your papa."

It was true. Andrew would like time to talk to his father. But the ride to the Greyson farm was the wrong opportunity. He needed someplace quiet where he could explain the situation and then glean the older man's sound advice.

They drove through the farmland, everything gray and wintry looking, trees bare except for the occasional flocks of small birds perched in their branches. In a few months the fields would turn green with new crops, and the trees would be in full leaf. For now, the world looked as barren as his marriage.

Above the noise of the car engine, his father said, "I'm sorry you had to give up your job. I know it was hard to find."

"It couldn't be helped."

"Helen and Madge will be thankful to have you home."

He didn't completely believe that. Mother Greyson perhaps felt that way. But Helen? "Did you see much of them while I was in Portland?"

"Not much."

Andrew glanced over at his father.

"Madge says Helen's friends have kept her occupied so she wouldn't spend too much time missing you."

He looked out the window. *Seems to have worked.* His mood

darkened, and he began to dread the moment when he would see his wife again.

"Gregory," his mother said from the back seat. "Look. The Maxwells are leaving."

Andrew's gaze shot to the farm a short distance up the road. A Ford truck, piled high with earthly possessions, was making its way slowly from the farmhouse to the road.

"It's true, then," his father said. "They've lost the place. I was hoping it was only a rumor."

"Should we stop and speak to them?" There were tears in his mother's question.

His father slowed the car, but he didn't bring it to a halt. "Better not. If they'd wanted to say goodbye, they would have. I imagine Timothy's pride is wounded. Mine would be."

"But we don't even know where they're going."

His father touched the brim of his hat as they passed the driveway. With sunlight reflecting off the windshield, Andrew couldn't tell if anyone inside the truck could see them or knew their loss was being acknowledged and mourned with them.

"Papa?"

"Hmm?"

"Are you good? Financially, I mean. You're not in any danger of losing the farm, are you?"

His father glanced at him. "We're fine, son. We've always been careful with our money, your mama and me. We can weather most anything that comes our way."

"You'd be in even better shape if you hadn't spent all that money on college for me."

"Education is never a waste, my boy. It isn't just about employment, after all. And don't worry. Your time will come. The right opportunity will appear when you least expect it. For now, your smarts are needed to help the Greysons."

His smarts? The word choice made him want to laugh. He didn't seem to be smart enough to help himself, let alone his in-laws. But he could work a farm. He knew animals and a fair amount about growing alfalfa hay. He knew how to repair a fence and keep a barn roof mended.

Now if he could just discover a way to mend his marriage.

Chapter 10

All week long, while Ridley repaired the fence or worked on the shed or mowed the grass or played with the dog, he found his gaze going to his neighbor's house again and again. He never saw Jessica herself. Hadn't seen her since she'd driven away on Tuesday. He wondered if she was all right, but he couldn't think of a reason to go knock on her door.

On Friday afternoon, with Kris unhappily shut in the house, Ridley was chopping away at an old tree stump when the UPS truck pulled into Jessica's half-circle driveway and stopped. He saw the driver, a woman, seem to struggle to remove a large box from the back of the truck, so he leaned the ax against the shed and headed in her direction. He arrived in time to help her get it settled onto the hand truck.

"Thanks," she said, the word coming out on a gush of air.

"I didn't do much. You did the heavy part."

"Thanks anyway. You must be Ridley, Jessica's new neighbor. I'm Carol." She grinned widely. "The UPS driver."

"Nice to meet you, Carol the UPS driver."

"Ha!"

"Need help getting that up to the house?"

"No, I've got it that far. But I'll bet Jessica will need help with it after that." Carol jerked her head toward the front door. "Follow me and we'll ask her."

What choice did he have? He followed. Not that he minded.

Carol rang the doorbell, and together they waited. It took about a minute before the door swung open. Jessica wore a paint-splattered smock, and her shoulder-length hair was captured in a twisted ponytail. Another splash of paint smudged her cheek.

She looked, he thought, adorable.

"What on earth?" she said, eyes on the box.

"Not sure," Carol answered, "but it's addressed to you." She pointed to the label on the side of the box.

"I didn't order anything." Now Jessica's gaze shifted to Ridley.

He shrugged, fighting a smile. "I didn't order anything either. I'm just here to lift and carry."

"I see." She looked at Carol again. "Then I guess you'd better leave it for me."

Carol took the hand truck up to the door, turned, and backed it over the step and into the house. Once there, she slid the hand truck away from the box that was nearly as high as her shoulders. She gave the box a pat. "Let me know what's in it. I'm dying of curiosity. You know how I am. I'd wait, but I'm running a bit late on deliveries." She flashed another broad smile in Ridley's direction. "Thanks for the help."

"Sure thing."

Both he and Jessica watched Carol push the hand truck down the walk, whistling as she went. Soon she was inside the vehicle and driving away.

"Let me get a box cutter," Jessica said into the sudden silence. "I confess I'm curious too."

While she was gone, Ridley laid the box down flat on the floor and slid it to a more open space in the room.

"How did Carol rope you into this?" Jessica called from her studio.

"She didn't rope me in."

"I'll bet." She walked back into the living room.

He held out his hand for the box cutter. "Let me."

She hesitated a moment, then gave it to him.

He worked quickly, soon discovering that there was a white box inside the brown shipping box. "Still a mystery." He glanced up at Jessica.

It wasn't a mystery for long. He tipped the shipping box and let the other box slowly slide out onto the floor.

"A crib," Jessica whispered. "My mom must have ordered it for me. She told me she wanted to help with the nursery."

"Where is it? The nursery. I imagine it's best to assemble the crib in the room it'll stay in."

"Oh, you don't have to—"

"I want to, Jessica." He tilted his head to indicate her condition. "Besides, you shouldn't do it, even if you're able."

Her expression told of the argument she was having within herself. He'd guess she rarely, if ever, asked for help from anybody. Had she been that way before the death of her family or was that something new? Just one more thing he'd like to know about her.

At last, as if defeated, Jessica pointed. "First room on the left at the top of the stairs."

It didn't take Ridley long to get the box up the stairs and into the appointed room. It was empty of furniture, the off-white walls bare and, if he wasn't mistaken, recently painted. He set the box in the middle of the room and ripped open one end. By the time Jessica appeared in the doorway, a tool chest in one hand, he had all of the parts out of the box.

"This shouldn't be too hard to put together." He picked up the written instructions and perused them. He'd never assembled a baby's crib before, but if he could take a computer apart or build a bookcase or repair a shed, he could manage this.

Especially for her.

The thought caused him a moment of alarm. It had been only three days since he'd decided he was a poor judge of character when it came to women. Just because he found Jessica sweet and funny, just because he felt sorry for her with all that had happened, didn't mean he wanted to let himself care too much. Not with his life turned upside down.

"I got rid of Angela's bed and her old crib too." Jessica set the toolbox beside him. "I got rid of all her clothes and toys after the funeral. I didn't think there was any reason to keep any of it. I was trying to purge the pain by cleaning things out. And then I discovered I was pregnant."

Ridley sat back on his heels and looked at her. "That's rough."

"Yeah." She smiled sadly.

The other night he'd upset her by mentioning her husband in passing. So what could he say now? He didn't want to repeat that mistake. He decided to go back to work on the crib.

"The walls in here used to be pink. It was Angela's favorite color . . . along with red. She loved red too." She drew in a breath and released it on a sigh. "I don't know the baby's sex, so I went with eggshell for the walls."

Ridley didn't know much about pregnancy, but he was pretty

sure it was easy these days for a woman to know if she was having a boy or a girl, at least by the time she was as far along as Jessica. He wondered why she didn't know. Again, that seemed dangerous ground. He chose not to ask.

∽

Jessica leaned her shoulder against the doorjamb and watched as Ridley opened the toolbox. He selected the tools he would need and set them on the carpet. Then he dumped the screws and washers and whatever else was in the small plastic bags onto the floor and began to sort them into appropriate piles.

I should go, she thought. But despite herself, she remained. Why, she couldn't say for certain. It wasn't because she needed him to put the crib together. Even six and a half months pregnant, she could have managed the task. At a slower pace, no doubt, but she could have assembled it without a problem. Perhaps she stayed because there was something pleasing about watching him work. It was more than the flex of his muscles or the way he held his mouth when he concentrated. Although that part was nice too.

Maybe I just miss having a man around the house. Any man.

She frowned, wondering if that was true. No, she answered herself. It wasn't true. She wasn't that kind of woman. She would rather be alone than have just any man.

Only Ridley wasn't just any man.

How can I be sure of that? I thought Joe was special, and look how that turned out. And what does it matter anyway? Ridley's here for the summer and then he's gone.

She pushed away from the jamb. "I'd better get back to my work. If you need anything, holler."

He glanced at her. "I'll do that."

It surprised her, how reluctant she was to leave the baby's room, but she made herself do it. She went down the stairs and into her studio. But instead of returning to her painting, she went to the bookcase and picked up her great-grandfather's Bible. She remembered the day of her grandmother's funeral and her mom's words of encouragement. Her mom had always been her chief cheerleader in life. Even that crib Ridley was assembling upstairs was her mom's attempt to lift her spirits, perhaps even to inspire her to look toward the future with hope. Her mom and Grandma Frani had been alike in that regard. Had her great-grandfather Andrew been the same?

She moved to her work area and settled onto her chair, letting the book fall open on the desk before her. Psalm 139. The first two verses were underlined.

O lord, thou hast searched me, and known me.
 Thou knowest my downsitting and mine uprising, thou understandest my thought afar off.

While she preferred to study a more contemporary version, there was something beautiful about the language of King James. It summoned an image of Andrew Henning, sitting at a small table, lamplight spilling a pool of yellow light onto the pages of this Bible.

For there is not a word in my tongue, but, lo, O LORD, thou knowest it altogether.
 Thou hast beset me behind and before, and laid thine hand upon me.

"O God," she whispered, "there isn't a word in my mouth that You don't know. You have put a hedge around me. Your hand is upon me. Help me to remember that whenever I forget how much You love me."

It was the first real prayer she had prayed in months, and something shifted in her spirit as she spoke the words aloud. A broken, secret place way down deep inside began to heal. She couldn't have explained how she knew that was true, but she knew it all the same.

KUNA, IDAHO
Monday, April 20, 1931

They buried Frank Greyson on a beautiful spring day, the pungent scent of turned earth conveyed upon a breeze. The sun shone warm upon the mourners as new leaves in the trees swayed in a gentle dance.

Andrew's father-in-law had lingered longer than the doctor expected, but he'd never regained his ability to communicate following his stroke. His passing seemed a mercy, as it had been hard on everyone watching him lie there, trapped in a once-robust body that had now betrayed him.

At the graveside, Andrew stood behind his wife, watching the slight shudder of her shoulders as she wept. He almost put his hand on her waist, an offer of comfort, but he stopped himself. The gesture wouldn't be welcome. He knew why, although he hadn't admitted it to anyone but himself.

His wife was in love with another man.

While the minister spoke, Andrew's gaze swept over the people standing opposite him. Was the man among those who mourned Frank Greyson? Was he a friend of the family? Was he someone Andrew spoke to on Sundays after church? The questions plagued him. Had plagued him for several weeks. But all he had were questions. Never any answers. Helen had given him no clue as to the man's identity. Had she been discreet out of respect for her father? Or did she have other reasons?

Sorrow welled inside Andrew and tears stung his eyes. He blinked them back, ashamed to give into them. Ashamed that the tears were about Helen and not her father whom he'd loved and respected.

He heard those around him murmur "Amen" and realized the minister had closed the graveside service with a prayer. People approached the family to offer their condolences, and again Andrew watched every man who took Helen's hand and spoke words of comfort.

It seemed forever before the family stood alone at the graveside—Helen and her mother, Andrew and his parents. In silence they made their way to the waiting automobiles. Andrew shook his father's hand and hugged his mother while Helen helped her own mother into Frank's 1929 sedan. As Andrew slid behind the wheel, his wife beside him, he knew they couldn't go on this way much longer. Something had to change.

"Open rebuke is better than secret love."

It took him a moment to remember where he'd read those words. Proverbs, of course. While still in Portland, he'd been challenged from the pulpit to read a chapter of Proverbs every day throughout 1931. He was nearly finished with his fourth time through the book, but he didn't recall that verse having made any special impact upon him when he'd read it last. Yet now the words spoke in his heart as if long memorized.

He knew what they were saying to him. He couldn't be passive if he hoped to save his marriage. He must take action.

Chapter 11

Jessica hadn't been inside Hope Springs Community Church since the Friday of the funeral. At first it was because she couldn't bear to remember that horrible day, those two coffins sitting at the front of the sanctuary. Then she didn't return because she felt distanced from God, remote, cut off. And finally it was because she didn't think God wanted her to be there. She had failed Him, failed to be faithful.

Nerves tumbled in her belly as she got out of her car on Sunday morning. She'd arrived late on purpose, wanting to enter the sanctuary without being seen. At least not seen right away. Her plan worked too. She slipped into the back pew after the greeting time and while one of the elders was giving announcements. No one else was in the back row so she didn't have to smile at anyone. She could simply sit and give herself time to feel at home again.

"Hey, there," came a soft voice from beside her.

Her eyes widened as she looked at Ridley. Nerves erupted inside her for the second time that morning.

He whispered, "I wondered if you went to church here." Then he turned his attention toward the front of the church as Mick Phelps stepped behind the pulpit.

Jessica did the same. At first it was difficult to focus on what the pastor said. It was as if she'd fallen out of the practice of listening. But little by little, she began to hear the sermon. Not the words so much as the spirit behind them. It was enough for now.

At the end of the service, Jessica felt nerves begin to churn inside of her again. She wanted to flee before she had to speak to anyone. Even to old friends.

"Don't be in a rush," Ridley whispered. "It's a safe place."

She looked at him and saw understanding in his gaze. Despite having met each other less than two weeks before, he seemed to know her. Did she like it that he could read her so easily? She wasn't sure. She didn't think so. She'd been hiding her feelings for such a long time. Hiding them even from herself. Now, the way Ridley looked at her made her feel exposed, vulnerable, almost in danger.

"I'll bet you know everybody here," he said, no longer whispering.

"Just about." She picked up her purse and hung it from her shoulder.

"I attend a large church in Boise. Impossible to know everybody."

She might have asked the name of his church, but she was interrupted by the appearance of Billie Fisher.

"Jessica, I'm so glad to see you," Billie said. "I never called you this week about lunch. I'm sorry."

"It's okay."

Billie's gaze shifted to Ridley with obvious interest.

"This is my new neighbor. Ridley . . ." Jessica let her voice drift into silence, suddenly uncertain if he was still keeping his last name a secret.

"Chesterfield," he filled in for her as he offered Billie his hand.

She took it, smiling. "I hope you'll like living here." Judging by Billie's expression, Ridley's last name meant nothing to her.

"Actually," he answered her, "my folks bought the place, and I'm staying there for a few months."

Billie faced Jessica again. "Lunch Tuesday?"

Habit screamed for her to decline, but she forced herself to ignore it. "Sure. Where?"

"Meet at the Riverside? At noon."

"Okay."

Billie gave a little wave of goodbye, the gesture taking in both Jessica and Ridley, before she walked away.

"That went okay," Ridley said softly.

He was right. It had gone okay. Better than okay.

⁓

When Ridley looked at Jessica Mason, he was reminded of a wild colt, skittish and ready to bolt. But she'd relaxed a little after Billie Fisher left them. For some reason, that made him feel good. As if he'd had something to do with it.

Face it. He was attracted to Jessica. He had been from the first time they met. He liked her smile and her laugh. He wanted to see and hear both of them more often. Whenever he saw the sorrow come into her eyes, he wanted to erase it. He had an almost overwhelming desire to rescue her in some way.

Not the best of desires. In the twenty-first century, a woman didn't want to be rescued by a man. She wanted to be equal to him. Many, it seemed from his personal experience—much of it painful—expected to be superior. But while Jessica was strong, there was something fragile about her as well, and it seemed to draw him closer. It made him want to protect her from any more hurt.

He walked with Jessica out of the church, pausing when she

stopped to speak to someone, then moving on with her when it was time.

"Thanks for letting me sit with you," he said when they reached the sidewalk.

"Did I have a choice?" She tried to hide her smile but wasn't successful.

"Not really. But thanks anyway."

"I owed you for your help with the crib."

He shook his head. "You don't owe me anything, Jessica." It bothered him that she'd put it in those terms. Maybe it shouldn't, but it did. More rescuing impulses? He'd best put a stop to them. "I need to head home." He took a step back, then, before he could check himself, added, "If you want to ride into town together on Sundays, I'd be glad to drive. For as long as I'm in Hope Springs, that is."

"That's a nice offer, Ridley. I . . . I'll let you know."

He walked to the parking lot and got into his vehicle but didn't start the engine immediately. He was still mulling over his feelings for the pretty—and pregnant—widow he'd left at the front of the church. It went against reason to be interested in her. Sure, he could be kind and neighborly, but he was afraid that wouldn't be enough for him. Afraid that the longer he stayed in Hope Springs and the more he got to know Jessica, the more interested in her he was going to be.

A couple of weeks ago, he'd told his mom that he trusted God but he didn't think he could trust most people yet. Not soon, anyway. Had Jessica changed that? Was he ready to trust her? And if so, why? What made her different from, say, Selena or Rachelle or Tammy? Hmm. Interesting that all of the names that popped into his head belonged to women. Maybe it wasn't most people he wasn't ready to trust. Maybe it was most women.

His jaw set, he turned the key in the ignition and drove out of the parking lot. But instead of following the road home, he turned the opposite direction and drove through town. Before long he followed the river highway north, a CD playing over the stereo. For a long while he thought of nothing but the lyrics, singing along to his favorites, but eventually he realized he was hungry. Moments later, like an answer to prayer, he saw a sign for a restaurant up ahead. He slowed and pulled into the gravel parking lot. It was nearly full at midday. Not surprising for a Sunday during the summer.

Inside the log restaurant and gift shop, he found a place to sit at the bar. To his left was a mother and her young daughter. To his right a portly man with white hair and a full beard to match. Add a red velvet suit and the fellow would be a dead ringer for Santa Claus.

Ridley perused the menu and was ready to place his order when the server appeared. The waitress looked to be no more than sixteen and wore a snug white top and denim shorts, along with a very disgruntled expression.

"What can I get you?" She held a pencil over her small order pad, ready but disinterested. He could almost hear her tapping her toe on the floor in impatience.

"I'll have the Trapper Burger with the works and a Diet Coke."

"Fries or a salad with it?"

"Fries, please."

"Okay." She turned away without once meeting his gaze.

Ridley chuckled as he spun his stool around so he could look out the windows at the back of the restaurant. The river beyond the glass was wide and calm. Much different from the stair-step rapids that crashed and broiled a mile south of this area. Beyond the flowing water and a golden-hued meadow, aspens and pines stood thick on the side of the nearest mountain.

The man to his right dropped two five-dollar bills onto the counter and placed a fork on top of them. Then he left the restaurant—as well as the newspaper he'd read while eating. Ridley stared at the folded paper for several moments. He'd avoided all forms of the news for several weeks, but now the temptation was too strong. He reached for the newspaper and slid it toward himself.

Drawing a deep breath, he unfolded it and scanned the front page. A bit of national news. Discussions of water concerns in the northwest. A tease about baseball to draw the reader to the Sports section. It worked for him. Better to stick with baseball news for now. He'd risked enough heartburn looking at the front page. The Treehorn campaign was no longer on page 1. He could be thankful for that. Perhaps the vultures had moved on to some other poor fool by now.

He closed his eyes and gave his head a slight shake, not liking the tone of self-pity that crept over him on occasion.

"Here's your Diet Coke."

He opened his eyes again to see his sullen server as she set the sweating glass on the counter in front of him. "Thanks."

"No problem." From the pocket of her small apron she pulled a straw, wrapped in thin paper. "There you go." She set it next to his glass.

"Thanks again."

She finally lifted her eyes to meet his. She didn't actually smile, but her expression changed enough to no longer resemble a scowl. "I'll be back with your Trapper and fries."

He chuckled to himself as she walked away, disappearing into the noise of the kitchen. For some reason, the encounter made him feel . . . normal. It was hard for a guy to feel normal when he was hiding out.

Laughter faded but the smile remained as he picked up the newspaper and turned it to page 2. Local news. If he was going to read anything unpleasant with his name in it, this was where he would find it.

KUNA, IDAHO
Friday, April 24, 1931

Despite Andrew's resolve to confront Helen about their marriage, to discover the truth and then begin working to improve their relationship, opportunities to do so alone were nonexistent in the days that followed the funeral. There were other people in the house—bringing casseroles, paying their respects—and Helen always seemed to retire before him and to be asleep when he entered their bedroom.

But on this Friday evening, she went for a walk in the gloaming. She slipped away without saying a word to anyone, but Andrew saw her go and followed soon after. He didn't try to muffle his footsteps. It didn't matter. She didn't seem to hear anything. She walked with her head down, her arms crossed over her chest, her steps slow and languid.

It wasn't until she reached the grove of trees near a small pond that he called to her. "Helen."

She stopped but didn't turn.

"Helen. Wait."

Now she looked over her shoulder.

"We need to talk." He approached her.

Defeat was written in her expression, but she tilted her chin in a temporary show of defiance.

He stopped before her, looking at her, remembering how very much he loved her. His heart ached, so sure he was that she didn't feel the same. Finally he motioned toward a fallen tree that had become a bench of sorts over the years. The top had been carved flat with an ax and smoothed. "Let's sit." He gently cupped her elbow to steer her in the right direction.

She went without argument.

A pair of ducks floated on the surface of the pond. He and Helen were like them, he thought. Swimming in circles, feet paddling beneath the surface. He shook his head, disliking the image in his mind.

They sat, space between them. She kept her arms crossed, as if warding him off.

"Helen, what's happened to us?"

"What do you mean?"

"You know what I mean."

"It's been hard with you away, with Father so sick and then dying. We never have any money. It's been a struggle almost from the start. And I don't feel . . . I just don't feel—" She broke off abruptly.

He drew in a slow, deep breath and let it out. "Who is he?" From the corner of his eye, he saw her head turn toward him. He mirrored the motion, meeting her gaze. "Who is he, Helen?"

"What do you mean?" she repeated in a whisper.

"You know what I mean." A little louder he added, "You know *who* I mean."

"Andrew . . ."

"Be honest, Helen. At least you can be honest with me."

A glimmer of tears welled in her eyes. After a few moments, she lowered her gaze. "You don't know him."

"What's his name?"

"Henry."

"Henry what?"

"Henry Victor."

"How did you meet him? *Where* did you meet him?"

"He's a . . . a friend of Sarah Knight. I met him at her house the week after you left for Portland." Her voice fell to little more than a whisper. "I never meant for anything to happen, Andrew. I felt so lost after . . . after everything. After the baby and after you went away. Henry's handsome and funny, and he's so attentive. He thinks I'm beautiful."

"I think you're beautiful too." Pain tightened his chest. "Do you love him, Helen?"

"Yes. I think so. Yes."

He'd known it in his heart already, but it hurt even more to hear her confirm his suspicion. "What do you mean to do about it?"

"I . . . I don't know." She drew in a breath but still didn't look at him. "I didn't mean for this to happen, Andrew. It just . . . it just did."

It surprised him that he believed her in that regard. However, believing her didn't ease the pain of her betrayal.

"I'm sorry, Andrew," she whispered.

"Helen." Resolve stiffened his spine. "I meant what I said on our wedding day. I married you for better or worse. I married you until death do us part."

She sucked in a soft breath. "But if I love him—"

"I'm your husband."

"But I thought, once you knew—"

"I'm your husband."

She stood abruptly and moved away from the log bench, stopping at the water's edge, her back still to him. "You expect us to go on, as if nothing has happened?"

"No." He stood, too, but remained by the bench. "No, that's not what I expect. I expect we're going to have to work hard in order to put things back together. I expect we're going to have to learn to be patient with each other. I expect we'll have to forgive and to be forgiven."

At his last words, she spun around. "You mean *I* need to be forgiven."

"I need forgiveness too. If I'd done what I should have done, you wouldn't have sought comfort from another man."

"Maybe. Maybe not. I don't know."

He wished he could see her expression, but evening had come in earnest by this time, and his wife had become little more than a darker shadow against lighter ones.

"Perhaps you should go stay with your parents for a while," she said.

"I'm staying with you." He shook his head. He might not be certain about much, but he was certain of that. Separation wasn't the answer. In fact, it had been part of the problem. "No, my place is here. Besides, your mother needs my help. There's a lot to be managed, now that your father is gone."

She turned to face the pond again. "Why has God punished me this way?"

"I don't think He's punished you." He took a few steps forward. "Or us."

"First you lost your job so that we couldn't stay in our apartment. Then I lost the baby. And now Father is dead. You don't think that's punishment?"

"I don't think it's punishment." He wrestled for a moment with his answer before adding, "Papa says that God's with us through all the trials of life. He's here to comfort us, Helen, if we let Him." *Count it all joy*, he added silently, needing the reminder while struggling with how he was supposed to accomplish it.

"Let's not talk about it anymore."

He opened his mouth to insist they go on talking, then shut it quickly. In this she was right. He'd said enough for tonight. *God, give me wisdom.* Inhaling another slow breath, he said, "Let's walk back to the house. Your mother will be wondering what's happened to us."

Chapter 12

Ridley stepped into the narthex of the church and paused, listening to the silence. So different from yesterday when the entry, sanctuary, hallways, and classrooms had bustled with activity. Following the instructions he'd been given over the phone, he turned left and made his way to the church offices. When he entered, the woman at the front desk looked up with a welcoming smile.

"You must be Mr. Chesterfield," she said. "Pastor Phelps is expecting you." She pointed toward a connecting doorway.

Before he reached it, Mick Phelps stepped into view. "Good morning, Ridley."

"Morning, Pastor."

Mick motioned him to enter his office.

Ridley drew in a deep breath as he stepped into the small room and sat on one of the chairs near the desk. The wall behind the desk was taken up entirely by bookshelves, and every shelf was filled with books, some of them stacked horizontally on top of the ones stored vertically. The titles he could read here and there told him the pastor's interests went beyond theological.

"You like to read?" Mick asked as he closed the door.

"Yeah, I do."

"Me too."

"I can see that."

The pastor chuckled. "Guilty as charged. My wife and daughters know they can never go wrong with buying me a book for my birthday or Christmas or our anniversary." He sank onto his own chair. "Biographies are my favorite, with histories running a close second."

"I'm partial to science fiction myself."

Mick nodded without comment.

"When I work out at the gym or go for a run, I listen to audiobooks."

"Ah. Another audiobook fan. I like them too. I have quite a collection if you ever want to borrow a listen. I download and keep them on an old iPod."

"Do you have good internet service here?"

The pastor cocked an eyebrow.

Ridley guessed what the look meant. "My folks' place isn't connected to anything yet. I've been in a black hole since I got here. No internet. No television. Not even LTE service on my cell phone."

"Except for the latter, I take it the black hole is by choice."

"By choice." He shrugged. "I came up here to get away from the news for a while."

"Well, the answer to your question is yes, we've got good internet service. Not perfect, but it meets our needs. I'm able to download books and music without extra data charges, and our service rarely goes down."

"That's good news."

"However, the network in our church could use a major upgrade."

"Maybe I could help with that. It's part of what I do, after all." As soon as the offer was out, he wondered if he should have said it was what he used to do.

Mick straightened in his chair. "That's quite an offer, Ridley."

He shrugged. "I like to help when I can."

"Even to just have your advice would be appreciated. You wouldn't have to do the work itself, unless you wanted to. I'm sure we could hire that out. But it would be nice to have an expert opinion about the best way to go. What equipment we should buy. Service choices. That sort of thing."

"I'm here if you need me."

The pastor leaned back in his chair, his expression suddenly sheepish. "I'll bet you didn't come to see me about books or internet service."

"No. I didn't."

"I'm sorry. Truly."

"No need to apologize, Mick."

"I do apologize, all the same."

"Accepted."

"So, tell me what brought you here."

"I was hoping for some advice." Ridley drew in a breath and let it out. "You know what's been in the paper or on the news in recent weeks."

"About you and Ms. Treehorn?"

"Yeah. The thing is I came up to Hope Springs to get away from the newshounds, and so I'd stop reading everything that was being said on social media. It was like driving by a wreck and craning my neck to see the carnage, only to find out that I was the accident victim. There's plenty of what you've read or heard that's got just enough truth in it to be hard to dispute outright. And yet it really isn't the truth either. I don't know if it's better to let things go and wait for it to all blow over or if I should . . . I don't know . . . Try to do something about it." He raked the fingers of one hand through his hair. "I thought I'd decided to do nothing, to say nothing. I thought I'd made up my mind. But now I'm wondering if that's the right thing to do."

"Ridley, would you mind if we stop for a moment and ask the Lord for wisdom in this matter?"

"No." He let out a sigh. "I think that would be a good thing to do."

⚬⚭⚬

The Riverside was a rustic restaurant in a beautiful setting. It had been built in the 1920s and had long been a popular stopping point for travelers driving the east-west river highway. But in recent years what caused people to make a special trip to eat at the Riverside in its out-of-the-way location was the chef, Philippe Benoit. His specialty dishes were North American Elk, Muscovy Duck, and Sautéed Idaho Trout, to name only a few.

Jessica entered the restaurant a little before noon on Tuesday. The last time she'd been to the Riverside had been with her mom and grandmother. Over a year ago already. She'd been clueless about the heartache that awaited her before the end of the year. How could she have known? On the other hand, she hadn't been unaware that her marriage was in trouble, that Joe was gone more from home, and when he was there he still seemed far away. But she hadn't said anything to her mom and grandmother at that luncheon. She'd smiled and pretended all was well.

"Jessica."

She looked across the open room and saw Billie already at a table for two overlooking the river. She put on a smile and made her way there.

"I'm so glad you could make it," Billie said when she arrived.

"Me too. I haven't been here in a long time."

"The truth is I'm a wretched cook and would rather eat here than at home. It isn't like we have a lot of dining choices, living in Hope Springs."

"No. That's true."

"The Burger Joint doesn't serve salmon or calamari."

Jessica laughed softly. "No. They don't."

"Then let's look at the menu and decide what we want to indulge in."

Unless the menu had changed since her last visit, Jessica knew what she wanted—the grilled steak sandwich with mushrooms and caramelized onions. Of all the amazing choices on the Riverside's lunch menu, that was her favorite. After months of staying home and eating her own inadequate cooking, she felt like splurging. It wasn't as if she had to watch her waistline. It had disappeared a couple of months ago.

Their server, a fresh-faced young man in black slacks and a crisp white shirt, arrived with tall glasses of water, lemon wedges sitting on the rims. "My name is Evan, and I'll be your server today. Would you like to know the specials?"

"Please," Billie answered, looking interested.

Evan rattled off several options, ending with, "Would you like a little more time to make up your minds?"

"No." Billie glanced at Jessica. "I think we're ready."

Jessica nodded.

Billie ordered soup and salad.

"I'll have the grilled steak sandwich," Jessica said when the server turned toward her. "And a glass of lemonade, please."

After the young man walked away, Billie leaned forward on her chair. "Jessica, I'm not very good at small talk, so I'm going to get right to the point. How are you? Really."

The frankness caught her off guard. Perhaps that's why she answered honestly. Or perhaps it was her more recent decision to stop pretending. "I have good days and bad days."

Billie waited, her expression patient.

"Most of them are good now. The house doesn't feel as empty as it did at first. I still cry when I remember happier times. I still miss holding Angela close." She glanced down at her expanding belly. "But I'm looking forward to meeting my son or daughter."

"You don't know what you're having?"

"No, I wanted to be surprised." She shrugged. "Silly, I guess."

"Not silly if that's how you want it."

Jessica ran the pad of her index finger around the top of her water glass. "My pregnancy came as such a shock. At first I thought I'd missed my period because of grief. We'd wanted—" She stopped and drew a breath. "I'd wanted another baby, but I gave up on it happening. Then when it did happen—" She broke off a second time, unable to continue. She hadn't lied yet, but if she continued, she would have to lie.

"I'm so sorry, Jessica. So very, very sorry."

She inhaled deeply and let it out. "It's okay, Billie. You didn't ask anything you shouldn't. But let's talk about you now. Are you enjoying the summer off?"

"Yes. But it's funny. I start missing my students after only a week or two without them. By July I'll be playing with lesson plans and going through all of my supplies for the umpteenth time. And by the first of August, I'll be anxious to get started again."

"In other words, you really don't take the summer off at all."

Billie laughed. "I suppose not."

Jessica felt a sting of envy but hoped it didn't show on her face.

Still, Billie must have sensed it was time to change the subject again. "Tell me about your new neighbor."

"Ridley?"

"Is there another one I don't know about? Yes, Ridley."

"He's nice. Single. Taking the summer off work." That seemed a polite way to say it. "He rescued a stray dog when he first got here. He's been repairing the outbuildings and fence, and he painted his mom's kitchen yellow. Plus, he put together the new baby crib for me when it arrived. He's been very kind to me."

"My goodness. That doesn't sound like the man we've heard about on the news."

"You recognized his name. I thought maybe you didn't."

"Are you kidding? My entire family are political junkies, and not all of us on the same side of the aisle either. You can't read about Tammy Treehorn without hearing about Ridley Chesterfield." Billie cocked her head slightly to one side, her gaze searching. "It seems you like him."

"I do like him."

Honesty had forced the answer out of her mouth before prudence could stop it. But then she realized she didn't want to stay silent. *I do like him,* she repeated silently, enjoying the way the words made her feel. She hadn't expected to like any man ever again. Not in the attraction kind of way. She still didn't expect to trust a man again. At least not any time soon. Yet she already liked Ridley Chesterfield . . . and she already wanted to trust him.

Evan arrived with their lunches. It gave Jessica enough time to think of a different topic of conversation. Thankfully, Billie followed her cue.

KUNA, IDAHO

Thursday, May 7, 1931

Andrew stopped on the porch of the Greyson farmhouse and turned to watch the sun set—a large orange ball, trees silhouetted before it, wisps of pastel-colored clouds feathering out against a darkening sky. A soft breeze brought the scents of rich soil and green grass, as well as the sounds of animals settling down for the night.

Andrew hadn't wanted to be a farmer, like his father and his father's father before him and his father's father's father before that. Not that Andrew didn't have a love of the land. He did. But his passion was numbers and problem solving. He'd dreamed of entering the business world. For a time his work goals had seemed within his grasp, but he didn't have time for dreams now. His days were filled with work from before sunup to after sundown. There were times when he wondered how on earth older men like his father managed to keep up with it all.

In the fading light, his gaze dropped to the toes of his boots. He would need a new pair soon. He didn't think these could be repaired again. But maybe . . .

With a sigh, he turned and entered the house.

His mother-in-law, washing a teacup in the sink, glanced toward the door. "Andrew, there you are. Would you like a cup of tea?"

"No, thanks, Mother Greyson. I think I'll wash up and head to bed." He looked toward the hallway. "Has Helen retired?"

"Yes." His mother-in-law's eyes were filled with concern. "Some time ago."

He gave her a nod and strode down the hall. His footsteps slowed as he passed the telephone. Earlier today he'd heard Helen talking to someone on it. She'd hung up the instant she saw him, but her flushed cheeks had told him everything he needed to know about who had been on the other end of the line. Henry Victor.

How long, Lord, do I put up with it? It's humiliating. I want an end to it.

Andrew had made a point of learning more about Henry Victor after Helen told him his name. Henry, known as Hank to his closest friends, was an attorney who lived and worked in Meridian. Andrew also learned that Henry Victor had spent a great deal of time in Kuna over the autumn and winter months. About the same period of time Andrew had worked in Portland. Henry Victor hadn't visited Kuna nearly as much this spring. Coincidentally, the period of time following Andrew's return from Portland.

Clenching his hands into fists at his sides, Andrew stopped in front of the bedroom door. No light spilled from beneath it, although he knew the light hadn't been off when he'd entered the house. If he went into the bedroom now, Helen would pretend to be asleep while lying on her side, hugging the edge of the mattress, putting as much space between her and Andrew as possible.

His heart aching, he moved away from the door and entered the small bathroom. There he washed quickly with the cold water from the tap. At least he didn't have to haul water from a well or from an outside spigot. He could be thankful for that.

Drying his face with a towel, he stared at his reflection in the mirror above the sink. His jaw was dark with the shadow of a beard. His features seemed sharper to him, gray half circles beneath his eyes. He looked far older than his twenty-six years. Did Helen think so too? Or did she even see him anymore?

Rather than lie in bed, sleepless, thoughts churning, he made his way to the living room and took up the book he'd left on the end table the previous night. He wasn't far into *The Maltese Falcon*, but he was far enough along for the story to have captured his imagination. Hopefully, he could lose himself in it again tonight. He'd rather think about the detective Sam Spade than about Helen and her lover.

Surprisingly, once he set aside the book and retired, Andrew slept hard, and when he awakened, the room still dark, he knew what he meant to do that day, as soon as his chores were finished. His decision never wavered throughout the morning, and by eleven o'clock he was driving the Greyson Model T toward Meridian. He found the law office of Henry Victor on Main Street and parked the automobile on the opposite side of the street.

The small town was quiet on this Friday morning. Two women stood outside a shop on the next block, talking to each other, and a few cars were parked on either side of Main Street. To the north, a flock of birds swooped above tall trees before disappearing into their leafy branches.

Andrew turned his eyes toward the office building across from him, unsure what his next step should be. Should he go in and pretend to be someone else until he got a good look at the man? Should he walk through the door and punch Henry in the nose? Should he try to reason with Henry Victor's better nature? Assuming he had a better nature.

He gripped the steering wheel, lowered his head, and closed his eyes, breathing slowly through his nose and releasing it through his mouth. Finally he whispered, "What do I do? Don't let me make a mistake."

He didn't know how long he sat like that, wishing for some

kind of divine guidance. A loud, audible voice would have been best. Something like he imagined had come to Moses from the burning bush. But he would have settled for a still, small voice in his heart. Neither happened.

At long last, he looked at the office opposite him again, drew another deep breath, and got out of the automobile. He glanced both ways, half hoping for there to be a rush of traffic. But the street remained empty. With nothing to stop him, he crossed the street and entered the law office.

A middle-aged woman with dark, bobbed hair turned from a filing cabinet. "May I help you?"

"I'd like to see Mr. Victor."

"And your name?"

"Andrew Henning."

"May I ask the nature of your business?"

"I believe Mr. Victor will know what's brought me here."

The woman raised her eyebrows, looking as if she might insist on a different answer. Then she said, "Have a seat, Mr. Henning. I'll see if he's available."

Andrew didn't sit down. Instead, he paced the width of the small reception area. He wondered if there was a back door, if Henry Victor would go out it rather than face him. But eventually, the door to his office opened again and the secretary reappeared.

"Mr. Victor will see you, sir."

Chapter 13

There was a dead pine tree at the back of the property, and on Wednesday Ridley decided to tackle its removal. After a quick trip into Hope Springs, he carried a new chainsaw and other tools out to the tree and set to work. By the time he brought it crashing to the ground, he'd worked up a good sweat. Shirtless, he stood back while wiping perspiration from his forehead with a rag.

"Nice job," a familiar voice said from behind him.

He turned to face Jessica. She wore a pair of bright-yellow shorts, a yellow-dotted cotton top, and sandals that revealed toenails painted the same shade of blue-green as her eyes. Her pale hair was pulled back in a ponytail. There was a sweetness about her that he could almost taste. That he would *like* to taste, heaven help him.

"Hey there." He reached for his T-shirt and slipped it over his head. When he could see her again, her gaze had shifted to the felled tree and her cheeks were flushed. He wondered if she might welcome his kiss. The thought made his pulse race even faster than when he'd held the chainsaw.

He cleared his throat. "How are you?"

"Good." She looked at him again. "But I'm afraid I need a favor."

"Whatever I can do."

"You're an internet specialist. Right?"

"IT work. Yes."

"Well, my network's been down since yesterday. I can't connect to the internet. I can't get my email or anything."

"You checked your modem?"

She nodded. "I've been over all that with my provider. My modem's good, they say. I guess it's my router, which is separate from my modem. Router. Is that the right word for it?"

"Probably." He ran the rag over his forehead again. "I can come have a look. Do you mind if Kris comes along? I shut her in the utility room while I was cutting down the tree. Didn't want her to get hurt. But she'll be eager for some exercise."

"I don't mind. She's always welcome at my house. We're old friends now."

"Great. I'll put away these tools and be right over."

Pink heightened her cheeks again. "Thanks. I really appreciate it."

"No worries."

Once he was back in the house, he peeled off his shirt for the second time and washed up in the sink. After a quick comb through his hair, he put on a clean shirt, grabbed a small box of tools, and headed out the door, Kris at his heels.

Jessica's back door stood open. He rapped on the jamb, and when he heard her call to enter, he pulled on the screened door and went in.

"I'm in the studio," she added.

He followed her voice.

The room had a well-used, delightful vibe that appealed to him. Tubes of paint were scattered on one of the counter tops. Beside the tubes were brushes, a mason jar of water, and a palette stained with a variety of colors. An easel was set up with the canvas facing the windows. A couple of drawers were half open, and a white smock hung from the corner of one of them. Jessica stood in the corner near her computer, looking as cute as she had outside, even though her expression was one of frustration.

"I really hated to bother you," she said as he stepped toward her.

"I don't mind. Let's have a look."

"I couldn't get anyone to come for a service call until next week. I can't be without the internet for that long."

Ridley used to feel the same way. But he'd been without it or television for over two weeks now, and he'd survived. Of course, he wasn't trying to run a business out of his home either.

"And," Jessica continued, "it's next to impossible to manage my order forms on my phone's email. Cell service is just too slow up here in the mountains."

"So you can't print them from your phone?"

She shook her head. "Even without fast service, my printer isn't Wi-Fi or bluetooth enabled."

"That's unfortunate."

"There always seems to be something else that's needed more than a new printer." She stepped aside, giving him room to begin work. "Can I bring you something to drink? Iced tea or water."

"No, thanks. I'm fine." He glanced over his shoulder. "Don't want to risk knocking liquid over by accident."

"Right. Well, I'll leave you alone. Holler if you need me."

"Sure thing."

About half an hour later, he went looking for her. He found her tossing a ball for Kris in the backyard.

"Bad news," he said when she noticed him. "I checked everything, but it's what you suspected. The router needs replacing. Where did you get this one?"

"I don't remember." She frowned.

He wondered if her husband had bought it for her. Most likely. "I could call the hardware store for you, see if they carry them."

"They don't. I already did that after talking to tech support."

"They're easy enough to buy in Boise." He waited half a breath before adding, "I'll be happy to drive you down to the valley, if you'd rather not make the trip alone. I know you're in a hurry to get up and running with your internet again."

⁂

Jessica's heart quickened at the offer. Not that she needed him to drive her to Boise. She'd made the trip often enough without a companion, and she was fairly certain she could buy a router without his assistance. But the idea of his company during the drive there and back was a pleasing one.

"Are you sure you wouldn't mind?" she asked.

"No. I don't mind." He glanced toward the dog. "You might have to make it up to Kris later."

"I will."

"Then I'll go lock her up. We'll take my car."

"Okay." She looked down at her shorts and comfortable summer top. "Give me a few moments to change."

"You look fine to me."

Her heart did another strange flitter. "I think I'll change anyway." She looked at him again. "It won't take me long."

He nodded, and something in his gaze said she would need to prove it wouldn't take her long.

She laughed as she turned and hurried away. In her room she changed into a loose-flowing, white summer dress and a pair of cute but sensible walking shoes. In the bathroom, she checked that her hair was still tidy, then applied a bit of mascara and some pink lip gloss. That was all there was time for. She grabbed a summer sweater on her way out of her room and was standing on the front stoop, waiting, when Ridley pulled up to her house in his Subaru.

He jumped out of the car and came around to open the door for her. "You, Ms. Mason, are a woman of your word."

She smiled. "Thanks for noticing, Mr. Chesterfield." She slid onto the passenger seat, frustration forgotten, feeling like a teenager playing hooky from school. Or was it more like a teenager on a first date? Her heart fluttered yet again.

Back behind the wheel, Ridley pressed a button on the car's CD player, and soft music came through the speakers.

"Classical?" Jessica looked over at him.

"Surprised, huh. What did you expect?"

"I don't know. Bruno Mars. Justin Timberlake."

Ridley laughed as he pulled out of the driveway and onto the road.

That wasn't a sufficient answer as far as Jessica was concerned. "Besides classical, then. Who are your favorite artists?"

"Toby Mac. Casting Crowns. Matt Redman. Chris Tomlin. Big Daddy Weave."

"Christian music."

"To start with. Yeah." He glanced at her, then back at the road.

That unwelcome guilt tugged at her conscience. She used to listen to praise music while she worked, but her studio had been silent for months now. For some reason, she'd fallen out of the habit of opening her music program on her computer. Just another indicator of the coldness of her heart, she supposed, and it made her yearn for the way she used to be.

"Ridley?"

"Hmm."

"May I ask you something . . . personal?"

"I guess. Sure."

"It's about . . . about your faith."

He looked surprised. "My faith?" Obviously, he'd expected her to ask something else.

"With what you've been through lately—on the news, on the internet, with your job—none of it seems to have shaken your faith." She sighed as she turned to look out the window. "Never mind." She wished she hadn't said anything. She'd revealed more about herself with her comments than she might learn about him.

After a lengthy silence, Ridley said, "It's people I lost faith in, Jessica. Not God. God didn't cause this situation. He didn't lie *to* me, and He didn't lie *about* me. People did that."

It wasn't God who lied. It was people. Jessica's breath caught. *God never lied to me either. Joe did the lying. Only Joe.* The truth of it shivered through her. Why hadn't she understood that before now? She'd acted as if God had lied to her, but He hadn't. He'd been there to comfort her through her tragic losses. He'd been near to walk with her, if only she would let Him.

Anger welled up next. Anger at Joe for cheating on her, for breaking their family apart even before she fully realized it, for taking Angela from her. But something in her heart insisted that being angry wasn't the answer. Maybe anger was a necessary step, part of the grief process, but she had to move on from there. *Forgive him. Forgive Joe.* She knew that whisper in her spirit. She recognized God's voice, despite having closed her ears to it for so many months.

O Father, forgive me for blaming You. She knew that was the place she had to begin. With her own confession and forgiveness. But it was difficult. So very difficult.

After a long while, she looked at Ridley. "Have you forgiven them?"

"Who?"

"The people who lied to you or about you."

"Not yet. I can't yet."

His answer confused her. "Why not?"

"I'm not sure *who* to forgive."

"Not sure?"

He shrugged, his head tipping toward her as he did so. "It's complicated."

She understood complicated and decided not to ask any more questions.

MERIDIAN, IDAHO
Friday, May 8, 1931

Henry Victor, attorney-at-law, was a tall man in his late thirties. His dark hair was sprinkled with gray, as was his mustache, giving him a dignified air. Andrew was no expert, but he suspected the man's suit was of the very best quality. His well-shined shoes weren't in need of repair. He must be doing well, despite the depression. That alone must have made him attractive to Helen.

"Mr. Henning." Henry Victor didn't offer his hand. Andrew wouldn't have taken it if he had.

"Mr. Victor."

"Have a seat."

"Thank you."

If the ability to hide one's thoughts and feelings made an

attorney successful, that explained Henry Victor's nice suit. His expression told Andrew nothing. He looked neither upset nor concerned to have his mistress's husband sitting opposite him.

"My wife thinks she's in love with you," Andrew said after a lengthy silence.

Henry's eyebrows raised a fraction, but otherwise the statement brought no reaction.

"Are you in love with her?"

"Would it make a difference if I were?"

"No. I suppose not. Your feelings do not change my desire to save my marriage."

Henry leaned back, his chair creaking softly. He steepled his fingers before his mouth. "Has she asked you for a divorce?"

Andrew perceived a slight change in the man's voice. Tension? Disapproval? "No," he answered. "She hasn't. Not yet." He feared she would but didn't say so.

Henry nodded.

"I'm here to ask you to stop seeing her. Divorce isn't an option in my mind, but as long as she thinks she may end up with you . . ." He let the words trail into silence.

This, at last, got a noticeable reaction. "End up with me?" Henry barked a humorless laugh. A moment later, he sobered. "Mr. Henning, I can assure you, I have no intention of marrying Helen, even if you granted her a divorce."

The urge to punch the man returned with such force that Andrew wasn't sure he could control the cold fury that curled his hands into fists.

Henry stood. "I will end my association with her. I give you my word."

What worth was the word of a man who would sleep with a

married woman? Andrew swallowed the question as he rose from his chair. All he could do was nod before turning and leaving the office.

The receptionist glanced up from her desk, and Andrew thought he saw pity in her eyes. He hoped he was wrong. The fewer people who knew of Helen's indiscretions, the better.

But that left him wondering—how few were those who knew?

Chapter 14

Jessica expected Ridley to take her to one of the large office-supply stores in Boise. Instead, he drove to a small strip mall on the north side of town and parked in front of a business called Mac's Electronics.

"The owner's a friend of mine," he said, as if she needed an explanation. "We'll find what you need here." He got out and before she could open the passenger door herself had come around and opened it for her.

"Thanks."

He offered his hand to help her out of the car, and she took it. Her skin seemed to tingle at the touch. She let go the instant her feet were firmly on the ground.

Inside the shop, the displays were few. Jessica decided the store couldn't do much in the way of retail sales with so few products to offer. A counter off to her right had a sign above it that said *Repairs*. She assumed repair work was the larger part of their business.

"Mac?" Ridley moved toward a doorway in the rear.

"Be right with you," a voice responded. A woman's voice. A

moment later she appeared in the doorway. "Ridley!" She threw her arms around him and gave him a tight hug. "My goodness. It's good to see you."

"Thanks, Mac. Good to see you too." He took a step back, then glanced over his shoulder. "This is my neighbor, Jessica. She's in need of a new router for her home office."

"Sure thing." Mac grinned at Jessica. "I'll be glad to get you set up. I'm McKenzie, but everybody calls me Mac. I've got what you want over here." She led the way to a display on her right. "Ridley, I heard you'd left town."

"I did."

"But you're back now." She reached into a cabinet beneath the display and pulled out a box.

"Nope. Only to see you. Then I'm gone again."

Mac stopped what she was doing and laid a hand on Ridley's upper arm. "I'm sorry it was so rough around here."

"Thanks." He covered her hand with his.

Jessica felt a strange sensation curl in her belly. Almost like . . . almost like jealousy. But of course it couldn't be that.

As if he'd sensed her inner turbulence, Ridley looked in Jessica's direction and offered a small smile. "I'm doing okay. I think the worst is over now. And I like where I'm at."

The strange sensation intensified, only this time it was nothing at all like jealousy. She turned, pretending interest in the nearest display.

In a short while, Mac carried the selected router to the register. Jessica met her there.

"So Ridley's your neighbor," the woman said as she put the boxed router into a paper bag.

"Yes. Temporarily."

Curiosity filled Mac's eyes.

Rather than answer the unspoken question, Jessica held out her business credit card.

"He's a super nice guy," Mac said in a low voice. "My husband and I have been friends with him for a long time." She set a chip reader onto the counter. "Just stick the card in there when you're ready."

Jessica did as she was instructed, suddenly liking the woman more than she had a short while before. It couldn't have anything to do with the mention of a husband, could it?

Mac asked if she wanted a receipt emailed or texted to her. Jessica chose email and gave her address. By the time she was done, Ridley had joined her at the counter.

"You ready?" he asked. "If it's all right with you, we'll grab a bite to eat on our way out of town."

"Sure." She took the sack by its handles.

Mac said, "It was nice to meet you, Jessica. Come again. And Ridley, don't be a stranger. We're here if you need anything."

"I know that, Mac. Thanks. Tell Todd hi from me."

"I'll do it."

They stepped out of the air-conditioned shop into the bright sunlight. Jessica reached into her purse for her sunglasses. Ridley already wore his. The dark glasses along with his muscular build made him look more like an action movie star than a computer nerd.

"What?" he asked.

Only then did she realize she'd been staring at him. "Nothing." She slipped her glasses into place.

"I'm starved. You?"

"Sure." It was a lie. She wasn't the least bit hungry. Not with that explosion of butterflies filling her stomach.

❧

After placing their orders, Ridley and Jessica parked in the lot of the fast-food joint that had been his favorite during his senior year in high school. In his mind, the thick, juicy burgers were the definition of comfort food. He didn't indulge often, but when he did, he enjoyed every bite.

"These are huge." Jessica unwrapped one half of the burger.

"I know."

"I'll never be able to eat it all."

He lifted his burger toward his mouth. "You might be surprised."

They were silent for a short while as they took their first few bites, but eventually Jessica said, "Mac seems nice. Where did you meet her?"

"We met at church. Her husband's on staff there."

"So she runs her electronics store all by herself? Not with her husband."

"No, not with her husband. But I think she's got a couple of part-time employees. She stays pretty busy, from what I can tell. I used to send her business whenever I could. There were lots of computers and networks to see to at my last job. Somebody always had need of something that Mac could help with."

He felt Jessica watching him. At first he tried to ignore it, but finally he turned to meet her gaze.

"The news made it sound like the Treehorn campaign let you go after the information leak. Is that true?"

"No, I quit."

"Why?" The question was soft and gentle.

"I'm not sure anymore. At the time, it seemed like I owed it to

Tammy. That maybe if I wasn't with the campaign any longer, she'd be heard over the noise. I don't think it worked out that way."

"You weren't a mole for the opposition." It was a statement, not a question.

"No." He released a laugh devoid of humor. "I'm no mole for the other guys. I believed in Tammy's platform. I believed in her personally." He looked out the window. "I sure wouldn't have given the files off that laptop to anyone outside the Treehorn campaign. It wasn't my job to read them, anyway, so at the time I didn't even know what was in them."

"Why don't you tell the press that?"

"I did. At least I tried. Nobody seemed to listen." He took a deep breath. "Look. Can we talk about something else?"

"Sure. I'm sorry. I didn't mean to upset you."

He leaned slightly toward her. "You didn't upset me, Jessica. Honest. The situation is frustrating, and I'm not sure I've handled it right. But it didn't upset me to have you ask about it." For the briefest of moments, he wanted to lean even closer and kiss her. He quashed the desire. It would be unwise for himself and unfair to Jessica. He straightened in his seat and picked up the remainder of his hamburger.

Silence filled the interior of the car for a second time. Ridley was trying to figure out a way to break it when Jessica released a little gasp. Her right hand went to her abdomen. "Oooh," she breathed.

"You okay?"

"Yes. Just a little pain."

"What kind of pain?" he asked, alarmed.

She looked at him and, seeing his expression, laughed. "Don't panic. Nothing is happening. Little pains come with being pregnant."

Her left hand joined her right. "When this one isn't jabbing me, he likes to press on my lungs so I can hardly breathe."

"He?"

Still smiling, she gave a small shrug. "I don't like calling my baby 'it' most of the time, so I take turns using 'he' or 'she.'"

Sunlight caught in her blond hair, and the desire to kiss her returned, even stronger this time. An invisible cord drew him toward her as his gaze moved to her mouth. One touch of her lips on his, and he would be a goner for sure.

As if suddenly realizing what Ridley was about to do, Jessica sucked in a breath and moved closer to the door. "I'd better use the restroom," she said, a quaver in her voice, "before we start the drive home. Be right back." She opened the door and got out, moving faster than he'd thought she could.

No longer hungry—not for food, at any rate—Ridley wrapped the remainder of his burger in the paper it had come in and stuffed it into the white sack sitting on the console between the front seats. Guessing Jessica was finished, he did the same with her leftovers, then got out of the car and threw the sack into the nearest trash receptacle.

Staring toward the foothills to the north, he silently berated himself. Talk about bad timing. Jessica was still grieving the loss of a husband and child, and he'd tried to put the moves on her. How thoughtless could he be? And as if grief wasn't complication enough, she was also about seven months pregnant. The last thing he needed was to lose his head over someone like her. Only, at the moment, he didn't think there was anyone else like Jessica. She was one of a kind. Fragile, yet strong. Uncertain, yet courageous.

"Get it together, Chesterfield," he muttered beneath his breath.

He turned and saw her walking toward him and his car. And he knew. He knew it wasn't his head he was in danger of losing to her. It was his heart.

KUNA, IDAHO
Monday, May 11, 1931

Henry Victor kept his promise. Three days after Andrew went to see the attorney in his Meridian office, Helen returned from a trip to town, and the devastation written on her face—although she tried to hide it—told Andrew all that he needed to know. She said nothing before going into their bedroom and closing the door, but he knew all the same. She had been to see her lover, and Henry Victor had ended the affair.

It surprised Andrew that he ached for her, that he was sorry she had to experience this pain. He'd experienced many emotions over the past months—anger and sorrow, humiliation and indignation, perhaps regret most of all—but pity for his wife hadn't been among them. Until today.

"Dinner will be ready in half an hour," Madge Greyson said as she stirred something in a pot on the stove.

He suspected then that his mother-in-law had known about Henry Victor and also knew what had happened that afternoon. "Thanks, Mother Greyson. I'll finish my chores." He headed outside.

But he didn't attend to any chores. Instead, once in the barn, he climbed the ladder to the loft. With a heavy spirit, he walked to the loft door and looked out at the sun, riding low in the western sky.

"Likewise the Spirit also helpeth our infirmities: for we know not what we should pray for as we ought: but the Spirit itself maketh intercession for us with groanings which cannot be uttered."

Remembering the first time God had impressed that verse upon his heart, Andrew dropped to his knees. That first night, he hadn't known how to pray, because Helen was losing their infant son. Now he was in a similar place—a moment desperately in need of prayer, an urgent need for the Holy Spirit to intercede for him. A groan tore from someplace deep inside, and he leaned forward until his forehead touched the straw-strewn floor of the loft.

"God . . . O God . . ." It was the only prayer he could form. "God . . . O God . . . O God . . ."

He didn't know how long he stayed like that, how long he whispered the same words over and over and over again. But when at last he straightened, the light in the barn had changed, turning from a yellow glow to a reddish orange. Dinner must be ready by now. Had anyone called for him to return to the house? Had *Helen* called for him? Would she ever call for him again, even now that Henry Victor was out of the picture?

He drew in a slow breath. "Can she learn to love me again?"

He heard no answer, of course. All he could do was stand in faith, trusting that God would see him through whatever was yet to come.

Chapter 15

Except for church on Sundays, Jessica rarely saw Ridley in the week and a half that followed their trip to Boise. Several large custom orders came in—she was so thankful for her restored internet—and she found herself rising early and working late in order to fill them. Ridley knew how busy she was since he'd checked to make sure the new router was working. She'd told him about her influx of business, and he'd promised not to bother her while she strove to meet the deadlines.

Trouble was his not bothering her bothered her.

Far too often, when she heard the pounding of a hammer or a bark from the dog, she left her work and went to the studio window, hoping for a glimpse of Ridley. She was seldom that lucky. As was the case right now.

And she knew it was better that way. She was about eight weeks away, if the baby came on time, from being a single mother. And he was not much longer away, if he only stayed for the summer, from going back to his life in Boise. Or perhaps even farther away if his notoriety kept him from local employment, as he'd mentioned to her once.

With resolve, she returned to her stool and set to work. An hour later, she'd mostly succeeded in pushing Ridley's image from her mind when the doorbell rang. Her pulse quickened as she whisked off her paint-splattered smock, thinking it might be him. She brushed hair from her face with the back of her hand as she hurried to the front door.

As she pulled it open, she lifted her eyes. But she looked too high to meet her mother's gaze.

"Hi, honey."

"Mom." It wasn't disappointment she felt. And yet . . . "I didn't know you were driving up today." She took a step back, opening the door wider.

"The trip wasn't planned. I hope it isn't inconvenient. Is it?"

"No. Of course not. Come on in."

Her mom stepped inside, and the two of them embraced. Before her mom pulled away, the baby gave Jessica a sharp jab.

"Oh, my!" Her mom leaned back and laughed. "That was some kick. Do you put up with a lot of that?"

"A lot."

"Are you getting enough rest?"

Jessica nodded, but it was a half-truth. She spent at least eight hours in bed every night, but she didn't spend all of that time asleep. Not as of late. She could blame some of her restlessness on her pregnancy. The remainder she would have to blame on thoughts about her attractive next-door neighbor.

"I have a few things out in the car for the baby's room, but I'll bring them in later."

"Can you stay the night?" Jessica asked, but she already knew the answer.

"I came prepared to stay, but only if I won't be in the way."

"You won't be. I'm finishing up with a big order, but we can visit while I get the last of it done. If that's okay with you."

"Sure."

Jessica turned toward the kitchen. "Would you like something cool to drink? I could use a little break before going back into the studio."

"I'd love something. Whatever you have. Just water would be fine."

"I've got iced tea in the fridge. It's decaf."

"Perfect."

Jessica took the pitcher of tea from the refrigerator and set it on the counter. "Did you decide about going to Tampa for Trish's play?"

"Yes, I'm going, but it'll have to be alone. Your dad couldn't get away from work." Her mom sat at the table. "I wish you could go with me."

"Me too." She poured the tea into two tall glasses. "How long are you going to stay?"

"Just a week. You know what your grandmother liked to quote about houseguests."

Jessica smiled as she carried the glasses to the table. "They're like fish. After three days, they begin to smell." She sat across from her mom. "But that doesn't apply to mothers."

"Of course it does." Her mom took a sip of tea. "And don't worry. I'm only staying with you one night. Your father and I have plans for the Fourth."

"I wasn't worried."

"You know, in aristocratic England of the Victorian and Edwardian periods, houseguests came and stayed for weeks and weeks. Months, sometimes. I suppose that wouldn't be so bad if a person had thirty or forty bedrooms for them to stay in. Not to mention servants out the ying-yang to cater to them all."

Jessica smiled, her heart flooding with love for her mom—for no particular reason other than that she was her mom. Although she was also terribly fond of the random facts her mom liked to share every now and then, thanks to her voracious reading habit.

A frown creased her mother's brow. "What is all that barking?"

Jessica rose and moved toward the back door. The barking grew louder, and then Kris came into view. Quieting, the dog ran up to the screened door, sat, and pawed at the jamb. When the sheltie saw Jessica, she gave a quick yap, then closed her mouth, wearing a look of expectation.

"Mom, come meet Kristin Armstrong."

"Kristin Arm—Jessica, what on earth?" Her mother rose and followed Jessica to the door.

"Kris for short." She pushed open the screened door, and the sheltie padded inside with a prance worthy of the show ring.

"You got a dog? You didn't tell me you were getting a dog."

"I didn't. My neighbor got one."

Her mom's eyes widened even more. "You have a neighbor? Someone's moved in next door?"

"Yes." She heard Ridley calling for the dog. "And you're about to meet him." She stepped onto the porch. "She's over here, Ridley."

He raised an arm and waved before heading in her direction, long strides eating up the distance. "Sorry about that," he called as he neared. "She's been good about staying close to home. I thought she was through with running off. I guess she got bored, waiting for me to play with her. Hope she didn't interrupt your work."

"She didn't interrupt. I was taking a break."

Her mom stepped to her side. "Your new neighbor, I presume," she said softly.

"Ridley, this is my mom, Pat Alexander. Mom, meet Kris's owner, Ridley Chesterfield."

He held out his hand as he put a foot on the bottom step. "Nice to meet you, Mrs. Alexander."

⌒➰⌒

"And you." Jessica's mom shook his hand, questions in her eyes. He couldn't tell if it was because she'd recognized his name from the news or because she was simply curious about the man staying next door to her daughter. Funny thing was he didn't really care anymore, and that was unexpected.

Jessica said, "We were having a glass of iced tea. Would you like to join us?"

"Sure." He grinned. After all, he'd hoped for that kind of invitation. "If I wouldn't be intruding."

Jessica tipped her head toward the kitchen. "Come on inside."

It had been a long twelve days, making himself stay out of her way. He'd seen her on Sundays, of course. In fact, she'd ridden with him in his car to church. But they'd come straight back after the services so she could get in a few hours of work in the afternoons.

"Sugar or lemon or both?" Jessica poured tea into a glass.

"Lemon would be good."

Jessica turned from the counter, the glass in one hand. His heart hiccupped in his chest. She looked adorable in her coral-colored leggings, loose-flowing cotton top, and bare feet. And the sight of her made him realize he'd missed her even more than he'd thought.

Pat said, "Let's take our drinks into the living room where we'll be more comfortable." The older woman reached for the two glasses on the table, but he intercepted her.

"Allow me."

It wasn't long before they were all settled in the living room, each with their own beverage.

"When did you move in next door, Mr. Chesterfield?"

"Call me Ridley. Please. And the answer is about a month ago."

Pat sent her daughter a glance. "That long." Looking at him again, she added, "I'm relieved to know Jessica has a neighbor at last. I hated her being out here alone all of these months."

"Mom," Jessica said softly.

"Well, I can't help it. I like knowing there is someone nearby, in case there's an emergency."

"Anything she needs, Mrs. Alexander, all she has to do is ask."

"Mom, Ridley didn't buy the house next door. It belongs to his parents. He's only there for the summer." Jessica glanced at him.

Funny, how tempted he was to say that it wasn't true he was only there for the summer. Only it was true. Eventually he would have to go looking for a job. Eventually he would have to leave the peace and anonymity he enjoyed in this remote mountain community. He had a house of his own in Boise. He had a life there too. Or at least he used to. In fact, he'd spent the last week giving serious thought to what he wanted to do next in terms of a career. His gut told him that what he'd been through in recent months would influence his decision. He just didn't know what that meant yet.

Pat set her glass on a coaster on the coffee table, drawing him from his thoughts. "When do you expect your parents to move in?"

"Not for a number of years. They plan to vacation here in the summers until they retire. Then they'll live here full time."

"Are they in Boise now?"

"Arizona."

Kris trotted into the living room and pushed her muzzle

beneath Jessica's hand where it rested on the arm of the chair. Jessica immediately began to stroke the dog's head.

"Looks like the two of you are good friends," Pat said.

"Kris loves your daughter." Ridley looked at Jessica, and he felt that now familiar quickening in his heart. "Maybe because she gave her a name." He grinned, as if sharing a secret with her.

Jessica met his gaze and returned his smile.

After a period of silence, her mom said, "If you two will excuse me, I think I'll bring in my things from the car."

Although he heard Pat's words, he was too taken by Jessica's eyes for the meaning to penetrate. Her mother had already risen and taken a step away from the sofa before he realized what he'd heard her say. He stood quickly. "Let me help you."

"Oh, heavens. I don't need help. Sit there and enjoy your tea. Visit with Jessica. I'll only be a moment." She slipped out the door.

Willing to be dissuaded, Ridley's gaze returned to Jessica. "She's staying, I take it."

"For the night. She said she brought things for the baby's room, but that was just an excuse. She worries about me."

"I got that." He almost said that he was going to worry about her, too, once he wasn't staying next door. A foolish inclination. She wasn't his responsibility.

"She doesn't need to worry," Jessica said. "Not anymore. I'm stronger now. Stronger than she knows. Stronger than I knew until . . . until recently."

KUNA, IDAHO

Tuesday, June 23, 1931

Sweat trickled down Andrew's spine as he pitched hay from the wagon onto the growing stack north of the barn. Emil, the hired hand, stood on the top of a ladder, pushing the alfalfa hay even higher with his pitchfork.

The weather had been kind to them for this first cutting. It had been warm and sunny for weeks. Rarely even a cloud in the sky. Abundant sunshine was the most important ingredient for a successful hay harvest. Rain was the enemy when it came time to cut, dry, and stack.

"When we're done with this wagonload, Emil, we'll call it a day."

"Sounds good to me. I'm beat."

Andrew wanted a bath more than anything. Chaff had worked its way beneath his shirt and the band of his trousers and into his socks. It was everywhere on his sweaty body, pricking his skin, making him itch.

Half an hour later, Emil bid Andrew a good evening and walked away from the farm toward his home a mile away. Andrew watched until he disappeared from view, then went to the pump, removed his hat, and bent over to wash the hay out of his hair. Afterward, he gave his head a good shake, like a dog coming out of the creek. When he straightened and turned toward the house, he saw Helen standing on the porch, watching him. He expected her to look away when their gazes met. She usually did. This time she didn't. Then he expected her to go back into the house. She didn't do that either.

Pushing his hair back from his face with one hand, he moved toward the porch. "It's a hot one."

She nodded.

He touched his sweat-dampened shirt. "I'll take a bath before dinner."

Another nod.

It had been like this between them for more than a month. He said something. She nodded or shook her head. When they were in the same room, he treated her like a fragile figurine, afraid that she would break with the slightest wrong move. Much of the time, she shut herself away from both him and her mother. When they did see her, she was listless, aimless. Andrew and his mother-in-law didn't talk about Helen, except to exchange glances of concern. He couldn't bring himself to tell Mother Greyson what he knew. He supposed it was the same for her.

"I've got a buyer for the hay," he said, encouraged that she hadn't left the porch.

"Good."

The barn loft had become his prayer closet. Every day he made his way there, as soon as the morning milking was done. He prayed many things up there on his knees amidst the hay and dust, but mostly he prayed for Helen. He prayed that she would forgive him for stopping the affair. He prayed she would ask to be forgiven, by God if not by him. He prayed she would find contentment. He prayed she would learn she had a choice to be happy. He prayed she would find her way back to the Lord. He prayed she could learn to love him again, that she would believe love could blossom between them as if something new.

Andrew was no saint. He struggled at times with anger, with frustration, with resentment, with wanting to throw up his hands and walk away and never look back. He struggled with an ache in his chest that sometimes seemed too much to bear. He prayed about all of that too.

He hadn't been the patient sort in his youth. He'd been in a hurry to grow up. He'd been in a hurry to finish school. He'd been impatient to begin a business career, something that would take him to the city and away from the farm. For that matter, he'd been impatient to marry Helen.

But he had to be patient in this. Yet he couldn't stand still either.

Running his fingers over his wet hair again, he asked, "Would you care to take a walk this evening when the temperature cools?"

"No." She lowered her eyes. A lengthy silence followed. Then, "But thank you for asking . . . Andrew."

His breath caught at the sound of his name on her lips. He couldn't remember the last time she'd spoken it. Many weeks. Before he'd gone to see Henry Victor. In his heart, he grasped that slender thread of hope like a drowning man grasps a lifeline.

"Another night," he said.

The slightest of smiles tugged at the corners of her mouth. There and then gone. "Perhaps." She turned and went inside.

Chapter 16

"I like your neighbor," Jessica's mom said the next morning as they sat at the breakfast table.

It had surprised Jessica that her mom hadn't mentioned Ridley after he and Kris went back to their place yesterday. She hadn't mentioned him as she presented Jessica with canvas bags full of baby clothes and more, and she hadn't mentioned him during dinner or the evening spent watching a favorite movie.

It seemed the avoidance of the topic was over.

"He seems nice. What do you know about him?"

Defensiveness rose in her chest. "He *is* nice." She ignored the question.

"You must know *something* about him," her mom pressed.

Jessica released a soft breath. "Do you know who Tammy Treehorn is?"

"Of course. She was the candidate I planned to vote for, although she's withdrawn from the race now. Just as well. Poor woman. I felt sorry for her. How many of us would like our mistakes to be plastered all over the news?"

"Ridley worked for her. Some people blamed him for what happened. For the information that came out about Ms. Treehorn."

"*He* was to blame for that?"

"No, but I guess some people pointed the finger at him."

"My goodness." Her mom gazed down into her coffee mug, allowing silence to fill the room.

"It wasn't the accusations saying he did something underhanded that bothered me. Which I don't believe, by the way. Not after getting to know him. It's how vicious people have been. Especially on the internet. Everyone's become so cruel anymore. You can't just disagree with one another. If someone doesn't agree with you, then he is an enemy that must be silenced. Or worse."

Jessica had never been as politically active as her parents, and she'd cared even less about politics and government in recent months. She'd been in too much of a fog to care. Even with the fog lifting, she couldn't bring herself to be concerned for anybody involved in the Treehorn campaign. Anyone except Ridley.

Why was that?

"Honey."

She took a sip from her own mug. "Mmm?"

"Be careful."

"Careful?"

"You shouldn't become involved with anyone right now. Especially not anybody with troubles of his own, which he certainly has. You're too vulnerable. You've been through so much in the past year."

Jessica shook her head. "You said you liked him. And last night you said you were glad I had someone living next door."

"I *am* glad of that. I've hated you being out here, all by yourself, so far from town."

"Besides," Jessica continued as if her mom hadn't spoken, "I'm not involved with him. Ridley is my neighbor. That's all."

"Okay. Okay. I'm sorry I said anything."

Jessica was sorry too. She rose and carried her mug to the sink. After rinsing it, she put it in the dishwasher. As she straightened, her gaze lifted to the window.

Morning light showed how badly the old swing set needed a coat of paint. Two summers ago, Joe had promised he would get around to painting it. He never had. He never would have gotten around to it . . . even if he'd lived.

On the heels of that thought came another. She would have been okay. She and Angela would have survived his going. It wouldn't have been easy, but they would have survived. God would have seen them through, just as God was seeing her through now.

"Mom." She turned and leaned her backside against the counter. "You don't have to worry about me. Not about me being alone and not about any involvement with Ridley Chesterfield." She drew in a slow breath. "I may be vulnerable, but I'm not weak and I'm not foolish."

৩৩৩

Standing on the sidewalk across the street from the Tammy Treehorn campaign office, wearing dark glasses and a baseball cap pulled low on his forehead, Ridley watched and waited for employees and volunteers to leave for lunch. But nobody came out and nobody entered. So different from the last time he'd been on this sidewalk.

For the past two weeks, ever since his visit to Mick Phelps's office, Ridley had been contemplating this trip to Boise. Not that the pastor had advised him to meet with Tammy. Mostly Mick had listened and then asked questions to help Ridley discover the answers for himself. His main takeaway from that meeting, however, had been that he could trust God to guide him, both into the known and the unknown. And this morning God had done just that. Which was why he was here now. It was time.

Drawing a determined breath, Ridley crossed the street to the glass door of the office. Inside, there were only two young women seated at desks. They looked to be barely more than eighteen. He recognized one of them as Tammy's oldest daughter, although he'd never been introduced to her. Most of the remainder of desks were missing papers and file folders. The office felt almost . . . abandoned, and it saddened him to see it that way.

He nodded toward the two young women and pointed toward the back of the building, hoping he looked like he knew exactly what he was doing and where he was going. It worked. Neither of them called after him to stop. Perhaps neither of them cared.

His luck continued to hold. When he rapped on the door to Tammy's office, she responded, "Come in."

He opened the door, stepped inside, and closed it before she looked up from a stack of papers on the desk. Remaining near the door, he removed his dark glasses.

Tammy's eyes widened. "Ridley."

"Ms. Treehorn." He'd called her by her first name in the past, but now that didn't seem right.

"I didn't expect you. Did we have an appointment?"

"No." He gave his head a slow shake. "We didn't. When I tried to make one, I was told that wasn't possible."

"By who?" She stood.

"Rachelle."

She motioned for the chair across the desk from her own. "When was that?"

"Right before I resigned. Bob Tate told me the same about a week later."

"I'm sorry, Ridley." Tammy leaned back in her chair. "Of course it was possible for you to meet with me. I would have welcomed it."

He'd suspected as much. He should have persisted.

He took the offered chair. "Let me just say what I came to say. I recovered that data off the laptop, but I didn't pass it to the opposition. I followed protocol."

"You gave the data files to Kurt Cooper." She wasn't asking a question.

Something inside of him eased. "Yes."

She turned her head and looked out the window. Her expression seemed bruised. "I never lied about the abortion," she said softly. "I simply kept it to myself. But that's the same thing as a lie, I guess. A lie by omission."

He didn't know how to respond, so he said nothing.

Tammy met his gaze again. "I was sixteen and so, so stupid." She sighed, then added, "And I wasn't a Christian at the time, so my choice didn't seem wrong."

"I'm sorry."

"Oh, Ridley. You are not the one who should be sorry. This is on me. I know you took a lot of heat from all quarters, from both sides of the aisle. There were people who wanted to blame anybody but me. That wasn't right. My silence wasn't right either. Not about the abortion and not later when it came out the way it did. I listened to my advisors, and I should have gone with what my convictions told me was right. With what my faith told me was right. I hurt my family. I hurt my party. I hurt all the people who believed in me.

Including you." She lowered her gaze to her hands, now folded atop her desk. "The truth will out."

He leaned forward. "Do you know who leaked the story?"

"Not for certain, although I have my suspicions. No one has taken responsibility. Perhaps no one ever will. Most everyone has moved on to other jobs. I've become a punchline, to be pointed at whenever another scandal derails a politician."

"I haven't been following the news lately. Have you officially left the race?"

She nodded. "It was the best thing to do. For me and for my family. For the party too." She pointed toward the front office. "I've got a skeleton staff helping me clear things out."

"I noticed."

"My daughter and one of her friends." She showed a quick but sad smile. "They're home from college for the summer."

"Ah."

"Ridley? I will do whatever I can to make certain it's known that you did nothing wrong. And I will write you a letter of recommendation." She issued a short laugh. "For whatever that might be worth."

"I appreciate it, Tammy. I really do."

He'd come for answers, not an apology. Although the apology was appreciated. Still, Tammy said she couldn't tell him who had tried to put the blame on him, smearing his reputation. He found he believed her. Not only that, he realized it didn't matter to him what others said nor who had caused them to say it. Knowing who was to blame no longer mattered to him. He could trust God with whatever he didn't know. He knew the truth about himself. He'd always known it. He would be okay, whether or not Tammy was able to clear his name with the media. His future was in God's hands. He would let the Lord take care of his career, whatever that would eventually look like.

Ridley stood. "I hope it all works out for you. I hope you find a way to use your talents and make the difference you want to make."

"Thanks, Ridley. I appreciate your good wishes. Especially given the circumstances. I hope the same for you too."

He took a step away from the chair, then stopped. "I've had to remember something in the last weeks. 'There is now no condemnation for those who are in Christ Jesus.' God's all about second chances, even when we mess things up because we weren't listening to Him."

"Thank you." A smile flickered across her lips and was gone. "It's a good reminder."

KUNA, IDAHO
Saturday, September 26, 1931

The wedding of Martha Standish and Eddie Edwards took place at two o'clock on a mild September afternoon. Flowers of autumn—bright yellows, brilliant oranges, deep reds—covered the altar and were tied to the pew ends with satin ribbons. Since first grade, the bride had been a close friend of Helen's. The groom had played baseball with Andrew when they were young boys. In fact, the two of them had smoked their first—and for Andrew, his last—cigarettes behind the barn of the Henning farm.

Andrew sat with his wife and mother-in-law about midway down the center aisle, and while he pretended to listen as the minister spoke the words of the marriage ceremony over the couple, his thoughts were far away. He was remembering his own wedding that had taken place in this same church. He had been working in Portland, Oregon, on his and Helen's first anniversary. Would she want to even acknowledge, let alone celebrate, their second anniversary when it arrived in a few short weeks?

He remembered promising himself on his wedding day that he would never let Helen regret marrying him. He hadn't kept that promise. She had regretted her choice, regretted it many times, regretted it enough to break the vows they'd spoken. And when her affair with another man had ended, she'd stayed with Andrew, he feared, only because she had nowhere else to go.

He glanced to his left. Helen looked lovely in lavender. It was the perfect color with her hair and complexion. The dress wasn't new. She hadn't had a new dress since before he lost his job at the start of the depression. That was a long time for a girl like Helen. She deserved finer things than he'd been able to provide.

He looked straight ahead again, reminding himself that despite the depression that dragged on and on, they were okay. So many were in much worse shape than they were. The hay cuttings this past growing season had brought in enough to buy the essentials that the farm itself didn't supply for the family. And while his marriage to Helen wasn't what it once was, it was better than it had been in the spring. He had reason to hope.

With God, all things are possible.

Sometimes he repeated those words to himself a dozen times a day. He supposed it was part of the practice of bringing into captivity every thought to the obedience of Christ, the way Second Corinthians told believers to do.

As if in answer to his current thoughts, Helen's gloved fingertips touched the back of his hand where it rested on his thigh. He looked at her and saw a flicker of emotion hidden in the depth of her eyes. Perhaps guilt. Perhaps regret. Perhaps an apology. And perhaps she had remembered that she'd loved him on the day of their own wedding. Hope soared in his heart at that last possibility.

With God, all things *were* possible.

Chapter 17

It was a cliché, but Ridley felt like a new man as he left Boise and drove toward Hope Springs. Lots of negative feelings, even ones he hadn't known he harbored, had been left on the floor of the Treehorn campaign office.

How did that other cliché go? He spoke the answer aloud: "Today is the first day of the rest of my life." He laughed to himself. But the truth was that's how he felt.

For the rest of his time in Hope Springs, he meant to spend it mapping out his future, finding that new calling. Actually, he probably didn't need to stay in Hope Springs any longer. He could go home to Boise if he wanted. Only . . . that didn't seem to be what he wanted. Not yet.

Back in Hope Springs, he noticed Jessica's mom's car wasn't in the driveway. Was Jessica alone again, or had the two of them driven into town?

Last week, Jessica had asked him if he'd forgiven the people who lied about him. He'd answered that it wasn't possible because he didn't know who to forgive. He would have a different answer for her now. He was able to forgive the person or persons who remained nameless. He'd also forgiven Tammy for her silence in the wake of the debacle, and he'd forgiven himself for not listening to his gut when it told him something wasn't quite right.

Okay, Lord. I'm really letting go of it all. You know my future. You can show me what it is and how I'm supposed to get there. I trust You.

He let Kris out of the house and threw a ball for her, hoping to wear her out a little. Between every throw, he glanced across the field toward Jessica's house. Was she there? Would she see or hear him with the dog and come outside? He'd like to tell her about his day, about his thoughts, about his feelings.

Oh, he knew none of that was a good idea. After all, where could it lead? Jessica's heart was taken by a man who no longer lived. She still wept or withdrew when Joe Mason was mentioned. It was possible she wouldn't ever be ready to love again. On top of all that there was the matter of her pregnancy. How would the baby impact any future relationship? How would it impact him if he chose to pursue something more with Jessica? And, of course, there was the problem with location. This was her hometown, but it wasn't his. His stay was supposed to be temporary. Would she consider living elsewhere? He didn't know. He'd never asked. Why would he? He had no reason to ask.

He motioned for Kris to join him, and the two of them went inside. The dog paused in the utility room, lapping water from the bowl next to her empty food dish. Ridley kept walking. He passed through the kitchen and went into the living room. His eyes moved to the mantel. His mom had said she planned for a TV to hang on the wall above the mantel. Fortunately, cable television was available, even this far out from town, and now that he didn't feel the need to isolate himself from the rest of the world, he decided that would be his next project for the folks. That and the internet.

Which took his thoughts back to Jessica. Had he asked her yesterday if her new router continued to work properly? He couldn't remember. He did remember that he'd liked her mom. And he hoped she'd liked him. She'd seemed glad to have him living next door.

He shook his head. What good was it to stand there and think about Jessica when he could walk right over to her house and talk to her? Maybe it was temporary. Maybe they only had the summer. But he liked her company. Was it a crime to like a woman's company without a promise of tomorrow? No. No, it wasn't a crime.

"Come on, Kris." He headed out the door again, the dog at his heels.

⌒ↂↄ⌒

Through a nap haze, Jessica heard Kris's sharp bark, the one meant to get attention. The one that meant, "I've come for a visit. Let me in." Amazing how quickly Jessica had learned to interpret the dog's language.

Releasing a soft groan, she used the back of the sofa to pull herself to a sitting position. A moment later she stood.

"Anybody home?" Ridley called, followed by a soft rap.

Pressing on the small of her back with her fingertips, trying to stretch out a few kinks, Jessica moved toward the kitchen, stopping when Ridley and Kris came into view beyond the screen door. "Hi." She sent them a sleepy smile.

Ridley grinned back. "Did we wake you?"

"No," she lied, knowing he wasn't fooled. "Come on in." She motioned him forward before turning so he wouldn't see her yawn.

"Is your mom still here?" The screen door announced its opening.

Jessica faced him again. "She left right after lunch."

"Sorry I missed her." He moved into the center of the kitchen and stopped.

She smiled again, feeling happy for no explainable reason. "She'll be back again. Probably after her trip to see my sister."

"I forgot to ask yesterday if your internet's still working as it should. No trouble with the new router?"

"It's working. No trouble."

"Good. Good."

She stifled a second yawn. "I think I could use a cup of coffee. My doctor allows me twelve ounces of caffeine a day, when and if I want it. I want it. You?"

"Sure. If you're going to make it."

"I am." She headed for the coffeemaker, slowing as she passed between Ridley and the counter. Funny how his nearness made her breath catch, how afraid she was that her enlarged belly might rub against his arm. Her awareness of him had always surprised her. Right from the very start.

Jessica had loved two men in her life—her dad and Joe. In very different ways, of course. Her dad had spoiled her rotten, had thrown her into the air as a toddler, had rubbed her back when she was sick in bed and had to stay home from school, had held her when she shed teenaged tears because she thought herself ugly, had grinned with pride as he'd walked her down the aisle. And Joe . . . Joe had loved her for a season, then had broken her heart. Would she ever want to risk another broken heart?

"You shouldn't become involved with anyone right now," her mom's voice whispered in her memory. *"You're too vulnerable."*

"Can I help?" Ridley asked.

"No, thanks."

163

She heard him move and couldn't stop herself from glancing over her shoulder. He had stepped to the nearby counter and leaned his backside against it. He seemed comfortable while she felt as if the kitchen was shrinking in size. She looked forward again. Soon she had the ground coffee out of the fridge and the reservoir in the coffeemaker filled with water. It wasn't long before she pressed the button for it to begin brewing.

"Did you make the deadline on those orders?" Ridley asked, breaking the brief silence.

She looked over her shoulder a second time. "Yeah. I did. And I'm not going back into my studio until Monday. A whole weekend off."

"Good for you." He smiled.

The look made something inside of her melt like butter.

I like him. I like him so very much. Trying to sound normal, she asked, "What did you do with yourself today?"

"I drove down to Boise to see Tammy Treehorn."

Surprised, she turned to face him. "You did?"

"I did."

"And?"

"And I think I took care of that forgiveness matter you asked me about. Not just Ms. Treehorn but the unknowns too."

"That's good. I'm glad for you." She *was* glad for him. She also envied him, although she couldn't tell him how she felt. Not without explaining why—which she couldn't do. It was one thing to tell her mother about Joe's unfaithfulness, another to share it with someone outside her immediate family. But her heart told her she would never be completely free of the hurt until she forgave Joe. She'd made strides—back to God, back to her faith, back to a kind of peace. Still . . .

"Something's wrong," Ridley said softly. "You look unhappy."

"Do I?" For some unknown reason, she touched her mouth with the fingertips of her right hand. "I'm not. Not really."

His gaze lowered from her eyes to her lips, and she felt her breath catch. She saw his desire to kiss her and knew she wanted the same. Knew she wouldn't resist him, even if she should. He pushed away from the counter and crossed the kitchen with only a few, measured strides. She tipped her head back so she could hold his gaze.

"Jessica," he whispered.

She almost couldn't hear him over the pounding of her heart.

He cupped the sides of her head with his large hands. Tenderly. Gently. Her eyes fluttered closed, and her breath came out on a sigh mere seconds before his lips pressed against hers. There was an explosion of color behind her eyelids. His arms moved to embrace her. She swayed into him, truly weak in the knees. She would have collapsed if he hadn't been there to hold her.

Perhaps that's why the baby kicked. Perhaps her baby feared she would fall. Or perhaps it was her rapid heartbeat that alarmed the little life. Whatever the reason, the hard jab to her abdomen brought her to her senses. It made her remember all the reasons her mom thought she was vulnerable and should be careful. She drew back, her breathing quick and shallow as she opened her eyes to stare into his. "I think . . . I think the coffee is ready."

"Yes." His voice sounded gruff. Maybe the baby's kick—which he couldn't have helped but feel—had brought him to his senses as well. He took a step back from her.

She busied herself with pouring coffee into two oversized mugs, hating that her hands remained unsteady when she carried them to the kitchen table. Silently, he followed her there, and they sat in chairs opposite each other. She stirred a little sugar into her coffee, not because she wanted the sweetener but because she wanted a reason not to look at him yet.

"Was that an unforgivable mistake?" he asked at long last.

She lifted her gaze. "Not unforgivable."

"But still a mistake."

"I'm not . . . I don't . . ." Not knowing what to say, she let the words die in her throat.

He nodded. "Bad timing on my part."

"Bad timing," she echoed in a whisper.

They sipped their coffees during another long silence.

"Jessica." He set down his mug.

"Hmm?"

"I'm sorry my timing was off." He leaned forward. "But I don't want that to ruin things between us."

What is there between us, Ridley? she wondered as she looked into his eyes, her pulse quickening again.

He pushed his chair back from the table and stood. "I'd better go feed Kris. She's gotta be hungry."

Jessica looked at the dog, who lay peacefully on the floor nearby. Kris didn't look the least bit hungry or in a hurry to go home. But that excuse was as good as any to let him leave.

She gave him a wobbly smile. "You can tell me about your trip to Boise later."

"Yeah." He didn't return her smile. "Later."

⁂

The next day, Ridley threw himself into repairs with even more intensity than when he'd first arrived in Hope Springs. Only this time he wasn't an hour's drive away from what he wanted to escape.

The focus of his troubled thoughts and feelings was living right next door.

That kiss. That blasted kiss. Why had he given in to the desire? He should have known he was moving too fast for her. And there were numerous reasons that he shouldn't *move* at all. Reasons he'd gone over in his head time and time again. The first of which, it was obvious she wasn't ready to fall in love again.

Love? The word reverberated in his mind, in his heart. Was that what he felt for Jessica Mason? Was it love?

He'd hoped to one day find love with the right woman. He'd hoped to marry and have a family. But Jessica was already pregnant. Her child would be a reminder of the husband she'd loved and lost. Did she have it in her heart to love again? Or perhaps he should be asking, did he have it in himself to love her baby as his own? Because that's what a relationship with her would require. He couldn't spend his life wondering if he measured up to Joe Mason, and he would have to be able to love the child she carried exactly the same as he would love any children they might have together later. He wanted to believe it would make no difference to him. But how could he be sure?

Maybe he couldn't measure up to Joe Mason.

He'd come to Hope Springs to get away from his career troubles, and now it seemed he'd landed in a completely different kind of problem. One of a romantic nature.

Jessica . . .

Jessica . . .

Jessica . . .

It would be easier to walk away, to leave Hope Springs and go back to the life he knew.

Definitely easier.

Definitely.

KUNA, IDAHO

Christmas Day, 1931

Andrew finished up his evening chores. Christmas or not, the animals had to be tended to, especially in the cold of winter. When he opened the barn door, he found snow falling. It had been doing so long enough for the world to have turned white. He paused and watched it for a while, letting the silence settle over him.

It had been a good day. The Christmas service at church this morning. His parents over for dinner in the afternoon. A few gifts to open beside the Christmas tree in the living room. Shawls for his mother and mother-in-law. A new pipe for his father. A bracelet for Helen. Mother Greyson had knitted him a scarf and hat, and his parents had given him a pair of gloves.

Pulling his coat collar close around his neck, he strode toward the house. He shook off the snow and stomped his boots before stepping inside. The kitchen was dark except for the faint orange glow showing around the door of the stove. He stepped over to it and warmed himself, then moved to the living-room entrance. Helen sat alone in the room, seated close to the lamp, her sewing box beside her.

"It's snowing," he told her.

"I saw." She set the sewing box on the floor near her feet. "Mother's gone to bed. She said it was early but she couldn't hold her eyes open another minute." She patted the sofa. "Would you like to join me?"

Pleased by the unexpected invitation, he moved across the room and sat where she indicated.

"It was a nice Christmas," she said, her gaze on the small tree in the corner. She and her mother had decorated it a few days earlier with ornaments made of paper and strings of popped corn.

"Yes, it was nice."

"It was good to have your parents here."

"Yes."

"I hope they didn't think ill of me, that I didn't give you your gift along with the others."

He hadn't expected a gift from her, but he didn't say so.

"It wasn't something I could wrap."

He turned his eyes on her again.

"Andrew . . . I'm going to have a baby."

His heart seemed to stop, then race. "Are you . . . are you sure?"

She nodded. "I'm sure."

For many months, beginning even before his father-in-law's death, they'd shared a bed without intimacy, but there had come a night in the autumn—not long after Martha and Eddie Edwards's wedding—when she'd allowed him to draw her into his embrace. Their relationship had been different after that. Still tentative at times, but different. Better. Did she love him again? He didn't know. She hadn't said so. But the sadness in her eyes was seen much less often.

"Helen . . ." He hoped his love came through in his voice before he leaned in and kissed her. When he pulled back again, he asked, "When?"

"Early July."

"An Independence Day baby?"

"Maybe."

"Are you . . . happy about it?"

She nodded.

"*For who hath despised the day of small things?*" The verse from Zechariah played in his mind. It came with a new understanding and appreciation. They had taken many small steps toward each other over recent months. They had experienced numerous small beginnings. He wasn't to despise how little they might be nor disparage how long it had taken them to happen.

And now all of those steps and new beginnings had brought them to this moment. They were to have a baby. He and Helen.

He could do nothing but rejoice and thank God for bringing them this far.

Chapter 18

Between Billie Fisher and Carol Donaldson, Jessica hadn't had a chance of staying home from the Independence Day celebrations in town. It was her own fault. She'd stopped being a complete recluse, let herself go to lunch with a friend and to church on Sundays, and suddenly no one honored her desire for privacy. And perhaps that was just as well. Being with friends might keep her from thinking too much about Ridley . . . and that kiss. Oh, that kiss.

Hope Springs had a nice-sized park with a band shell, a large covered picnic area, and some tall trees for shade. The temperature had risen to 80 degrees by the time Billie and Jessica arrived in town on the Fourth. Billie had insisted on driving out to get her, probably so Jessica couldn't change her mind and not go at the last minute.

"Look." Billie pointed. "There's Carol." She waved her arm before going to the back of her car and pulling items from the trunk—a couple of blankets, a rolling cooler, and two camping chairs. She hadn't allowed Jessica to bring anything other than her favorite brand of sunscreen.

They joined Carol on the grassy edge of the park, exchanging hugs.

Carol said, "I staked out a good spot for us near the band shell that will be in the shade the entire afternoon."

"That's great," Billie replied. "Let's go."

Carol smiled at Jessica as they walked. "I hope you're taking a rest now that you filled those orders." She looked at Billie. "You should have seen the number of boxes and padded envelopes I picked up at her house over the last week. I thought she was single-handedly trying to make sure I keep my job."

They all laughed, but Jessica thought her friend might be half serious.

The park bustled with activity. Several food trucks sat parked on the east side, all of them doing a brisk business, and it appeared a three-legged race was underway at the southern end of the park. The sandpit at the north end hosted a volleyball game.

It had been announced the previous week that there would be no fireworks display due to the extremely dry conditions. The mountain areas had experienced an unusually wet spring, but rain hadn't been seen in many weeks, meaning there was plenty of dry fuel should a spark land in the wrong place. Instead of fireworks, lights had been strung from tree to tree and all around the band shell. Later there would be music and dancing. Not that Jessica would take part in the latter.

After leaving their gear at the spot Carol had chosen, the three women made their way first to one of the vendors to buy flavored snow cones. Jessica chose the rainbow—the sign said the flavors were cherry, lime, pineapple, and blueberry.

"Your lips are going to be an interesting color when you're done." Billie laughed.

"Jessica Mason! Is that you? I haven't seen you since the funeral."

Recognizing the voice, she tried not to cringe as she turned around. "Ellery. Yes, it's me." She forced a smile. Ellery Wallace was *not* one of her favorite people.

Strikingly beautiful with delicate features, dark hair, green eyes, and a tall, lithe body, Ellery had a toxic personality, loving to pit one person against another for her own amusement. "Good grief!" Her eyes widened. "Look at you. You've gotten so fat!"

"Thanks." Jessica couldn't hold her smile in place any longer.

"A woman gets larger when she's having a baby," Carol said dryly, drawing closer to Jessica's right side.

"Pregnant?" A little of the color left Ellery's cheeks. "I hadn't heard. Did Joe know before—" She broke off.

Jessica was taken aback by the unfinished question. Her mind went momentarily blank.

Billie stepped forward on Jessica's left side. "Is that boyfriend of yours with you, Ellery? What's his name? Ted?"

Ellery flicked her ponytail over her shoulder. "He's around."

"I thought maybe the two of you broke up," Billie added.

"We didn't break up." Ellery's expression hardened. "He wanted to play volleyball. I don't like sand."

"Hmm," Billie and Carol said in unison.

Ellery sent them each a scathing look. Then, an icy smile curving her mouth, she said to Jessica, "Good luck with the baby." Head held high, she swirled around and walked away.

Beneath her breath, Billie hissed like a cat.

Jessica lightly slapped her friend's arm. "That's not nice."

"*I'm* not nice?" Billie tipped her head in the departing Ellery's direction. "She had her claws out the instant she saw you. Did you do something to her?"

"We've always been civil to each other, although I admit I've never liked her much."

Carol grunted. "Unlike most of the men in this town. She plays guys like a maestro with a violin. They never see her nasty side until it's too late."

"Not *most* of the men," Jessica countered.

"Sometimes you're just too nice for your own good, my friend." Billie took hold of Jessica's arm. "Come on. Let's go watch the games."

The threesome headed toward the gathering of people at the south end of the park. Jessica felt the warmth of the sun on the top of her head. More than that, she felt the warmth of this community. She heard voices raised in conversations and lots of laughter, and pleasure washed over her.

"Thank you." Stopping, she looked from Billie to Carol and back again. "Thank you both."

"For what?" Carol asked.

"For not letting me slip away completely."

Carol patted her back and Billie squeezed her arm. Then the three of them moved on.

⁊⁊

Thanks to Mick Phelps, Ridley found himself about to run in the last three-legged race of the afternoon. His partner was a little red-haired girl whose father, he was told, was currently deployed overseas. Cassie was her name, and she informed him she was nine years old and fast as a fox.

"We'll win if you can do your part," she said, eyes narrowed as she gave him a once-over.

"Don't worry, Cassie. I know how to run a three-legged race."

"I hope so." Clearly, she didn't believe him.

He wanted to tell her there were other things he could do at this moment rather than listen to a nine-year-old insult him. Then again, he supposed that would make him sound like a nine-year-old himself. Chuckling at the thought, he said, "I promise to do my best."

Standing next to the girl, Ridley took the provided strip of heavy cloth and tied their ankles together. Of course, three-legged races were best run with partners of equal height, but since every other pair in the race had the same disadvantage—one adult and one child—he wasn't worried about it. If he had to, he'd carry Cassie across the finish line. Hopefully in first place, because he liked to win every bit as much as the girl seemed to.

They were getting into place at the starting line when he looked up and saw Jessica on the sidelines with two other women. He searched his mind for the names of her friends, but before he placed them, Jessica looked in his direction. Surprise overtook her expression, followed by amusement. She whispered something to Carol—he'd remembered names by this time—and the two of them laughed.

"Cassie." He looked down at his racing partner. "We *are* going to win this thing."

She grinned, and the freckles across the bridge of her nose and her cheeks seemed to jump about in a wild dance.

"Ready!" a voice to his right shouted.

Cassie's right arm went around his waist. His left arm went around her shoulders.

"Start with our outside feet," Ridley said.

"Right," Cassie replied.

"Set!"

He leaned forward slightly.

"Go!"

They bolted from the line like a racehorse from a starting gate. Ridley was fast, but it was trickier than he'd expected running with someone almost half his height. Still, Cassie was a game little thing. She ran more like a gazelle, making her strides surprisingly long.

"Hold on, Cassie," he shouted to her. "We've got the lead."

"I'm holdin' on!" Her knuckles pressed into his back at his waistband.

With a slight turn of his head, he saw a father-daughter team he'd spoken with earlier not far behind them. *Oh, no, you don't.* Gritting his teeth, he put everything he had into the last ten yards of the race. Three strides beyond the finish line, he tripped over Cassie's foot and the two of them pitched forward into the grass. He pulled back on the girl, trying to take the brunt of the fall himself— and did, if his right elbow and both knees could be believed.

Cassie didn't care. She was screaming and laughing and hooting with joy. "We did it, Mr. Chesterfield. We did it. We won." She managed to twist around and untie their ankles before Ridley could right himself. "We won!"

"Yeah, I know." Sitting up, he brushed grass and dirt from his elbow. A bit of skin came with it.

"You okay? You need help gettin' up?"

He hadn't known how ancient a smart-mouthed nine-year-old could make him feel. "No, thanks. I'm good." He stood up and brushed at his knees with both hands. More skin and a little blood this time. It made him wish he'd worn Levis instead of Bermuda shorts, but he hadn't anticipated being coerced into a three-legged race by a pastor.

A short while later, he and Cassie got their first-place ribbons. The ribbons came with safety pins, and Cassie pinned hers to her blouse. Then she thanked him for the race and ran to join her mom.

Ridley stared at the ribbon in his hand. Why not? He pinned it to his T-shirt. When he turned around, he found Jessica and her friends standing nearby. He'd lost sight of them when the race started and had assumed they'd moved on to other spectator sports when it was over. He was entirely too pleased to find Jessica had stuck around.

"Congratulations," she said, laughter in the word.

"Thanks."

She pointed at his knees. "You need to get that cleaned up."

"I'm okay."

"Come on. You don't want it to get infected." She motioned with her hand. "First aid's right over there." Then to her friends she added, "I'll meet you back at our chairs."

"Okay," the other two women said in unison. They each acknowledged him with a wave but didn't linger to talk to him.

"How did you get roped into that race?" Jessica asked as she and Ridley started for the First-Aid Station.

"Pastor Mick."

She laughed again. "I should have known."

"The kid's dad's deployed overseas. She needed somebody. I couldn't say no."

"Of course you couldn't." Jessica reached out and lightly tugged the blue ribbon attached to his shirt. "And look, you won. You earned the wounds on your knees."

He held up his arm. "And this one too."

"Ouch." But her smile said she wasn't too concerned with his pain level.

Over the past two days, he'd almost convinced himself he could leave Hope Springs and never look back, that the kiss he'd shared with Jessica hadn't altered his world. But he was a fool to believe it, even a little. He was a goner, and somehow he was determined to find answers to whatever problems stood in his way—in their way.

Perhaps it was ridiculous to think one had anything to do with the other. But if he could manage to win a three-legged race with a nine-year-old stranger without breaking his neck, maybe he could make a future with Jessica Mason and the baby she carried.

KUNA, IDAHO
Wednesday, April 27, 1932

The new filly was born at dusk. Andrew stood outside the stall, not wanting to worry the mare but making sure he could lend a hand if one was needed. It wasn't. The birth was of the textbook variety, and the mare was soon washing her offspring clean.

"Andrew?"

He turned at the sound of Helen's voice and watched her approach. Above her protruding stomach, she carried a mug in both hands.

"I brought you some coffee." She stopped beside him.

"Thanks." He took the mug. "Have a look."

Helen peered over the top rail of the stall. "Oh, Andrew. Look at her. She's a beautiful little thing."

"*You're* a beautiful little thing," he said softly, eyes on her and not the mare and foal.

"I'm anything but little these days."

He wanted to object, to argue with her. He knew she felt unattractive in this last stage of her pregnancy, but she was wrong. She was gloriously beautiful. So beautiful he couldn't find the words to describe how she appeared to him.

"Belle was Dad's favorite mare." Her eyes seemed to reveal the memories of years past. "He would have loved to see this new filly."

"I'm sorry he isn't here."

Helen looked at him. "He died easier knowing you would take care us, of Mother and me and the farm and everything. He trusted you, Andrew. I . . . I didn't appreciate it then. I was so confused after we lost the baby. To escape the pain, I closed myself off from you, and I tried to find happiness elsewhere. But Dad was right. He told me I'd married the best of men. He was right."

Emotions welled inside, almost choking Andrew. He moved the mug to his left hand and slipped his right arm around his wife's shoulders. Then he turned his gaze back onto the mare and foal. They stood like that, in silence, for a long while, allowing a few words to accomplish another level of healing between them.

At last, Helen took a step away, taking her warmth from his side. "I need to go inside." She gave him a fleeting smile. "And your coffee's growing cold."

He didn't care. "Probably." He took a sip. "Already cold." He returned her smile.

She rested a hand on her belly, and a look of apprehension passed suddenly over her face. He'd seen it a lot lately, and he understood. She was close to seven months along. That's when she'd lost baby Ralph, and she had begun to fear that it would happen again. Not that she'd told him in so many words. He just knew. Maybe because, sometimes, he was afraid of the same thing.

"I'll be in soon," he told her.

After Helen left the barn, Andrew bowed his head and prayed for her protection, for her life and for the life of their unborn child. It had become a frequent prayer. Not that he didn't believe the good Lord had heard him the first time, but until their child was born, he'd determined to be like the persistent widow in the book of Luke who pounded on the judge's door until she received what she wanted.

Setting aside the mug, he tended to the remainder of his duties in the barn, then headed for the house. He'd stomped off the dust and straw from his boots and removed his jacket before he heard a deep voice coming from the living room. Curious to see who it was, given the hour, he headed in that direction. Once there, he discovered their neighbor from across the way.

"I'm gonna have to sell the last of my cows," Luke Adams said as he slowly inched his fingers along the brim of the hat that he held between his knees. "I don't see any way to avoid it." He noticed Andrew in the doorway and gave him a weary nod. "I've come to the end, I think. The farm will go next."

"I'm real sorry to hear it." Andrew crossed the room to sit on the couch next to Helen. "Is there anything we can do to help?"

It was the sort of question neighbors had asked neighbors a lot since the beginning of the depression. Of course no one had believed the economic situation would drag on so long, hadn't known so many would be affected by it. Certainly that was true for Andrew, and he was supposed to understand about money, given his education. The country had been promised by many a politician that better days were coming, that the end was in sight. Tell that to men like Luke Adams who'd worked hard all their lives, building up dairy farms, grocery stores, insurance agencies, and the like, only to face losing everything.

"No," Luke answered at last. "Nothing anybody can do, far as I can tell."

Helen asked, "How is Agnes?"

"She's takin' it mighty hard. We're not young. Hard to start over at our age. Don't know what we'll do or where we'll go."

Andrew's mother-in-law said, "Tell Agnes that Helen and I will come calling tomorrow."

"I guess that's really why I came over. She could use some comfort from other womenfolk. I'm at a loss what to say to her. I spent the last two years telling her we'd be all right. And now . . ." He ended with a shake of his head.

Uncertainty shivered through Andrew at those words. He'd said much the same thing to Mother Greyson and Helen. He still believed they were true. But what if there was a drought? What if a crop failed? What if sickness took the livestock? What if—

"Therefore I say unto you, Take no thought for your life, what ye shall eat, or what ye shall drink; nor yet for your body, what ye shall put on. Is not the life more than meat, and the body than raiment?"

The words of Christ that echoed in Andrew's heart calmed the tremble of uncertainty inside him. Yes, life was more than meat and clothing. And even if they were to lose everything, would it make God's words any less true? No.

"Luke, if you do think of something you need, anything at all, all you need do is ask."

"I appreciate it, Andrew. Thanks."

Chapter 19

The nurse at the First-Aid Station was busy tending to an older woman who said she felt faint, but Jessica wasn't in need of assistance. She'd attended enough of these events—and cleaned up more than one scraped knee—to know what to do. She instructed Ridley to sit on one of the benches beneath the shade of the open-sided tent. Then she got some supplies from the first-aid kit and sat beside him.

"I've been hurt worse, you know." He slid his sunglasses up to the crown of his head, then took a wet wipe from her and began to cleanse his right knee.

"Football?"

"Baseball. Basketball. Hiking."

"Ah. Accident prone?"

"No, ma'am."

Finished with the wipe, he exchanged it for some antibiotic ointment, followed by various sizes of Band-Aids.

She'd been afraid seeing him again would feel awkward, but it didn't. It felt natural, and she was thankful the kiss they'd shared hadn't ruined their fledgling friendship. She would hate to lose that.

"Thanks, Nurse Mason, for your help." He grinned at her as he wadded up the packaging from the first-aid supplies. He turned and tossed it all into a nearby receptacle.

She started to push herself up from the bench. Before she could manage to rise, he was on his feet and helping her with a hand at her elbow. It surprised her, the difference it made. "Somebody called me fat today. I guess she was right. It's getting harder and harder to get up from a chair."

"You're not fat, Jessica."

"I *feel* fat."

"Well, you're not."

The appreciation in his eyes told her he meant what he said. And just like that, she believed him. For a moment, she felt attractive and . . . desirable. A corresponding sensation spiraled through her, causing her breath to quicken.

"Come on," he said, lowering his sunglasses into place. "I'll walk you back to your friends."

"Okay."

They left the First-Aid Station, their pace unhurried.

"Have you attended a lot of these community events?" Ridley asked, his gaze sweeping the park.

"I've been to all of them since I moved here. Is that a lot?" She shrugged. "I suppose so."

"No fireworks this year, I hear."

"Nope. No fireworks. Fire danger is too high this summer, and there are too many open fields near the park. No one wants to take the risk. It's bad enough when all the campers pour into the mountains for the holiday. There are always a few who are careless."

"Too bad. I love fireworks."

"Me too."

"Did Angela like them?" There was great tenderness in his voice.

She smiled, glad that this time she could remember her daughter without weeping. "Yes, she did. She loved the games too. She would have beaten you in that three-legged race today."

He laughed softly.

"Or she would have nabbed you for her partner before Cassie did."

"Wouldn't she have raced with her dad?"

She felt her smile slip away. "He wouldn't have been here."

"I'm sorry. I didn't mean to—"

"Joe stopped coming to events like this a couple of years ago. He said he had to work on holidays to . . . to make his bosses happy. But now I think he . . ." She let the words drift into silence, having said more than intended.

"I've bungled it again."

She stopped walking and put her hand on his forearm, stopping him too. "No, Ridley, you haven't bungled it. It's okay for you to ask questions." Silently she added, *I need to learn to talk about my family, about the life we had. Both the good and the bad.*

He studied her through his dark glasses. She felt his stare more than saw it. Could he read her thoughts? Of course not. Yet in an odd sort of way, she wished he could.

Ridley turned his head. "Listen."

She paused. All she heard was the general hubbub of voices in the park. Then it came to her. The sound of musicians warming up their instruments.

"Come on." He reached for her elbow. "I'd like to see this Hope Springs orchestra."

Her arm tingled at his tender touch. *"Be careful,"* her mom's voice whispered in her head. She silently replied with the same words as before: *"I'm not foolish."* She prayed they were still the truth.

Walking beside Jessica toward the band shell, Ridley thanked God that he hadn't stayed at the house today. He'd almost convinced himself he should skip the festivities. After all, he'd managed to avoid Jessica for the past two days. Better to keep on avoiding her. And yet, here he was, strolling through the busy park with her, feeling like a million bucks because she was at his side.

The ensemble he'd labeled an orchestra wasn't large, but they proved themselves talented when they began to perform in earnest.

"Nobody's dancing," he said to Jessica.

"Too early. Wait until dusk. That dance floor they've put down will be packed with couples."

He wondered if he'd be able to convince Jessica to dance with him.

"I'd better get back to Billie and Carol. They'll be wondering what's happened to me."

"They know you're with me."

She cocked her head to one side, looking up at him.

He thought how easy it would be to lean down and kiss her again. But the timing wasn't any better today than it had been two days earlier. So instead, he looked around and asked, "Where are they?"

"Over there." She pointed.

He took her arm once again and escorted her across the grass. Carol and Billie and a few other people were seated on camp chairs and blankets in the shade between two tall, gnarly trees.

"There she is," Billie said, seeing their approach.

"We stopped to check out the musicians." Jessica glanced at Ridley.

He helped her settle onto the vacant chair, then took a step back, wondering if he should leave. But before he could decide on his own, Billie spoke up, introducing him to those he didn't know. After he shook a few hands, he was invited to sit down and join them. He didn't need to be asked a second time. He sank onto the edge of the nearest blanket and observed the group of friends as they conversed, joked, and laughed.

He guessed that Carol Donaldson was the oldest. She was probably a few years older than Ridley. The rest all seemed to be within a year or two of thirty, either way. Besides Carol, Billie, and Jessica, there were two married couples sharing the blankets and chairs. He didn't recognize the four from church, so he assumed they weren't members. Gordon and Marie Jones owned a small cattle ranch at the north end of the long valley, and Ian and Vicky Coleman managed a hot springs resort about fifteen miles to the east of the valley.

It was clear Jessica had been missed from their ranks since the death of her husband and daughter. She wasn't as alone and friendless as it had sometimes appeared to Ridley. He was glad of that.

The afternoon shadows were beginning to lengthen when the Joneses and the Colemans excused themselves, saying they were expected elsewhere. For some reason, it made Ridley worry he might be in the way of the remaining friends. After all, he was the one who had crashed their plans.

"Maybe I'd better go too," he said, ready to rise.

Jessica sent him a fleeting smile. "You don't have to leave, Ridley. You might get roped into another competition, and I'm not sure your knees could take it."

His knees were fine, but it was as good an excuse to remain as any other. He settled back onto the blanket.

"I'm getting hungry," Carol said. "Anybody else?"

"I could eat," Billie answered.

Carol stood. "Corn dogs or corn dogs?"

"Well, if that's our choice—" Ridley got to his feet. "—then I'll help you get the corn dogs." He looked at Jessica. "One or two? With or without mustard?"

"One with a light strip of mustard on one side."

He looked at Carol. "Picky, isn't she?"

"Terribly."

Chuckling, they walked off in the direction of the food booths. "You know what, Ridley? You're good for Jessica."

He gave a slight shrug, not sure what to say in reply.

"She's happier today than I've seen her in a long, long time."

"That's not because of me. That's the Fourth of July fun."

"No. Believe me. It's you."

He sobered, wanting to believe her but having trouble letting himself hope. After all, what had changed between Tuesday and today? Nothing. The timing was still off. The circumstances were more than a little complicated. Friendship might be all that could exist between them.

Carol and Ridley stood in line for quite a while, but at last they had their order of corn dogs and were heading back toward the shaded area where Jessica and Billie awaited them. They were almost to their destination when Carol's pace slowed, and Ridley heard her say, "Not again."

He looked at her, then followed her gaze. Another couple stood near their chairs and blankets talking to Jessica and Billie. "Who is it?" he asked Carol.

"Ellery and her latest boyfriend." Irritation was clear in her voice. "Ellery's no friend to Jessica. Don't be fooled by her."

They crossed the remaining ground. "Here we are," Ridley announced.

The newcomers turned toward him. He gave the woman a quick glance—dark hair, green eyes, tall and slender—before stepping past her to hand a corn dog to Jessica, keeping the other two he carried for himself. "One light strip of mustard. As requested."

"Perfect." Her smile seemed a little tentative. His gut told him it had something to do with the woman Carol had said was no friend. He looked in Ellery's direction. An unusual name, he thought, but it went with her striking beauty.

"You're new around here." Her smile could only be called dazzling. "I'm Ellery."

"Nice to meet you." He held up a corn dog in each hand, an excuse not to shake hands. "I'm Ridley."

Her gaze slid to Jessica, a question in her eyes, but apparently one she didn't intend to ask.

Ridley looked at the man beside Ellery and gave him a nod.

"Ted Daniels. So you're new to Hope Springs too?"

"Yeah. I've been here about a month."

"It's not a bad place. I moved here in January. Small, but it grows on you."

"I like it." His gaze returned to Jessica, and he wished he could announce to everyone that she was the reason he liked Hope Springs.

"Come on, Ted." Ellery hooked her arm through his. "Their corn dogs are getting cold. Better let them eat." She turned her boyfriend away from the group, then looked back over her shoulder, her eyes on Ridley. "See you on the dance floor."

KUNA, IDAHO
Monday, July 4, 1932
Andrew sat on the edge of the bed, elbows on thighs, head in his hands. The night had been a short one. Helen had been up and

down numerous times, and even when she slept, she was restless, sighing, groaning softly. He lifted his head and looked over his shoulder. Now she slept soundly. Bless her.

He rose and dressed in the predawn light, making as little noise as possible. Then he slipped from the bedroom. As usual, Mother Greyson had managed to rise even earlier. The scent of coffee greeted him in the hallway and drew him into the kitchen. He poured himself a cup, stood near the table, and blew on the hot beverage until he could drink it to the last drop.

"Thanks, Mother Greyson." He felt slightly more alive now than he had when he first awakened.

As he went about his morning chores, he talked to God, thanking Him for another fine day, for good weather, for the most recent hay cutting, for the general health of both the farm and his family. He prayed for his wife and unborn child. He prayed for his mother-in-law and for his parents. He prayed for Luke and Agnes Adams, wherever they were now.

When he tossed hay into the pen, Belle's filly trotted over to greet him. Just over two months old, she behaved more like a puppy than a horse. She loved to follow him about whenever fences didn't separate them.

"Andrew!"

He looked toward the house. Mother Greyson stood on the porch, waving a towel above her head. There followed a second of wondering what she needed. In the next instant he was running toward her.

"Has it started?" he asked when he reached the bottom step.

"Yes."

"Did you call the doctor?"

"Not yet." She gave him a patient smile. "It will be a while yet."

He remembered the last time, and dread clawed at his chest.

"Helen is fine, Andrew. I just wanted you to know. Finish your chores, then come in and have your breakfast."

The morning chores were finished, he could have told her, and he wouldn't be able to eat a bite, no matter what she said. Not now.

If Andrew lived to be a hundred, he would never forget the moment when—twelve hours later—Mother Greyson placed a tiny bundle of humanity into his arms, wrapped in the pink-and-white striped blanket that she'd knitted for the infant earlier in the summer. His mother-in-law had also knitted a blue-and-white striped one. "We'll put that one away for another time," she told him with a wink.

What did he care about blankets? All he had eyes for was his daughter. Francine Madge Henning. An awfully long name for such a small thing. Six pounds of perfection as far as he could tell.

"Are you disappointed she isn't a boy?" Helen asked from their bed. "Every man wants a son."

He looked at her, feeling as if he might explode from sheer joy. "Are you joking? She's exactly what I prayed for."

"You're going to spoil her, aren't you?"

"Every chance I get." He pulled back the blanket for a more thorough inspection. "I've never really looked at a baby's hands before. They're amazing. Look at those little fingernails."

"Andrew?"

"Hmm."

"Thank you."

He raised his eyes to meet her gaze.

"For loving me despite . . . despite all the mistakes I made. All the reasons I gave you not to love me."

He offered her a soft smile, knowing that he could never put into words the lessons God had taught him over the past year and a half. Not without her misunderstanding or being hurt by them. Some lessons a person had to learn for themselves and not from hearing the experiences of another.

For himself, Andrew had learned that love was far more than an emotion, much more than a feeling. Emotions and feelings weren't bad starting places, but it took more than that to last. Lasting love was a decision. Love was a commitment. He didn't love Helen today because the swirl of romantic love he'd felt at the beginning had endured. He loved her today because he'd determined to love her, no matter what. The words of the marriage ceremony were far more than he'd thought on the day he repeated them to the minister. Love, like marriage, was for better or worse. They'd been through some of the worst.

Holding his child, he figured they were in for some better.

Chapter 20

The instant Ellery and Ted were out of hearing distance, Carol said, "What did she want this time?"

Attempting not to look interested, Ridley stared at the ground as he took a bite of his corn dog.

"To insult you again?"

"No," Jessica answered. "Not to insult me. I think she wanted to prove to Billie that she and Ted are still a couple. You know, about what Billie said earlier."

Ridley looked up in time to see Billie and Carol exchange a meaningful look. What was going on? Whatever it was, he was in the dark, and he suspected Jessica was in the dark as well. His gaze went to the last place he'd seen Ellery and Ted, but the crowd had closed in and they were no longer in sight.

He finished off his corn dogs, washing them down with a cold soda Billie had produced from the cooler.

When Jessica finished eating, she excused herself and made her way to the public restrooms at the opposite side of the park. Watching her walk away, he thought that no one would know she was pregnant from that view. She was shapely but slender. How could anybody call her fat? The question had no sooner formed in his mind than he guessed it was Ellery who had said those words to Jessica. No wonder Billie and Carol didn't like the woman.

"So, Ridley . . ."

He looked at Billie.

"What do you think of the way we celebrate the Fourth?"

"It's been fun."

"Not too quaint for you?"

He chuckled as he shook his head. "No. It's nice."

She stared off into the distance. "Some people aren't cut out for life away from a city. I guess it's too quiet or something." Then her gaze moved in the direction where Jessica had disappeared from view. "And some people aren't as happy away from the mountains and small-town life." Her eyes moved back to him. "Jessica's one of those people. She grew up in Boise. You probably know that. But she found her true home when she moved to Hope Springs. She'd never be as happy somewhere else as she is here."

Ridley knew a friendly warning when he heard one. Was it a warning he needed? Maybe, if bad timing between him and Jessica wasn't enough of a problem.

"On the other hand," Carol piped in, "telecommuting is all the rage. As long as you've got good internet service, you can do just about any work here that you can do somewhere else."

Ridley grinned at her. He didn't believe Billie Fisher was against him, exactly, but he knew Carol Donaldson was for him. However, that didn't solve the problem of bad timing.

"Tell me something, Billie," he said as he stood. He took a couple of steps and dropped his empty soda can into a recycle receptacle before he faced her again. "What was Jessica's husband like?"

From her expression, he saw that he'd surprised her. It took her a long while to answer. "Joe was . . . charming and quite easy to like. At first." She glanced toward the restrooms, then back at him. "He was also selfish and thoughtless. Especially around those who loved him and would cater to him."

Ridley was more surprised by the answer than Billie could have been by his question. He'd expected to hear about a paragon of virtue.

"He was a fun dad. You know the kind. Sweep in and do all the entertaining stuff and then leave and let the harder stuff fall to the mom."

Ridley ran a hand through his hair, trying to readjust the image he'd had in his head for several weeks.

"Jessica deserved better."

"Yes," he said beneath his breath.

Carol spoke up again. "Joe was a particularly good *friend* of Ellery Wallace, but I don't think Jessica knew that."

The new picture in his mind of Joe Mason was now complete. No wonder Billie and Carol had closed ranks around Jessica when Ellery came calling.

Softly, Billie said, "Shh. Here she comes."

He turned his head and watched Jessica's final approach.

"You'll never guess who I was talking to," she said as she arrived.

Jessica mentioned someone Ridley didn't know, at which point he tuned out the conversation. He was trying to reconcile in his mind how any man could be unfaithful to Jessica. If that was true, it made no sense to him. He'd assumed she'd been married to a great guy, a great husband, a great father. But if Joe Mason had been unfaithful, it could explain why Jessica had pulled away from

Ridley's kiss. Perhaps it was more than just bad timing. Perhaps it was caution. Perhaps she'd known more than Carol thought.

What was it his grandmother used to say? Once burned, twice shy.

❧

It was such a very long time since Jessica had enjoyed herself as much as she enjoyed herself that day. She'd walked in the park and loved the feel of the sun on her head. She'd people watched to her heart's content. She'd sat in the shade and talked with friends. She'd laughed often. She'd eaten a corn dog and slurped a snow cone and drank ounces and ounces of cold water, making for numerous trips to the restroom.

But she didn't fool herself. What had made the day perfect was Ridley's addition to their small company, and some of the delight had disappeared when he'd said he had to get home to let Kris out of the house and feed her.

With the arrival of dusk, the strings of lights came on all around the band shell. Two singers joined the musicians on the stage. Couples began to fill the dance floor, from little kids to octogenarians. It wasn't long before two men she didn't know—brothers by the look of them—approached to ask Billie and Carol to dance. Jessica could tell her friends were going to decline the invitations, probably because they didn't want to leave her sitting there by herself. She was having none of it.

"Go on. I'm fine. It'll be fun to watch you from here."

Billie gave her a questioning look. "Are you sure?"

"I'm sure." She smiled as she motioned them away.

After a while, she struggled up from the camp chair and stepped to the edge of the blankets, her fingers pressed against the small of her back. She knew better than to sit for so long without rising and moving around.

The musicians played a rock tune from forty or fifty years ago. She saw Billie wave at her from the dance floor and quickly waved back to let her know she was fine.

"Care to dance?" came a soft voice from behind her.

She sucked in a breath. "Ridley?" She turned around.

He stood close, the lights overhead revealing his smile and a sparkle in his eyes.

"I didn't think you were coming back."

He shrugged. "Kris can manage without me for the evening. I gave her a good run before I left again." He glanced toward the band shell, repeating, "Care to dance?"

"I don't know." She glanced down at her protruding abdomen. "I probably shouldn't."

"We'll wait for a slow one. Dance with me."

She didn't seem to have the strength to decline a second time. "Okay."

Applause broke out as the rock song ended. Ridley cupped her elbow with the palm of his hand and ever so gently steered her toward the dance floor.

A laugh bubbled up from inside. "How do you know this will be the slow one?"

"They wouldn't dare play another fast one."

"Wouldn't they?"

As if in answer, the band began to play a familiar Rascal Flatts song. A slow one.

Ridley drew her into his embrace, and his grin said, *Told you so.*

When they started to dance, he didn't just sway in time to the music or move in slow circles in the same small space. He glided her around the floor with style, his hand on the small of her back gently steering her in the direction she should go. She felt beautiful and feminine and anything but over seven months pregnant.

"I can't believe how much I wanted to dance with you, Jessica."

She pressed her forehead against his shoulder. *How much?* She wanted to know. She didn't want to know.

"But I didn't know it until this moment."

God, is this supposed to happen? Is it okay for me to feel this way about him?

Ridley's mouth was near her ear, and when he spoke, she felt the warmth of his breath on her skin. "I know our timing is off. I know things are complicated in both of our lives, and I don't know what the future holds for either of us. But Jessica, I care about you. Can't we see what comes next? No expectations, but at least open to the possibilities."

That was the moment her mom would have called her foolish. The moment when Jessica drew her head back, met his gaze beneath the twinkling lights, and nodded.

KUNA, IDAHO

Saturday, October 8, 1932

Twelve million Americans were now out of work, according to the newspapers. About 25 percent of the normal workforce, the experts said, couldn't find jobs. Andrew thought he'd understood the severity of the great depression, already three years gone, that gripped the nation and much of the world. He'd seen neighbors lose their farms, and he'd watched prices for his own crops fall. His family was used to counting pennies and being careful not to waste.

But reality hit him afresh one October morning when he accompanied his father into Boise to deliver canned vegetables to a church's soup kitchen. That's where Andrew saw the long line of people already waiting for what would be their one meal of the day. Men with haggard faces. Women with hair askew. Children with frightened expressions, eyes seemingly too large for their faces.

He remembered a line outside this very same church that he'd seen on the day he'd become unemployed. Those people had been hungry, too, but the line had been much shorter that day.

"There's so many of them," he said, keeping his voice low.

"It's overwhelming, isn't it?" His father lifted a crate from the back of the truck. "So many without homes. So many without food."

"There has to be some way we can make a difference." Andrew picked up a second crate and followed his father into the church.

"Your mama and I donate as much produce as possible. Fresh fruits and vegetables in the summer. Preserved the rest of the time. What we can, we give." He looked toward the door, as if he could see the line that had formed beyond it. "It's only a drop in the bucket. Never enough."

Andrew grew alfalfa on the Greyson farm, as his father-in-law had before him. But hay was a worthless crop to hungry people, and that knowledge made Andrew feel impotent. He'd been so busy trying to take care of his wife, child, mother-in-law, and himself, he'd almost forgotten about those even less fortunate. When he lost his job and couldn't afford to pay rent, he'd had a place to go for food and shelter, unlike those outside this church. He and Helen had never been homeless. He might have had worn soles on his shoes and pants that required patches, but he'd never gone hungry.

The director of the soup kitchen came over to speak to Andrew's father. Leaving them to it, Andrew returned to the truck to bring in the last of the crates. On his final trip in, three kids caught his eyes. They were grouped tightly together, the tallest in the middle, an arm around each of the younger ones. Their blond hair and sky-blue eyes declared them siblings. Their clothes were dirty and ill fitting. The oldest, a boy, was barefoot. The middle child was a girl, the youngest another boy.

Andrew glanced around, then approached them. "Is your mama or papa here?"

"No, sir," the oldest boy answered, gaze averted.

"Are you here to get something to eat?"

"We don't have no money."

"You don't need any money."

Glancing up, the boy gave Andrew a skeptical look.

Andrew set down the crate, then crouched to open it. "Do you like cherries?"

The youngest boy's eyes widened at the sight of the jar in Andrew's hand but didn't answer.

"What's your name?"

The little guy pressed himself to his brother's side.

Andrew glanced at the long line, stretching to the end of the block and turning the corner. "How about helping me take this crate inside?" he said to the older boy. "I'll pay you a nickel." He could ill afford to give away a nickel, but he figured it would work better than anything else.

"A nickel?" The boy's tone said Andrew was crazy.

"A nickel."

The boy moved his siblings aside and reached for the crate.

"What's your name?" Andrew asked.

"Ben. Ben Tandy."

With his hands, Andrew guided the younger two into place

behind their brother. He ignored the glances of the folks in the front of the line as he herded the small family into the soup kitchen before its opening.

When his father saw them, he said, "And who's this?"

"Ben helped me with the last crate. This is his sister and brother. I thought maybe they could wait in here until the kitchen starts serving."

"I imagine that would be all right." His father gave him a quick nod before taking the crate from Ben's hands.

"Come with me, kids." Andrew led them to some wooden folding chairs in one corner. Ben sat on one. The younger pair shared another. Andrew looked at the girl. "My name's Mr. Henning. Care to tell me yours?"

"Louisa." After answering, she hid her face in her little brother's hair.

"And who's this guy?" Andrew touched the youngest boy's knee.

Ben answered the question. "He's Oscar."

It felt like a victory to have all of their names at last. Andrew reached into his pocket and found the promised nickel. He handed it to Ben. "This is yours."

The boy hesitated a few moments before taking the coin and shoving it into his pocket. Andrew could only hope there wasn't a hole in it.

Chapter 21

Daylight had flooded Jessica's bedroom by the time she opened her eyes the next morning. Her feet hurt from dancing. Her back ached from sitting in the camp chair. And her skin told her she hadn't used quite enough sunscreen.

She didn't care. She felt happier than she'd felt in ages.

Like a caress, Ridley's voice whispered in her memory: *"Jessica, I care about you. Can't we see what comes next? No expectations, but at least open to the possibilities."*

Possibilities. For so long, she hadn't felt as if they existed for her. And suddenly they did. The possibility that she might take a risk on love. The possibility that a man could make her a promise and she might trust him to keep it. The possibility that she might be able to believe in a whole family of her own again.

She released a soft groan as she rolled onto her side, then sat up and lowered her feet to the floor. Hopefully a shower would revive her and make her body feel as good as her spirits.

Her phone rang before she could stand. She glanced at the caller ID, then answered, "Hi, Mom." Her eyes moved to the clock, surprised to find it was after eight.

"Good morning, sweetheart. How are you? Did you have a good time yesterday?"

"I had a great time. Billie Fisher came to get me, and she and Carol pampered me the entire day. I didn't have to carry anything or get my own food. In fact, except for walking back and forth to the restroom, I didn't have to get out of my chair unless I wanted to." She decided against telling her mom about the times she'd wanted to be out of her chair. Especially when she'd been dancing with Ridley. There might come a time for that discussion, but it wasn't now.

"I'm so glad."

"What did you and Dad do?"

"The usual. Neighborhood potluck in the common area. Fireworks at dark."

"I think I told you the town council here opted against fireworks this year because of the danger. Except for the safe ones and sparklers for the kids, of course."

"But it sounds like their absence didn't spoil anything."

Again she thought of Ridley with his arms around her, turning her around the dance floor beneath tiny white lights, and smiled. "No. It didn't spoil a thing."

"Any chance I can talk you into coming to Boise for Sunday dinner? Or if not Sunday afternoon, then in the evening on Monday or Tuesday. I'll be flying to Florida on the eighteenth, and I'm not sure if or when I'll have a chance to drive up to see you before then. So much to organize before I go."

Jessica could almost hear her mom's mind whirring with to-do lists. "Can I let you know tomorrow what day works best for me?"

"Well . . . yes . . . I guess that would be all right."

Now it was disappointment she heard. "I'm sorry, Mom. You know what. Let's do Sunday. Usual time?"

"Oh, good. Yes. Just plan to be here before two."

"Would you mind if I brought someone with me? I'm getting to the place I don't want to make that drive by myself."

"Of course I don't mind. Your friends are always welcome."

"Thanks. I don't know who'll be free at the last minute, but I'll find somebody." It was Ridley's image she saw in her mind. "Can I bring anything for the dinner?"

"No, honey. Just yourself and your friend. Your dad's going to barbecue chicken and roast corn on the cob. I'll make a key lime pie for dessert."

"Yum."

"Knew you'd like it."

Jessica ended the call a short while later and hurried into the bathroom. Half an hour later, showered and dressed for the day, she made her way to the kitchen. Soon after, decaf coffee filled her favorite mug, an egg was boiling on the stove, and bread was in the toaster.

After breakfast, her coffee mug filled for the second time, she sat at the table with her great-grandfather's Bible open before her. She had come to love these moments spent in the old King James Bible, reading Andrew Henning's scribbles in the margins, paying close attention to the words he had underlined. She rarely knew the reasons why he marked certain passages, even when he'd jotted something in the margins. And yet she felt a strange connection to him, as if he were more than an ancestor. Almost as if their lives had converged in some way.

Flipping the fragile paper, looking for pencil and pen marks, she stopped on a page in Psalms. Along the top of the page Andrew had written a note:

Our daughter, Francine Madge Henning, was safely born today, July 4, 1932. My first little arrow. May I be deserving of this reward.

A pencil mark pointed to two underlined verses.

"Grandma Frani?" Jessica whispered, for some reason awestruck to see the notation. She knew her grandmother's birthday had been the fourth of July, but seeing it written on that page, eighty-seven years later, seemed both strange and wonderful. If she closed her eyes, she could imagine Grandma Frani's father sitting at a table much like hers, writing those words, excitement and joy flowing through him.

She read the underlined verses:

Lo, children are an heritage of the LORD:
And the fruit of the womb is his reward.
As arrows are in the hand of a mighty man;
So are children of the youth.

A smile bowed her mouth. Ah. That's why Andrew had called his daughter his first little arrow. Precious. No wonder her grandmother had been exactly that. Precious.

She leaned back in her chair and placed her hands on her abdomen. "My little arrow," she whispered. "May I be deserving of you."

Early in her pregnancy, after the shock and surprise, she'd had to work through so many other emotions. Knowing Joe had been unfaithful had made her wonder how she would feel about the baby after its birth. Would she love him or her as much as she'd loved Angela?

Tears pricked her eyes. *As much as I still love Angela.* She smiled through her tears, knowing the answer was an unfaltering yes. She would love this baby—already loved this baby—with her whole heart. Although anguish soon followed the moment of its conception, this child was God's gift.

Once more Ridley's image came to mind. Her pulse quickened, wanting something she didn't quite dare put into words. And yet it forced her to wonder: Was he the sort of man who could love her baby unconditionally? She thought he was. "But how can I know for sure, Lord?"

⌒⌒

"Hey, Steve. It's Ridley Chesterfield." Ridley had worked for Steve Knight for five years before leaving to join the Treehorn campaign, but the two men hadn't spoken in well over a year.

"Ridley." He heard the surprise in his former employer's voice. "How you doin', buddy?"

"Okay, now. I had some rough weeks, but I seem to be past the worst of it."

"I heard you'd left town."

"I did."

"You coming back?"

Ridley looked out the window, toward Jessica's home. "I'm not sure."

"Are you working?"

"Not yet. Not sure what I'm going to do. Nothing to do with politics, that's for certain."

Steve chuckled. "Sounds wise to me."

"Listen, when it comes time for me to look for employment, can I still depend on a good recommendation from you?"

"You know you can."

He didn't confess that he wasn't nearly as sure of people as he used to be. "Thanks."

"You bet. And make sure you look me up when you come back to Boise."

"I'll do it."

He said goodbye and ended the call. After setting down the phone, he went into the kitchen to pour himself another cup of coffee. An idea was trying to solidify in his mind, had been swirling in the background of his thoughts for days. A longing had been growing in his heart. He kept thinking of how wrecked he'd been in those first days after the accusations against him had been made. He'd been caught unawares by how deeply hurt he'd been, for his good name to be besmirched, for his integrity to come into question, for the inability to set the record straight. He'd hated that he had no control over the media, hated even more knowing that once something appeared on the internet, it never actually went away. Search engines were relentless. Now he wondered how he might turn his own experiences to use for good in the lives of others. Because that's what he'd begun to believe he was supposed to do. Was there a way? And if so, what was it?

He didn't know, but it seemed to him that God was trying to tell him something. That the answer was waiting for him to discover it.

"Rest in the Lord *and wait patiently for Him."*

He nodded, eyes closed. The words from a psalm were good ones to remember. Rest in the Lord and wait patiently. God would direct his path. He believed it more today than ever before in his life. But that didn't mean he was very good at waiting.

Kris scratched at the back door, drawing Ridley's attention. Carrying his coffee, he went to let the dog out. Warmth from the morning sun told him the day promised to be hotter than yesterday.

Yesterday . . .

He looked toward Jessica's house again. Memories of their time on the dance floor washed over him. She'd felt so right in his arms. But he couldn't forget the warning of her friend either. Jessica wouldn't be happy away from Hope Springs. If living in this small mountain community was a condition for her happiness, then how could he play a part in her life? Was he *supposed* to be a part of her life?

"No expectations, but open to possibilities." That's what he'd told her.

If she was nervous or scared, he understood. He was a little scared himself. Or at least uncertain. After all, sharing her life would mean sharing the life of her unborn child. Was he in the right place to take on a ready-made family? For some reason he didn't doubt that he could be a good father to Jessica's baby. He knew in the deepest core of his being that he could—and would—love it. But perhaps loving meant giving up whatever he might want. Did it?

"God, I need answers about that too. Because I've got it bad for Jessica, and I don't want to do the wrong thing for any of us. Help me know what to do next."

KUNA, IDAHO
Monday, November 21, 1932

The three Tandy orphans came to live on the Greyson farm the third week of November. Andrew had expected investigations and paperwork to drag out for many weeks, perhaps for months, but he supposed orphans were another depression problem that had overwhelmed government and charitable agencies.

Helen had been reluctant at first when he'd suggested taking these children into their home. More than a little so. But she'd come around once he showed her where and how they'd been surviving after the death of their parents—first their father the previous winter, then their mother a few weeks before Andrew found them outside the soup kitchen.

When Andrew brought the children to the farm, Mother Greyson took one look at them and said, "Well, we'll need to fatten you all up." Then she headed to the kitchen to cook something that would do just that. That was the sort of woman she was. No point wasting a minute when she could do something to help.

Helen, cradling Francine in her left arm, held out a hand to Louisa. "We're glad you've come to stay with us."

The little girl glanced at her older brother, as if for permission, then shyly took Helen's hand.

After giving the children time to get their bearings, Andrew led the way to what had been Francine's nursery. Their daughter was now in residence in her parents' bedroom. Two beds, recently purchased at auction, had been moved into the small room, one for the two boys, the other for Louisa. Clothes—not new but newer—had been laid out for each of them on the beds. Clothes that would fit better than what they wore now.

Ben eyed Andrew with suspicion before entering the room. "This is for us?"

"Yes. We thought you'd all like to share the same room. If that's all right."

The boy grunted but a little of the tension seemed to leave his slight shoulders.

"The bathroom's right across the hall."

Helen passed Francine into Andrew's arms, then led Louisa to her bed. "Can I help you put on your new dress?"

Louisa shook her head, then seemed to think again, and nodded.

"I thought this blue would match the color of your eyes. I was right." Helen sat on the bed and began to unbutton the dress Louisa wore.

"Ben, why don't you let me show you the place? The little ones can check it out later, but you ought to see it first, being the oldest."

"Didja bring us here to work for you?" Suspicion returned to his eyes. "I heard that's what you'd want. Labor for nothin'."

"No, we brought you into our home to be part of our family. Everybody does their part, of course."

"Yeah, right."

Nine years old with an enormous chip on his shoulder. But Andrew couldn't blame the kid. Ben had carried lots more than a chip on those narrow shoulders for the past ten months or so.

"Come with me. You don't have to do anything but watch and listen." Andrew looked at Helen. "You okay with these two and the baby?"

She nodded, so he laid Francine on the bed near her hip.

A short while later, Andrew and Ben entered the barn. Andrew showed him the gelding that was in the stall, then told the boy what he was doing as he treated the animal's wound. From there he showed Ben the other horses as well as the cows, hog, and chickens. After that, they walked to the edge of the fields. A slight dusting of snow covered the ground.

"Hard to tell, but come spring this will all be green with alfalfa."

"What's that?"

"Hay. It's used to feed cattle. We sell it to farmers and ranchers."

"How come you don't grow stuff you can eat?"

"We've got a good-sized garden on the other side of the house. We don't go hungry on the farm." He looked at Ben. "What did your father do?"

Ben seemed to debate whether or not to answer but at last said, "He worked in a factory 'til it closed down."

"Where?"

"Seattle."

Andrew knew this already, but he hoped it would help the boy to talk about it. "What brought you to Boise?"

"Dad hoped for work. Didn't happen. Then he got sick."

Andrew knew the family had lived in a tent near the river all through the last winter. A hard, bitter cold one. No wonder the father had taken ill. "So you've never lived on a farm before now."

"Nah."

"I think you'll like it if you give it a chance."

"I doubt it."

"I doubted I wanted to live here too. Except I grew up on a farm and knew what it was like. I wanted to get away. I wanted to live in the city and wear a suit to work." He shrugged. "Things didn't work out that way. I had to come back to the farm. Turns out I'm not sorry. God knew what was best for me and my family."

Ben grunted.

Andrew put his hand on the boy's shoulder. "Give us a chance. Give the farm a chance too. I promise it'll be better than going hungry, trying to get by on your wits, or living in an orphanage."

"We wouldn't've been in the orphanage if we'd never gone to that soup kitchen. Not if you hadn't seen us."

"I guess not, but that was for your own good."

"We was doin' all right."

"Your brother and sister were hungry, even if you weren't."

Ben scowled, refusing to admit that he'd been hungry too.

"They needed a decent place to sleep and a way to keep warm and dry. The nights were turning way too cold again."

"Nobody's gonna separate us." The boy's hands fisted at his sides, and he stuck out his chin in defiance. "I promised Mom we'd stay together always."

"Nobody will separate you, Ben." He spoke gently, hoping the boy could hear honesty in his words. "I promise. That's one reason you are here with us. So the three of you can stay together. Always."

Chapter 22

Jessica worked in her studio that day, but she chose her tasks well. It was repetitive work that required little concentration. A good thing, for her thoughts weren't on the details. She hummed music that she and Ridley had danced to. She paused frequently and remembered the feel of his arms around her. She heard the sound of his laughter echoing in her memory. Sometimes she thought she could still feel his breath upon her skin. It was all quite heavenly, and with the memories, the question about Ridley and her baby that she had pondered earlier was answered in her heart. She would trust God with it. She would allow Him to guide her into the future.

In early afternoon, she put away her art supplies, turned off her computer and the lights in her studio, and went to the kitchen, where she made herself a late lunch—half a tuna fish sandwich, a bowl of mixed fruit, and a glass of milk. As she drank the last of the milk, she found herself wishing for a chocolate-chip cookie. Then she wondered if Ridley liked chocolate-chip cookies.

There was one sure way to find out.

An hour later, she carried a plate of still warm cookies across the field to his house. Kris announced her before she could rap on the jamb of the open door.

"Kris, knock it off," came Ridley's voice from inside. But when he stepped into view and saw her, he grinned. "Hey."

"Hey." She stepped inside without waiting for an invitation. "I baked cookies. Would you like some?" She held the plate a little higher. "Chocolate chip."

"My favorite." He came to her, taking the plate while keeping his gaze on her, his smile still in place as he gently drew her into the kitchen. "How's your day been?"

"Good." Her stomach tumbled.

"Get any work done?"

"Yes, some." *But I thought about you all the time.* The gleam in his eyes made her wonder if he'd read her silent thought.

He set the plate on the counter. "I've been busy too. Come see."

She followed him into the living room, and when he pointed, she followed the motion with her eyes. There, on a formerly bare wall, hung a large-screen television. In the nearby corners stood speakers on stands.

"Cable company comes next week to hook it all up. Internet too. When the folks come in August, my stepdad won't be able to complain he has nothing to watch."

"And you won't mind having it either."

He chuckled. "To be honest, yeah, I'll like having TV and internet again. You know that I came up here to get away from it, but I've been thinking that my trouble was like a flash in the pan compared to what some people go through in the media." There was a subtle change in his expression, as if he'd made a discovery.

"Knowing what happened to you, I pity the people it happens to, whoever they are. Even if they actually did something wrong."

"Exactly." He stressed the word and nodded, speaking to himself and not to her. "Exactly." Then he drew a breath and focused his full attention on her again. "Now, how about I try out those cookies."

She smiled at him. "Of course."

For the second time in a matter of minutes, she followed him to the other room, watching as he pulled off the cellophane and picked up a cookie. He took a bite, closed his eyes, and tipped his head slightly back. After a long while, he released a soft, "Wow."

A bit dramatic, but she loved him for it.

Loved him for it . . . A fluttering in her chest caused her breath to catch. Loved him for it? The words wouldn't leave her head.

"That's not from a plastic container you bought at the grocery store," he said, a twinkle of amusement in his eyes.

She shook her head.

"Thanks for sharing with me."

She released a nervous laugh. "I can't afford to have too many sweets around the house." She patted her belly. "I get cravings."

He echoed her laugh before eating the remainder of the cookie and reaching for a second.

"Speaking of food . . ." she began.

He looked at her, waiting for her to go on.

"I'm expected to Sunday dinner at my parents' house. Would you mind going with me?"

"I'm invited?"

She almost said yes, but honesty forced a longer reply. "I told Mom I don't want to make the drive into Boise by myself at this stage in my pregnancy. She told me I could bring a friend."

"Ah."

"But you're the friend I want to take."

"I'll be glad to go with you."

The nervousness vanished, leaving only her happiness behind. "If we leave right after church, we'll be there in plenty of time."

"Sounds good. I'll need to come home first to let Kris out. Sounds like it could be a long day."

"We can bring her with us. The backyard at home is fenced, and Mom knows Kris. We always had dogs when my sister and I were kids. It'll be fine."

"You're sure?"

"I'm sure."

"Then it sounds like we're set for the day."

❧

Strange, wasn't it, the way the mind worked. First, his own comment: that his troubles were like a flash in the pan compared to what some people went through in the media. It was as if his words had turned on a light in a once dark room. And then Jessica's comment—that she pitied the people such things happened to, no matter who they were, even if guilty—had seemed to change a simple light into an intense spotlight. And just like that, God began to form the shapeless clay of his desire to help others into something concrete. Something he could see.

After Jessica went home, he sat at the kitchen table and scribbled in a notebook with a mechanical pencil, sometimes writing long paragraphs, sometimes drawing mind maps, sometimes jotting down bullet points.

What if there was a place people could go when their lives were falling to pieces? A place like Hope Springs had been for him. A sanctuary. A safe place to wait and heal. What if he could help provide peace and good counsel to people of all ages and all circumstances? News articles from the past flashed in his mind. Not about him. About others. A teenaged girl being bullied on social media until she took her own life. A CEO accused of wrongdoing who'd lost everything, including his family, before being proven innocent. News pieces that he'd read and then moved on from, like nearly everybody else except for those who kept churning out the stories. What if . . . ?

He reached for his phone and hit Chad's number in his Favorites list.

"Hey, buddy," Chad answered. "I was just thinking about you."

"Oh, yeah?"

"Yeah. Selena called me again."

Hearing his friend's comment took some of the wind from his sails. "What did she want this time?"

"She's still trying to find you. She told me to tell you, next time we talked, that she's sorry and wants you back."

"You're kidding."

"Nope."

He pictured Jessica, and a slow smile curved his mouth. "It'll never happen." Even if he didn't care for Jessica, he wouldn't have tried to pick things up with Selena again. She'd been all wrong for him. He'd begun to suspect it before the breakup, but Jessica had shown him what he wanted for his future. He wanted someone loving and kind. He wanted someone who would let a dog pounce on her while covered in shampoo and be able to laugh about it. He wanted someone whose friends would do everything they could to protect her. He wanted someone who would bake him chocolate-chip cookies for no other reason than to please him.

"Ridley? You still there?"

"I'm here."

"Anything you want me to tell her if she calls again?"

"Just tell her it's over and I wish her well."

"Got it."

"Now for the reason I called you." Ridley lowered his eyes to the notebook open on the table before him. "I've got some ideas about what I want to do next. It's for a kind of retreat center. Not retreat as in a vacation or a spiritual retreat like the men's group at church does. More like retreat as in getting away from a crisis. A sanctuary of sorts. I'd like to bounce a few ideas off you. Have you got time to listen?"

"Sure thing. My time is yours."

KUNA, IDAHO
Tuesday, July 4, 1933

At his March fourth inauguration as the nation's thirty-second president, Franklin D. Roosevelt had said, "The only thing we have to fear is fear itself." Listening to the speech on the radio, Andrew had felt disinclined to agree with the man, no matter how stirring the words. There seemed an abundance of things to worry about or fear.

For one, bank holidays might have stopped another run on the financial institutions, but they'd done nothing to help the precarious nature of the times for ordinary men and women.

For another, while the country waited for enough states to approve the Twenty-first Amendment, allowing the return of legal beer and liquor, little attention was paid to the rise to power of Adolf Hitler in Germany, the wars in the Far East, or the disintegration of the League of Nations. Andrew had noticed all of those in passing when he read or heard about them in news reports. But, like others, he'd quickly forgotten them. They'd seemed too far away to disturb his little corner of the world.

On the Fourth of July, Andrew set aside his worries about the poor income from the first harvest of the season—the worst prices since the start of the depression—to celebrate Francine's birthday. His darling daughter, whom everyone now called Frani, was a year old. All of the grandparents—Andrew's mother and father and Mother Greyson—were present for the party. And of course Frani's foster siblings Ben, Louisa, and Oscar were there. Along with Helen and Andrew, they all made for a merry band.

Helen had planned out every detail of the party. The table had been carried outside, along with chairs and a bench, and set in the shade of the willow tree. Paper hats awaited all participants at each place setting, and there was a three-layer cake with thick frosting and ice cream for dessert. They had to eat the ice cream very fast because of the intense summer heat, but no one complained about that.

Andrew took photos of the family with Frank's old box camera. He didn't know much about photography and could only hope he managed to take a few good pictures. He wouldn't know the results until he took them into Kuna to be developed.

Sitting in her high chair, Frani seemed to enjoy being the focal point of the day. From the start, she'd been a good-natured baby, rarely crying or fussy. As a toddler, she bubbled over with joy, giggling over the smallest things. She had a special affection for Ben. Now that she was walking, if still a bit unsteadily, she tried to follow him everywhere. The boy pretended he didn't return Frani's feelings, but Andrew knew better. Ben had a soft spot for all of the younger kids. He took his role as big brother seriously and was protective, often bossy, but always loving.

Look at us, God. This family that's been cobbled together. It wasn't all that long ago that I didn't think my marriage would survive, let alone that we could be happy again. That Helen and I would have a baby together. That we would be able to provide a home for three unhappy orphans in their time of need. Look what You've done with us, Lord. It's a miracle, and I thank You for it all.

Chapter 23

"Are you comfortable?" Ridley asked as Jessica settled into the front seat of his car.

She offered a rueful smile. "It's getting harder every day to answer yes to that question." She tugged at the shoulder strap of the seatbelt, giving her abdomen a little more room.

Kris thrust her head between the driver and passenger seats, looking less than happy.

Now Jessica laughed. "I take it she's grown used to riding shotgun."

"Yeah." He closed the passenger door. "Bad habit too. I should make her ride in the back in a crate. It would be safer for her."

Jessica stroked the dog's head. "I'm sorry, girl, but this spot is mine for the day. I'll make sure you get a treat when we get to Mom's. Okay?"

Kris licked Jessica's hand, then disappeared into the back seat.

Ridley grinned as he hurried around the front of the car and got behind the wheel. He was looking forward to spending the day with Jessica. He also looked forward to meeting her dad. He already liked her mom and hoped the woman liked him a little.

Funny, he'd never much cared for meeting his girlfriends' parents or siblings. It felt like he was making some sort of commitment when that happened. But it was different this time. Maybe because he could imagine a future with Jessica, fuzzy though that image in his head was most of the time.

Ridley guided his automobile through Hope Springs and onto the winding two-lane highway that followed the south fork of the river. A playlist of Big Band standards played on the car stereo.

"You are even more eclectic in your music choices than you let on. Not just classical or Christian, huh?"

He glanced at Jessica, then looked back at the road. "Guilty. It was my grandfather who turned me on to this music. Glenn Miller was one of his all-time favorites. 'Stardust.' 'Moonlight Serenade.'"

"'In the Mood,'" she interjected.

He grinned. "Yeah."

"My grandma loved music from that era too."

"Maybe our grandparents were listening to their radios at the same time."

"Maybe."

"From things you've said, you were real close to your grandmother."

"Yes. We were close." Her voice softened. "If she'd lived, she would have turned eighty-seven years old on the Fourth of July. The other day I found a notation in her father's Bible dated the day she was born. He wrote that she was his first little arrow and prayed that he would be worthy of that reward."

"From one of the psalms."

He felt more than saw her turn her head to look at him. "Psalm 127. You know it?"

"My grandfather quoted it to me. About five years ago, I think.

Something about children being like arrows and a blessing from God. He was telling me it was time for me to settle down and have kids of my own."

Jessica laughed. "It obviously didn't do any good."

Not yet, he thought, keeping his eyes on the road despite wanting to pull to the shoulder and take her in his arms—a desire that was getting harder and harder to resist. And not just to kiss her once. To kiss her time and again. Today and tomorrow and the next day and the one after that. To sit beside her on the sofa and watch television while she cradled a baby in her arms. To have her trust him to care for her and for this baby and for any future babies. He'd never expected to want anything as much as he wanted those images to be his future.

"Have you ever come close?" she asked. "To getting married, I mean."

"I've never proposed to anybody. No."

"Have you been in love?"

A smile pulled at the corners of his mouth. It amused him that the woman he was undoubtedly falling in love with—had already fallen in love with—was the one who'd asked the question. Did she have no clue what she'd done to him?

"Too personal?" she asked as the silence between them lengthened.

"No. Sorry. Not too personal." He glanced over at her, but she was staring out the passenger window. *You're not ready to hear my answer just yet,* he silently told her.

"Love can be complicated." Her words were almost too soft for him to hear.

"Seems that way." *But not for long,* he added to himself. *I'm going to find a way to change your mind, Jessica Mason. I promise you that.*

⤳

Jessica's parents lived in the north end of Boise in a two-story home built in the thirties. They'd purchased and remodeled it as newly-weds, close to forty years before. Large, ancient trees shaded both front and back yards, and there were glorious bursts of color every-where, thanks to her mom's green thumb.

Jessica had waited until shortly before she and Ridley left Hope Springs before texting her mom that they were on their way, adding matter-of-factly that they were coming in Ridley's car and bring-ing his dog. Thus, neither of her parents showed any surprise over whom she'd brought with her to Sunday dinner. Ridley was greeted warmly and made to feel at home, and Kris was turned into the backyard along with a tasty treat that Jessica's dad had purchased at the grocery store especially for her.

"Ridley," her mom said, "would you like something to drink? We won't eat until two. Iced tea or lemonade. Or if you prefer, I've got Diet Coke."

"Lemonade sounds good, Mrs. Alexander."

"Pat, please."

Jessica headed for the fridge. "I'll get it, Mom. Dad, do you want something?"

"Lemonade for me, too, honey. Thanks."

Before long, the four of them were settled around a table on the patio. The forecast promised the temperature would top a hundred degrees, but the trees and a waterfall and small pond on the west side of the patio made it comfortable to sit outside for now.

"Were you able to attend the Independence Day celebration in Hope Springs?" her mom asked Ridley, getting the conversation started.

"Yes, I was. It was a lot of fun." His gaze flicked to Jessica.

As had become its habit, her stomach tumbled in response. She lowered her eyes to her glass of lemonade, watching beads of water slide down its sides.

"As far as I could tell," Ridley continued, "the whole town was in the park that day."

Her mom laughed softly. "I wouldn't be surprised."

"I even managed to win the last three-legged race of the afternoon. It was a narrow victory but a victory all the same."

Jessica lifted her eyes. "You didn't win it by yourself."

Her mom sucked in a breath. "Don't tell me you raced with him. Not in your condition."

"Of course not, Mom." She shook her head. "His racing partner was an adorable redhead." She smiled at Ridley.

"She was cute, wasn't she?" He laughed before taking a sip of lemonade.

"Nine years old and about half your height." Silly though it might be, the memory of watching that race in the park felt intimate and special to Jessica. A memory the two of them shared.

Her dad cleared his throat. "Looks like your dog has her eyes on the goldfish in the pond."

Ridley didn't smile or wink at Jessica, but it felt to her as if he'd done both before he turned to look at her father. "Your fish should be safe. Kris doesn't think much of the water. She might bark, but she won't go in."

As if to prove Ridley's point, the sheltie stepped close to the pond, barked, then backed several steps away, snorting her displeasure before giving her head a vigorous shake.

Jessica's dad chuckled. "I see what you mean."

Her mom stood. "I'd better check on our dinner." She glanced at Jessica, a silent request to go with her, before walking inside.

"I'll give her a hand." She looked at Ridley, wondering if he minded being left alone with her father.

He seemed to understand and gave his head a nod to let her know he would be fine.

She rose and went inside. Her mom was in the kitchen, the oven door open.

"I thought Dad was barbecuing chicken."

"That was the plan." Her mom straightened. "But something's wrong with the grill, so pot roast it is. I hope you aren't disappointed. I still made the key lime pie."

"I'm not disappointed. I love your pot roast. Anything I can help with?"

"Not a thing. But you can sit at the counter and talk to me, if you want."

"Sure." She set her glass of lemonade, now half full, on the counter, then settled onto the nearest stool. "Talk about what?"

Her mom sent her a pointed glance.

"He's still just my neighbor, Mom."

"Is he? That isn't what it looks like to me."

Jessica sighed. "Okay, maybe it's a little bit more than that. But like I told you before, I'm not foolish."

"Oh, honey."

"I'm not."

"I know you're not. But so much has happened in the last year. I can't help but want you to protect yourself from any more pain."

Jessica ran a fingertip around the edge of her glass. "I don't want to live that way, trying to protect myself from getting hurt. Because if I'm protecting myself from pain, I'm protecting myself from feeling other things too. Like joy. Like pleasure."

"Like love?"

She met her mom's gaze again. "Like love."

"Do you think you love Ridley?"

"I don't know. It's too soon to know. Besides, as you're well aware, it's complicated. He doesn't live in Hope Springs. He's only there for the summer." She looked down at her belly. "And that isn't even the biggest complication to a relationship."

"Maybe I shouldn't go to Florida."

Jessica rolled her eyes. "Of course you should go. Deidra needs to spend time with you as much as I do, and you shouldn't miss seeing Trish play Peter Pan."

"But it's so close to your time."

"Not really. You'll be back four or five weeks before the delivery. More if I'm as late as I was with Angela."

"Second babies often come sooner."

"But sometimes they come later."

"Oh, you." Frustration laced the two words.

Jessica grinned in victory. "Oh, me."

Her mom drew back slightly. "You *are* emotionally stronger. I can see that."

"I am stronger."

"All right. I'll try not to interfere again. Just . . . be careful."

"I will. I promise." Although she wasn't at all sure she could keep that promise. Was it possible to be careful while falling in love?

KUNA, IDAHO
Monday, December 31, 1934

A bitter wind whipped the corners of the Greyson home, and snow swirled beyond the window glass. Inside, the house lay silent. The kids as well as Helen and his mother-in-law had retired for the night. He was the only one likely to be awake to see in the New Year.

Not that he expected 1935 to be much different from 1934.

Many believed the depression was loosening its grip on the nation. The mood of most people seemed more upbeat. Perhaps it was the repeal of Prohibition that had made the difference. Or maybe it was all due to that adorable new Hollywood child star Shirley Temple.

Andrew chuckled before lowering his gaze to the ledger, open on the table.

Farmers in the Midwest had suffered through a brutally cold February, followed by searing temperatures in the month of July. Crops had withered in the drought that struck throughout the breadbasket of America. The silver lining for farmers like Andrew, living in other areas of the country, were the resulting agricultural price increases. His hay had sold for more this past growing season, bringing in a tidy sum.

But one good summer wasn't enough to ease his worries. There always seemed to be needs beyond income—Frani's stay in the hospital for a high fever last spring, Ben's broken arm in May, the loss of a milk cow in the fall, clothes and shoes for four growing kids. Andrew wasn't yet thirty, but there were days when he felt older than his father.

Last spring, when he'd read in the newspaper that Henry Ford had restored the five-dollars-a-day minimum wage to the majority of his workers, Andrew had been tempted to pull up stakes and move the whole lot of them to Michigan. But he'd had enough good sense to resist the impulse. If he'd had that thought, no doubt there were thousands, tens of thousands, of other men thinking the same thing. No, he and his family were better off right there in Idaho, on the farm.

Has the Lord failed to provide for us?

No. God had been ever present and ever faithful. As long as Andrew had the good sense to set his eyes and thoughts on the Father, he could enjoy peace.

He closed the ledger and pushed the book to the side of the table. He replaced it with his Bible. He turned to the title page and stared at his father's handwriting:

To our beloved son,
Andrew Michael Henning,
on the occasion of his graduation
from the university.
Follow God and you will never lose your way.
Papa and Mama
Kuna, Idaho
1929

He closed his eyes, remembering the day of his graduation. How proud his parents had been as he'd stood there in his cap and gown. How proud *he'd* been. How sure that he had life by the horns and nothing but good times and success ahead of him.

Success. He flipped the pages to the beginning of the book of Joshua, found the verse he wanted, and underlined the words with a pencil as he silently read:

> This book of the law shall not depart out of thy mouth; but thou shalt meditate therein day and night, that thou mayest observe to do according to all that is written therein: for then thou shalt make thy way prosperous, and then thou shalt have good success.

He had come to believe that God's definitions of *prosperous* and *success* differed from what most men believed. What mattered was not the size of his bank account. What mattered was the type of men and women his children became. What mattered was that he loved his wife as Christ loved the church, enough to die for her. What mattered was that he cared for the widow in his midst. What mattered was that he honored his parents. Now he needed to live in that truth, in that definition, every single day, depression or no.

He took the pencil and wrote their names in the narrow margin: Helen. Mama. Papa. Madge. Ben. Louisa. Oscar. Frani.

Chapter 24

Ridley and Jessica settled into a comfortable routine in the days immediately following the Sunday dinner with her parents. Mornings were spent alone, Jessica working in her studio, Ridley making more repairs around his parents' place. At noon, Ridley, with Kris at his heels, wandered over to Jessica's house where they ate lunch together and talked about little things, seemingly unimportant things. And yet those times together felt important to Ridley as he caught more glimpses of who Jessica was, who she had been, and who she wanted to be. With each glimpse, he fell a little more in love. He hoped she felt the same, but he didn't rush her.

After lunch, Ridley returned home with his dog. Now that the cable and internet had been installed, he spent the afternoons doing research on his retreat ideas. He had yet to share his ideas for the future with Jessica. He wanted his thoughts to feel more concrete before he did that. He didn't want to make promises he couldn't keep. She'd had enough of those in her past.

In the evenings, after the earth started to cool, they took long walks together down their country lane. They listened to the clapping of aspen leaves, stirred by a breeze. They watched the sky turn from azure to pewter as the sun settled beyond the mountains. They took turns throwing a ball for Kris to chase. Unlike their lunches, they talked little during these nightly walks. Instead, they simply enjoyed the presence of the other and the beauty of the valley that surrounded them.

Ridley heard Kris's whimper through a haze of sleep. He wasn't ready to wake up, not since it meant letting go of a dream that made him feel joyous. Sadly, the details of that dream had already slipped away. Turning onto his side, he opened his eyes. The dog's face was mere inches away, her muzzle now resting on the edge of the mattress. She whimpered again.

"I'm gonna install a dog door," he muttered.

Paws hit the mattress on either side of Kris's muzzle, and dark brown eyes pleaded with him.

"All right. All right." He tossed aside the sheet and sat up. "You win."

Clad in a T-shirt and shorts, he padded barefoot down the stairs and to the back door. He opened it, and Kris dashed outside, in a hurry to do her business. Waiting for the dog to finish, Ridley drew in a deep breath. He loved the smell of morning air in the mountains. The only thing that would make it better was if he was holding a mug of coffee.

Light had begun painting the valley with a buttery hue. It was early. Not yet six, he guessed. Birds chirped as they fluttered from branch to branch in the trees. For some reason, the sound made him think of his dream, and he smiled again. Not because he remembered the details. Only that he remembered it had made him happy. And if it made him happy, it must have been about Jessica.

Kris trotted back to the house and went straight to her food bowl, looking back at him to see if he followed.

"Not a chance, mutt. My coffee first."

She released a soft bark.

He laughed as he walked into the kitchen. It didn't take long to get his morning coffee started, but as he stood waiting, he felt a nudge in his spirit. It was as if God said, *No more waiting. It's time to act.* And just as quickly, he knew what his next step was supposed to be. It was time to discover how he could finance his dream.

A few hours later, he rapped on Jessica's back door. Her face revealed surprise when she opened it.

"Sorry to bother you," he said. "I need to drive down to Boise on business, and I was wondering if you could look after Kris until I'm home."

"Of course."

"Afraid I'll miss lunch, but I should be back before it's time for our walk."

A soft smile curved her mouth, letting him know she liked that he had called it "our walk."

He liked the sound of it himself. "I've left the key under the mat at the back door. She might need to be fed again before I'm back."

"I'll take care of it."

Instinctively, he leaned in and kissed her. He'd resisted the urge for better than two weeks—and it hadn't been easy. The first kiss they'd shared had been considered bad timing. He hoped the second wouldn't be considered the same. Her lips warmed beneath his, and he had his answer.

"Thanks," he whispered when they drew apart. "See you tonight."

He hardly remembered why he wanted to drive to Boise. He

would rather stay where he was, take her back into his arms, and kiss her until they both ran out of air. But he knew that wasn't an option.

He cleared his throat and made himself turn and walk away.

༄

Jessica was putting away her paints when the doorbell rang, causing Kris to bark. Her eyes went to the clock on her studio wall, and she was surprised to see she'd worked straight through the lunch hour. It was nearly two o'clock. No wonder her back ached.

"Be quiet, Kris," she commanded as she left the studio.

The dog obeyed, moving off to one side of the entrance and sitting on a throw rug.

"Good girl." Jessica was still looking at the dog as she pulled open the door. When she looked up to see her caller, she felt a jolt of surprise. "Ellery?"

"I hope it's all right that I dropped by without calling." Ellery flashed one of her gorgeous smiles.

"Of course. Come in." She widened the opening as she took a step back.

Ellery moved inside, her eyes sweeping the living room. She'd never been to the Mason home before this and seemed to take a great interest in everything.

Jessica wanted to ask what on earth she wanted, but good manners kicked in. "Could I get you some iced tea? It's decaf but it tastes the same."

"I'd love some."

Jessica's stomach growled as she walked to the kitchen. She tried to silence it with a bite of cheese from the fridge before she filled two small glasses with tea. The size of the glasses was intentional. She didn't want to encourage Ellery to remain longer than necessary. She set the glasses on the table, again thinking that sitting there would be less inviting than for them to be seated in the living room. "Ellery."

The other woman stepped into view. "This is kind of you, Jessica."

"Not at all." She returned to the kitchen for sugar and lemon wedges. "Help yourself." She set the sugar bowl and saucer of lemon slices on the table. "I'll be right back."

She went down the hall to use the bathroom. After washing her hands, she stared at her reflection in the mirror. What was Ellery Wallace doing in her home? She couldn't imagine. They weren't friends. Their paths had seldom crossed through the years, and certainly the woman had never been a guest here. Other than the Fourth of July, she hadn't seen Ellery since . . . since Joe's and Angela's funeral, and then only a glimpse of her at the back of the church. Jessica frowned, bothered by that memory.

She shook off the feeling and left the bathroom. After all, she would find no answers in that small room, staring at the mirror. Only Ellery could tell her why she'd dropped by out of the blue. For all Jessica knew, she wanted to order some original artwork.

Ellery hadn't waited in the dining room. She had carried her glass of tea into the living room where she was perusing a group of photographs. As Jessica stepped from the hallway, she saw Ellery run her fingertip along the frame of a photo. It was the only one of Joe still on display in the house. She'd put all others in a box not long after the funeral.

"That was taken last summer," she said, moving forward again.

Ellery drew her hand back, like a child caught in the cookie jar.

"Joe loved those wilderness trips. Packing in where few other people ever go."

"Did you like going with him?" Ellery turned her back to the photo.

"Yes."

"I've never cared for roughing it myself."

Jessica didn't know Ellery well, but she would have guessed that about her.

"When is your baby due, Jessica?"

"Around the first of September."

Ellery was silent a long while before saying, "You must have gotten pregnant just before the accident."

Resentment coiled in Jessica's chest. What business was it of Ellery's when she'd gotten pregnant? What made Ellery think she had a right to say anything about Joe or their baby?

And just like that, Jessica knew the answer. Almost as if she'd known it all along. She stepped quickly to the sofa and sat down, her right hand on her belly in a gesture of protection.

"He never told you about me, did he? He said he was going to, but he didn't." Ellery shook her head. "I guess he betrayed us both."

"Why did you come here?"

"I don't know. I just . . . I just couldn't believe it when I saw you in the park. I thought . . . He told me you never . . . He said he didn't . . ." Ellery let the words die unfinished.

Resentment was replaced by an unexpected wave of pity. Jessica wanted to hate Ellery Wallace, but all she felt was sympathy. Ellery wasn't a kind person or a generous person or even a friendly person. It should be so easy to hate her now that Jessica had discovered the truth. But hate wouldn't come. She felt sorrow, regret, pity . . . but not hate.

Drawing in a deep breath through her nose, Jessica gave her head a slow shake. "I'm sorry, Ellery, but I think you should go."

"Yes." Ellery set her glass on the coffee table. "I should go." She moved toward the door, then stopped and turned. Her chin lifted and a look of defiance entered her eyes. "He was going to marry me, you know. He promised to marry me and take me out of this town for good." With a slight toss of her head, she turned away a second time.

Jessica stood but didn't follow Ellery to the door and didn't bother to say goodbye. After the door closed, she sank onto the sofa again, mulling over the encounter. She was surprised by the calm she felt in its wake. It had to be the peace that passed understanding, for she didn't believe it would be possible otherwise. How very astonishing to discover the identity of her husband's mistress, only to also discover it no longer mattered to her. There was lingering sadness for what might have been, for what should have been. She had wanted a lifelong marriage, filled with memories and joy. She had wanted to watch Angela grow up in a home with both a mother and a father. That wasn't what had happened. Her life was very different from what she'd wanted, from what she'd planned. But God had brought her through the pain and heartache and loss. God would always bring her through. He was there in the joy, and He was there in the sorrow. He was there in the sameness and in the surprises. He was with her always, just as He'd promised.

It flowered inside of her then, the ability to let go of the past she could not change. The bitter root she'd held on to, even longer than she'd been aware, was gone.

"God, I forgive Joe," she whispered. "I truly forgive him. And I forgive Ellery. I'm even sorry for her. Father, please forgive me, too, for failing to always walk as You would have had me walk. I lay it all at the foot of the cross. Help me not to take it up again."

KUNA, IDAHO

Wednesday, August 28, 1935

A polio epidemic had struck the country in 1935, and President Roosevelt, himself a victim of infantile paralysis, led a drive to find a way to prevent or combat the disease. That summer the nation mourned the passing of Will Rogers in a plane crash in Alaska. And over all of that, the economic gains enjoyed in the previous year caused labor and capital to fight with each other harder than ever. To Andrew, it seemed more of a brawl of the no-holds-barred variety.

But for the Henning family, the biggest news of the year was the adoption of Ben, Louisa, and Oscar, which became final at the end of July. It didn't change the way Andrew felt about the children. They'd been his kids in his heart from the moment they'd come to stay on the Greyson farm. Actually, it was the Henning farm now. Mother Greyson had transferred the deed to him and Helen the previous year.

At twelve, Ben had become Andrew's trusted right hand, but at the moment, he was glaring at his dad. "School doesn't make that much difference. Not when I'm driving a tractor or pitching hay."

"School always makes a difference, son."

"Not to me. I'm not smart like Louisa and Oscar."

Andrew put a hand on the boy's narrow shoulder. "That isn't true. We all have different strengths. You may have to work harder at some things than your brother or sister, but you're smart and you need an education. No child of mine is going to leave school as long as I can help it."

"If I was home, you wouldn't have to hire help for the fall harvest. Haven't I been what you needed all summer?"

"You've been exactly what I needed all summer. You're a hard worker and you listen to my instructions. Those are important

237

attributes. But I also want you to be well read. When I talk to you about a story from the Bible, I want you to know the story already because you've read it for yourself. When I quote from Shakespeare, I want you to recognize what play it's from. That won't happen if you quit school at your age."

"Who cares about Shakespeare? Won't help you grow more hay on the same forty acres."

"Ben." He spoke the name softly and slowly. The boy knew that meant the conversation was over, and he was smart enough to heed the gentle warning. Andrew reached out and ruffled Ben's hair to let him know he wasn't angry. The boy gave him a reluctant nod before bending to pick up a board.

"Andrew!"

He looked toward the farmhouse and saw Helen standing beside the Ford, waving at him. "Finish up with that," he told Ben. "I'll be back." He strode toward his wife.

It pained him at times that he couldn't buy her lots of new clothes or give her a new car or spoil her with jewelry. But standing there in the same dress she'd worn to the wedding of Martha and Eddie Edwards—almost four years ago—with sunlight gilding her little straw hat, she looked like a queen.

"I didn't expect you back from town this soon," he said as he approached her. "Weren't you having lunch with Mae?"

"We had lunch, but I didn't want to dawdle." She looked as if she might jump up and down, the same way Frani did when she was excited. "I have something to tell you."

"What's up?"

"I went to see Dr. Russell."

"Dr. Russell?" Alarm skittered through him. The Hennings didn't go to the doctor for any old thing. "What's wrong?"

"Nothing's wrong."

"Then what—" He stopped, understanding hitting him like a two-by-four to the back of his head. "When?"

She laughed, the sound tinkling and merry. "February."

He picked her up and swung her around in a circle, his laughter joining hers. Then, just as quickly, he set her down. "Sorry. I shouldn't have done that. Are you okay?"

"Of course I'm okay. I'm not made of glass, and neither is the baby."

His gaze shot to the house. "Guess I'd better get to work on that attic room I've talked about. Frani's getting too old to stay in our room anyway, and I know Louisa'd give anything to stop sharing a room with the boys."

"How will we afford it, Andrew?"

"We'll afford it. I'll make it work somehow." In his mind, he started listing what he could sell or do to raise extra money.

"You're happy about the baby, then?"

"Of course I'm happy about it. Our quiver's not full of God's blessings yet. Not until He says so."

She shook her head, amusement remaining in her voice. "Some people would think four children is plenty, especially in times like these."

"Some people would be wrong."

Chapter 25

Feeling elated by his day down in the valley, meeting with a financial advisor and a Realtor, Ridley rapped on Jessica's back door.

When she saw him, she smiled. "I didn't expect you this soon. What time is it?"

"Not quite five."

"I haven't fed Kris yet."

"I can take care of that." He ran his hand over his hair. "How about I take care of you too? I mean, let me take you out to dinner."

"Oh, that's not necessary."

"Please. I'd like to tell you why I went to Boise and what happened."

She glanced over her shoulder. "I could fix us something. We could talk just as easily here."

"Jessica, let me take you out to dinner." He spoke softly but firmly. "Let's call it a date."

Pink rose in her cheeks. "A date?"

"Yeah. I think it's time. Don't you?"

Her answer was a tentative nod.

He took a step back, grinning. "I'll be back in half an hour. I hear the Riverside is nice."

"It is nice, but you don't need—"

"Good. See you soon." His gaze lowered to the dog, who sat on the floor behind Jessica. "Come on, Kris."

He fed the dog, showered, and dressed in record time. Before heading out to his car, he called the restaurant to make certain they weren't booked solid for the evening. They weren't.

He drove to Jessica's house, but this time he walked to her front door. His pulse quickened when he saw her in a lemon-yellow dress, loose and flowing and summery. She carried a white sweater over one arm and held a small clutch in her left hand.

"Yellow becomes you."

She flushed at the compliment.

"Shall we go?" He offered his hand.

She took it. Her fingers felt cool within his larger, warmer hand. He was reluctant to release his grip when they reached the car, but he had no other choice. He saw her settled into the passenger seat, then hurried around to get behind the wheel. As eager as he was to finally share his ideas about his future, he didn't want to do it while driving. He searched for something else to say, but his mind seemed suddenly blank.

It was Jessica who broke the silence in the car. "Do you remember the day you and I drove to Boise to get my new router?"

"Sure."

"And I asked you if you'd been able to forgive the people who'd lied about you."

"I remember." He glanced her way, but she was looking out the passenger window at the river.

"And later, you told me you'd found forgiveness for them."

"I remember," he repeated.

"I didn't tell you how very much I needed to be able to forgive someone too. I didn't tell you because I didn't think I could forgive." She drew in a long, deep breath. "My husband was having an affair when he died."

Ridley had guessed as much, that day in the park, but it made his heart ache for her, hearing her say it.

"He was leaving me for the other woman, but I didn't know until today who she was. Who she is." Her voice had lowered almost to a whisper. "She came to see me while you were down in the valley."

He released a breath.

"I never had a clue that it was Ellery. Isn't it strange that I didn't know?"

Nothing on earth would have made him tell Jessica that he was convinced her friends had known.

"Do you remember Ellery Wallace?" she asked. "You met her in the park on the Fourth."

"Yeah. I remember her."

She drew in another deep breath. "It was hard, learning the truth. Especially from her. But after she left I realized that I could forgive Joe for what he'd done. And her too. I'm not even sure how it happened. I offered my bitterness to God, and I felt Him take it from me."

"You've never seemed bitter."

"I was. Trust me. It was all twisted up with my grief. But I became an expert at hiding things long before Joe and Angela died. I was an expert at hiding my emotions, my hurt, sometimes even my happiness." She sighed. "I hid the truth from others and from myself. I tried to hide it from God too. But I don't want to hide anything anymore."

Ridley had never admired anyone as much as he admired Jessica Mason in that moment. However, he was beginning to question if this was the right time to share his own news. His excitement over the possibilities for the future might not be appropriate. She'd had a difficult afternoon, and he wanted to be sensitive to it. If he'd known when he first asked her out to dinner . . .

They arrived at the restaurant a short while later. Ridley pulled into a parking space and cut the engine. He glanced at Jessica, tenderness filling his chest. "Here we are."

"Good." She sent him a fleeting smile. "I'm hungry."

⌒≷⌒

It occurred to Jessica while they waited for their meals to be delivered—they both ordered the wild trout—that she felt an amazing lightness in her spirit. No, it was more than that. It was as if she'd opened a door to make room for life to enter again. She'd been opening that door, a little at a time, over the course of the summer, but today she'd thrown it wide.

After the server brought their salads, Ridley said a quick blessing, and they both began to eat. Jessica hadn't lied when she'd told him she was hungry. She took several bites before she was ready to talk again. Or rather to listen.

"You were going to tell me why you went to Boise and what happened there." She speared a cherry tomato with her fork.

"It can wait if you want."

She sensed the reason for his reluctance, and she smiled gently, appreciating his thoughtfulness. "I'm good, Ridley. More than good. And I don't want to wait to hear about whatever it is. Tell me. Please."

"Well—" He moved the salad around on the plate. "Remember last week when I told you that my troubles with the media didn't amount to much in comparison to what some people go through. You said you pitied them, whoever they were. Your reaction was what I needed to solidify an idea that had been trying to take hold in my mind. Something about what I wanted to do with my life from here on out. Something very different from what I used to do."

His excitement had returned. She saw it in his eyes and heard it in the timbre of his voice. He explained how he'd like to help people who were in the midst of media storms like the one he'd gone through, no matter the reason for it. "I got to thinking, maybe I could create a place for people to escape for a time, the way I did when I came here. A place where they could find peace in the midst of the storm. A place where they could get sound counseling and gain a bit of perspective. Maybe completely change the course of their lives. In a good way. And then I got to thinking, maybe that place could be here in Hope Springs. Kind of an appropriate name for the town, come to think of it."

"That's a lot of thinking," she said. "Does that mean you plan to stay in Hope Springs?" Her heart fluttered as she asked the question, her own hope rising.

"Maybe. If it works out." He grinned. "But I think it can be done. I've put my house in Boise on the market. There's good equity in it, even after a Realtor gets a chunk of the sale, and I've got some savings too. Not enough, of course. I'll need to find investors, but I've got a start on those too."

"You did all of that in one day?"

"Not all of it. Having internet helped me get a head start." He leaned forward. "There's some property on the north end of the valley that I want to look at tomorrow. Will you come with me?"

She couldn't have refused the invitation, even if she'd wanted to. And she didn't want to. Knowing Ridley had helped to change her world, her attitude, her outlook. Had he been part of God's plan to bring her out of her misery so that real healing could begin? So that she could find her way back to faith? So that she could reach a place of forgiveness? It seemed so to her. And now he was talking about staying in Hope Springs. Did she dare allow his plans to matter to her?

Smiling again, she answered, "Yes. I'll go with you."

"Ten o'clock too early?"

"No. Of course not."

"Great." His attention returned to his salad.

Jessica looked down, suddenly wondering if Ridley looked at her and saw only her or if he remembered there was another life inside of her. Even if he didn't, she must.

KUNA, IDAHO
Thursday, October 24, 1935

Andrew had counted pennies for what seemed an eternity, but for tonight he refused to do so. This was his and Helen's sixth wedding anniversary. When he considered all they'd been through, all that their marriage had survived, it seemed right they should celebrate in a special way.

He made reservations for dinner at an upscale restaurant in Boise. When they were newlyweds, he had promised Helen he would take her to the Ballentine. He'd expected to do so within a few weeks. A couple of months at most. He'd never imagined it would take him six years to keep his promise.

"You look nice, Dad."

Andrew met Ben's gaze in the mirror. "Thanks." He adjusted

his tie, then tugged at the hem of his suit coat's sleeves, pretending not to see the frayed edges.

"Louisa says Mom's about ready."

Nerves turned in his stomach. Like they had before his first date with Helen. At thirty, he'd thought he was too old to feel that way. Apparently not. Apparently love was no respecter of age.

"Did you tell her where you're takin' her?" Ben asked.

"No. Just that we're going out for dinner."

"Hope it's as good as you think it's gonna be."

Andrew laughed softly. "So do I, son. So do I."

He left their bedroom, his eyes going to the closed door of the girls' bedroom. That's where Helen had chosen to get dressed tonight. He supposed she had a surprise for him as well.

He was right about that. When she opened the door and walked down the hall, it was like the moment when he'd seen her walking toward him as a bride. Only she was more beautiful to him now than she'd been then. She wore a dress of midnight blue with a touch of white lace at the neck and the wrists. She must have made it when he was in the fields in the daytime, for he couldn't recall seeing her working on it.

"Ready, my love?" he asked.

She smiled at him, the look both tender and tentative. "I'm ready. Where are we going?"

"To Boise. But where exactly, I'm not saying." He checked his watch. "We'd better get started so we don't lose our reservation." He took hold of her arm at the elbow and escorted her out of the house.

The children and Mother Greyson all came to stand on the porch to wave them off. Ben had sprouted into a beanpole. At twelve, he was already taller than Andrew's mother-in-law but about half her width. Louisa, at nine, was the levelheaded one, and she loved mothering Frani. Right now she held her little sister's hand firmly within her own. Eight-year-old Oscar . . . Well, he was the outlaw in the family. If there was mischief to be found, he would find it, usually on his own. As if to prove the point, he stood slightly away from the others, his face scrunched in thought.

After helping Helen into the automobile and turning the crank, Andrew hurried around to get behind the wheel, pausing long enough to wave to his family. Love welled inside of him. *Thank You, God.* It was a lesson he'd learned. Or at least had started to learn. The beauty of a grateful heart. The satisfaction of learning to be content, whether in plenty or in want.

They talked of many things on the drive into Boise. About the children, their schooling, the need for new clothes for everybody, Louisa's crooked front tooth. About Mother Greyson's failing eyesight. About the barn cat's new litter of kittens.

Southwest Idaho was enjoying a prolonged Indian summer, and just before the sun set, a golden haze blanketed the land. It lasted only a short while. Evening moved in quickly, and the first twinkle of stars appeared in the sky before they arrived at the restaurant.

Helen gasped when she saw where they were. "Andrew, is the Ballentine your surprise?"

"A man should keep a promise to the woman he loves. Even if it takes six years to do it."

"But we can't possibly afford to—"

"Don't say it, Helen. Don't mention money tonight."

"But, Andrew—"

He held up an index finger, stopping whatever else she might have said. Then she smiled, and he knew she wouldn't argue further. He also knew she was more pleased than she could say. He was rather pleased himself.

Chapter 26

Ridley and Jessica left her house at ten the next morning. They drove with the windows down, enjoying the cool air whirling around them. It whipped Jessica's ponytail against her neck and cheeks and made her feel young and carefree. They'd driven for ten minutes or so before Ridley turned the car off the main road and onto a dirt one, very similar to the one that ran in front of her home. Another ten minutes brought them to a gate across the road. A white-and-red sign announced the property was for sale and gave some particulars in smaller type. Ridley hopped out of the car and walked to the gate, slipping the chain over the post. It swung open with a loud *creak.*

"Is someone meeting you to show you around?" Jessica asked him when he got back in the car.

"No. I was given a key."

She turned her eyes up the long drive. Only in a place like Hope Springs would it be all right for them to look at a property without a Realtor or owner present. She wondered whom it belonged to. She wasn't familiar with this area.

As if hearing her thoughts, Ridley said, "It belongs to a family named Pearson, but I was told no one has lived in the house since Aaron Pearson died in 2007 at the age of ninety-two. I understand he was a small boy when his father built this house. Around 1925. The rest of the family—his kids and grandkids—are scattered around several states in the West. None of them in Idaho. Apparently the house has been on the market ever since Pearson's death. A couple of nibbles, but no offers. Which could be very good for me price-wise. Assuming the place isn't falling apart."

A bend in the drive parted a copse of aspens, and a red-brick house came into view. Perhaps mansion was more apt than house. Jessica was reminded of one of the stately homes on Warm Springs Avenue or Harrison Boulevard in Boise. But it seemed very out of place here, stuck in the middle of nowhere.

"Wow. I wasn't expecting that," Ridley said.

"You didn't see any photos?"

"Yeah, I did. But they weren't recent. I was afraid they wouldn't be accurate."

They parked in front of the house and made their way up the steps. Ridley tested some boards on the sweeping front porch with the toe of his shoe before pulling a key from his pocket and unlocking the door. Jessica's first impression was of openness, spaciousness. The second impression was of light. There seemed to be windows everywhere. Ridley exchanged a look with her before moving deeper into the entry hall, the soles of his shoes making soft sounds on the black-and-white tiled floor.

Jessica stepped to the right and looked into what appeared to be the living room. Sheet-draped furniture sat clustered before a large fireplace, and an enormous portrait of a man standing beside a white horse hung above the mantel. "Do you suppose that's Aaron Pearson or his father?"

"Probably the father. Whoever it was, he wanted to look like the lord of the manor. Wouldn't you say?"

She laughed softly. "A little."

They moved together toward the room on the opposite side of the entry. It turned out to be the dining room. The long table and chairs were also covered with sheets, but she guessed there had to be room for at least fifteen chairs on each side of the table. A party for thirty-two.

"Who on earth did they entertain?" She stepped to the center of the room and turned in a slow circle. "Can you imagine this place at Christmas?"

"I'm starting to."

They went into the kitchen next. Whatever it was like when the home was built, it had been completely modernized since then. Most likely in this century, judging by the supersized side-by-side refrigerator that hummed softly against the opposite wall and the state-of-the-art stove top and double ovens to its left. Jessica couldn't imagine that a man in his eighties or nineties would have cared about any of this. Who had made the decision for him? Or had it been done after his death in hopes that it would make for a quick sale? Obviously that hadn't happened.

She opened a door. An automatic light turned on, revealing a pantry as large as the baby's room at home. "Nobody's lived here in years, but they've kept the power on?"

"I guess the estate doesn't have to worry about money. Besides, it wouldn't show well if it was all dark and gloomy."

They finished touring the rooms on the lower level—den, office, library, master bedroom, two baths, and a maid's quarters— then they climbed the stairs to the second floor.

"There's a laundry room and a game room in the basement,"

Ridley said when they reached the top, "plus eight bedrooms and six bathrooms up here."

"Eight? Did the original Pearsons have a huge family?"

"I don't know that either. But it makes me think so. Why else build a mansion?"

"I'm going to do some research on the Pearson family when I get home. I can't believe I've never heard anyone talk about them or this place."

They took their time moving down the hallway, looking into each bedroom as they went. Even the smallest room was twice the size of Jessica's bedroom at home.

In the room at the end of the hall, Ridley pointed to a corner in the ceiling. "Looks like there's a leak in the roof. There's some water damage." He turned in a slow circle. "But overall, the whole place looks to be in great condition. Especially considering its age."

"Modern plumbing and electricity. Forced-air heating and cooling. Remodeling and updates and additions." She walked to one of the windows. The grounds swept slowly up to the pine-covered mountains. "And a beautiful view from every window. Perfect."

"Peaceful."

She fingered the drapes. "You'll have to replace these. They're very worn." She sneezed. "Not to mention dusty."

Ridley laughed. "Agreed."

They returned to the hallway and looked over the banister at the entry hall.

"This would be perfect for a retreat center," he said after a lengthy silence. "It's beyond anything I'd hoped for."

"Will your clients all be wealthy?"

He turned to look at her. "No. That wasn't my plan. I plan to have a sliding scale, depending on the client's income and ability to pay. And if I get the right kind of licensed staff members—a counselor and a psychiatrist for sure—then insurance would pick up a part for those who have it. I'll want someone who can do career planning as well, for those who need it."

She admired him more than she could put into words. He wanted to make a difference. How few people thought beyond their own desires and needs. But Ridley wanted to take his hard experience of the past few months and use it to help others. "It's an ambitious undertaking," she said.

He leaned toward her. "But an important one." Then he brushed her lips with his, ever so briefly, before adding, "And I'm glad I can share it with you."

❦

Did Jessica have a clue how much she'd come to mean to him over the past weeks? He hoped she knew, at least a little. Enough to encourage her but not so much it might frighten her.

He straightened. "I'd better have a look at the basement too. Want to join me?"

"Of course. This place has my imagination working overtime. I want to see every corner."

He gave her a smile, then took hold of her hand and held it all the way down the staircase, through the entry hall to the back of the house, and down the narrow steps to the basement. He flicked on a light switch at the base of the stairs.

A pool table stood in the center of the room to his right. A fireplace took up a good portion of the far wall. To its left was a door with a window in it. He crossed the room to look through the glass. Concrete steps led up to the backyard.

"An exit," he said as he turned around.

"Brr." Jessica hugged herself. "It's cold down here."

"No air conditioning required for this floor."

He pictured the room filled with dark leather furniture. A man cave. He smiled at the thought. Aloud he said, "It's like God made sure the house was here for the retreat center." He felt a sudden kinship with Esther from the Bible and added, "Like it was built for such a time as this."

She shivered and began rubbing her upper arms.

"Come on. Let's go up where it's warmer." He motioned for her to precede him, then followed her up the stairs.

At the top, Jessica moved to the center of the entry hall, stopped, and turned in a slow circle. "It does seem ideal for your intentions."

It was easy for Ridley to imagine not only the house working for a retreat center but also to see Jessica as part of it. Would she want to be? Even as certain as he was that this idea was God's will, risk remained. Would she want to take the risk with him? He drew in a deep breath, steadying himself. Jessica was facing single motherhood in a matter of weeks. This wasn't the time to ask her to be part of a risky undertaking. But maybe he could ask her to cheer him on from the sidelines while they awaited the right time.

"Jessica." He cleared his throat. "If I get the place, maybe I can hire you to take care of some of the blank wall space with your inspirational artwork."

She smiled at him. "I'd be honored, Ridley."

BOISE, IDAHO
Thursday, October 24, 1935

The Ballentine restaurant showed no signs that this city and the entire nation had been gripped by an economic depression for six long years. The tablecloths were still a bright white. The china was still gold trimmed. The wine goblets still shimmered in the light of the chandeliers and wall sconces.

A waiter in a black suit led Helen and Andrew to their table. He placed menus before them, then retreated to let them consider their choices. They both decided to have the boneless squab chicken stuffed with wild rice, new potatoes rissole, and asparagus tips in butter sauce. After ordering, they turned their attention to the man at the grand piano in a far corner.

"I always wished I could learn to play the piano." Helen's voice sounded wistful.

"Maybe someday you can. We could put a piano against that west wall of the living room." He pictured the spot in his mind's eye. It would be crowded, but it could work. "I'll bet Louisa and Frani would like to learn to play too."

"Maybe Oscar as well."

Andrew felt his eyes widen. "Oscar. He'd never sit still long enough to play a scale."

Helen laughed, but the sound died abruptly. Surprise, almost fear, swept over her face.

Andrew followed her gaze to a table not too far from the piano. There sat Henry Victor with a beautiful young woman. It had been nearly four and a half years since Andrew had seen the man in his Meridian office, but Andrew wasn't likely to forget his face. He looked back at his wife. "Are you all right?" He tried to sound normal but wasn't sure he pulled it off.

"Yes." She lowered her eyes. "I thought for a moment I saw someone I knew."

"At the Ballentine?"

She laughed again, but this time it was a humorless sound. "I was mistaken."

He'd never told Helen he'd met Henry Victor, that he'd gone to the man's office and confronted him. If he didn't tell her back then, how could he tell her now? He frowned, wondering if staying silent was the same as a lie or if it was a kindness.

"I need to powder my nose," she said, rising from her chair.

He got up too.

"I won't be long." She hurried away.

Andrew sat down while his gaze went straight to Henry Victor. If the man had seen Helen or Andrew, he didn't let on. His attention was fixed completely on the young woman with him. Andrew couldn't help but wonder if she had a husband at home.

Anger and jealousy swirled inside of him, catching him by surprise. After all this time, after the healing and the forgiveness, after one baby and another one on the way, after adopting three children with his wife, he wouldn't have expected to still feel that way. Their marriage was good, strong, better than ever. He knew in his bones that Helen loved him, that any feelings she'd once had for Henry Victor were over. And yet, the anger and jealousy twisted Andrew's insides into knots.

He looked toward the ladies' room, and a few moments later Helen came out. Although pale, she held her head up, her shoulders straight, as she walked toward him. She even managed a small smile when their gazes met.

He stood again and returned her smile. "Did I tell you how pretty you look tonight?"

"No, I don't think you did." When he pulled out her chair, she sat down.

"I must've been tongue-tied when I saw you walking down the hall at home."

"I love you, Andrew."

He heard far more than those four words. He heard, *I'm sorry.* He heard, *I never meant to hurt you.* He heard, *How can you forgive me?*

"I love you, too, Helen. More than you know." Silently, he added, *You are not only beautiful, you are brave. I'm proud to be your husband.*

Chapter 27

Late morning sunlight streamed through the windows of the studio and onto the large canvas on the easel. Jessica stepped back and stared at the painting. She'd been working on it for over a week, ever since the day Ridley took her to see the Pearson house. The painting was to be a gift to Ridley on the day his retreat center opened. There wasn't any great hurry since she expected that would be months in the future, but still she worked on the painting every chance she got.

Her phone rang, and she stepped to the counter to look at the display. When she saw it was her mom's cell phone, she answered on the next ring.

"Hey, Mom. How was the play?"

"Hi, honey. Trish was amazing. The best Peter Pan ever."

Jessica smiled as she settled onto a stool. "Couldn't be you're prejudiced. Just a little bit?"

"Of course I am. I'm her grandmother."

"Tell me more about it."

Her mom promptly obeyed, detailing the entire evening, from the early family dinner before the play to the celebration that followed after the last curtain call. "Now what about you, Jessica? How are you?"

"I'm good, Mom. I waddle more than walk now. Even worse than when you last saw me. And my house needs a good cleaning. I have a hard time bending over, so I ignore anything that is out of easy reach. Otherwise, all is well."

"What about . . ." Her mom hesitated. "Have you seen Ridley Chesterfield lately?"

"Seen him?"

"Honey . . ."

"Yes, I've seen him. In fact, I see him every day. He's my neighbor." She knew her mom wouldn't believe that excuse any more than she believed it herself. "He's planning to stay in Hope Springs, Mom."

"What?"

"He's trying to buy some property here. He wants to open a type of retreat center."

"Good heavens."

Jessica smiled again, imagining her mom's expression. "It's quite exciting to hear him talk about it. He's full of plans and ideas. And the property he's found is amazing. It's a home I'd never seen before. A mansion, really. It's been here almost a hundred years, and I didn't even know it existed. I couldn't believe it. It's far out from town, to the east, near the mountains."

"It sounds as if he's going to be very busy. Starting a new business is never easy. Whatever he's planning has to be a precarious undertaking."

Jessica hooked a lock of hair behind her ear. "Quite precarious, I'm sure." She longed to add that it wasn't any more precarious than making one's living as an artist, but good sense told her she'd said enough. Instead she changed the subject, asking questions about her sister and brother-in-law and what the family planned to do for the remainder of her mom's stay in Florida. Was it going to be a day at the beach or a day at one of the theme parks? It sounded as if they planned to squeeze in both.

After the call ended, Jessica rose from the stool, groaning as she rubbed her lower back. She picked up the stainless-steel tumbler she'd left near her paint palette and took it to the kitchen to refill with ice and water. Afterward, she went to the back door and stepped outside. Heat rose off the patio, forcing her to take a step back into the shade. Her yard was green, thanks to irrigation and sprinklers, but beyond the fence, July had painted the wild grasses in shades of tan and brown. The sun was an intense yellow in a cloudless blue sky.

She looked toward the neighboring house. No sign of Kris or Ridley. She leaned forward. Ridley's car wasn't in sight, but a blue pickup truck sat parked at the side of the house. She wondered whose vehicle it was and where Ridley had taken his guest. No doubt out to the Pearson place. She wished she'd been asked to go with them.

She'd told her mother the truth. She saw Ridley every day, if only for their evening walks. But the whole truth was she didn't see him as often as she wanted. She thought of him first thing when she awakened in the morning, and she thought of him last thing before she closed her eyes at night. Too many times a day, she looked out her studio window or went to her back door, hoping to catch a glimpse of him.

"I love him."

There. She'd admitted it at last. It was true. She'd fallen in love with Ridley Chesterfield. She wasn't *falling* in love. She was there already. She loved him. Maybe it wasn't smart. Maybe she wasn't completely ready for romance. Maybe there were obstacles and complications. But she loved him all the same. And although he'd never said as much to her, she thought he might love her too. At least a little.

The baby dragged a heel or an elbow across her belly, as if to get her attention. It worked. She cradled the sides of her stomach with her hands, knowing that she loved this child with all her heart, no matter the heartache that had accompanied its conception. She also knew that, despite all that Ridley had come to mean to her over the summer, one niggling doubt remained. The biggest of obstacles and complications: even if Ridley loved her, could he love her child—another man's child—as if it were his own? It was a question that had to be answered before there could be any hope of a future for her and Ridley.

❧

Chad Evers stared at the fireplace in the living room and whistled softly. "This place is unbelievable."

Ridley chuckled, enjoying his friend's reaction.

"And the owners have accepted your offer?"

"Yes. I didn't think they would right away. I lowballed my offer, expecting that we would have to negotiate back and forth for a while. I even made requests for some repairs. I never thought they'd go for them. Instead, they said yes to everything I asked, including the price."

"Unreal."

Ridley let his gaze roam the room. "But just like God." With every passing day, he became more and more convinced of that. He was experiencing Romans 8:28 in real time. All things were working together for good, including what he had considered the darkest moments of his life.

"My dad was impressed with the proposal you wrote up," Chad said. "I think you'll have the investors you need before long."

"I appreciate his help with that."

"You know Dad. He loves a challenge, and you've given him a great one."

Ridley laughed again. "I aim to please."

The two men left the living room and wandered through the rest of the house. Chad didn't look at everything in the same way Jessica had. He was curious, but he didn't care about the molding or the paint color choices or the window and floor coverings. He didn't care about the furniture that lay beneath the white sheets. Although he did seem to like the look of the pool table in the basement.

When they stood on the steps outside the front door again, Chad said, "You know, when all the trouble broke about Tammy and the campaign and you, I sure never imagined this was where you'd end up before the end of summer."

"Me neither."

"You look happier than I've seen you look in a long time. You've been reinvigorated by your plans. A whole different man than the guy I came to visit back in June."

Ridley grinned, but it was thoughts of Jessica and not plans for a retreat center that made him do so. Still, he kept that bit of information to himself as they went down the steps.

As Chad opened the passenger door, he looked at Ridley over the roof of the car. "My mom thinks she might know a vocational counselor who'd be interested in working with your clients a couple of days a week. She's in Mom's book club, I think."

"Great. Have your mom send me the counselor's contact information."

They drove back to Ridley's place, enjoying the beauty of the valley. After so many years of friendship, they felt no need to fill the silence with small talk. When they arrived, Ridley parked his car in its usual spot. His gaze went over to Jessica's house and he saw her taking sheets off the clothesline.

"Chad, come with me. I want you to meet my neighbor."

"Sure. Okay."

They started across the field. Before Ridley could call out to her, she saw them. She waved, then picked up the basket that held the sun-dried sheets and moved to stand in the shade while she waited for their arrival.

"Chad, this is Jessica Mason. Jessica, this is Chad Evers. We've been friends since high school."

Jessica put down the basket a second time. "Hi, Chad. It's nice to meet one of Ridley's friends."

"Nice to meet you too."

The two of them shook hands.

"Jessica's an artist. I'm going to hire her to do some artwork for the retreat center." He smiled at her. "She's really talented and very inspirational."

"Is that so?" Chad said.

Ridley was barely aware that his friend had spoken. "Chad and **I were out** at the Pearson house. I wanted to show him around. His dad's helping me with finding a group of investors."

"That's marvelous." Her gaze moved to Chad. "I trust you were duly impressed."

"I was. I still am."

She laughed.

Chad poked Ridley in the upper arm with his knuckles. "I'd better be heading back to town."

That, at last, forced Ridley to look away from Jessica. "So soon?"

"Afraid so." Again to Jessica, Chad said, "Very nice to meet you."

"I hope I'll see you again soon."

"You probably will."

Ridley gave Jessica one last smile, then walked away next to his friend.

They were almost to the back door of the house when Chad said, "An artist, huh?"

"Yeah."

"She's pretty."

"Yeah." Ridley grinned.

"She's also pregnant."

"I've noticed."

Chad stopped walking, forcing Ridley to do the same. His friend stared him in the face for a long while before saying, "Man, you've got it bad for her."

The words pleased Ridley. "Yes, I have."

"She isn't why you've decided to stay in Hope Springs, is she?" Chad's expression sobered. "I mean, you aren't doing this retreat center so you can be near her, are you?"

Ridley shook his head, but he considered the questions carefully before he answered. "No, Chad. Not that being near her won't be a perk, but the inspiration for the retreat center is something separate altogether. I think the center is why God brought me here in the first place."

"I take it there's no husband in the picture."

"She's a widow. Her husband and their daughter died in an accident back in December."

"That's rough. But don't you think you might be rushing it a bit? Maybe she's not ready."

"I love her, Chad. That's all I have to know. And I'm willing to wait until she's ready to love me too."

Chad put a hand on Ridley's shoulder. "And what about the baby?"

"Don't worry. I've given her baby plenty of thought too. I know they're a package deal. When I realized how I felt about her, I started some soul-searching of my own. You know, wondering if I was ready to take on that responsibility. And I discovered the answer is yes. When Jessica's ready to have me, I'm ready to have them both."

Chad took a step back. "Friend, when you change your life, you *really* change your life."

KUNA, IDAHO
Tuesday, December 31, 1935

Another New Year's Eve rolled around, but unlike the previous year, as the hour grew late, Andrew didn't sit at the table alone. Helen was with him. At nearly eight months pregnant, she often had trouble sleeping. The baby, she said, seemed to press upon her lungs, making it hard to breathe. About her only place of comfort was the rocking chair.

Tonight, as they stayed warm near the woodstove, Helen knitted something for the baby while Andrew read aloud to her from the short novel *Goodbye, Mr. Chips*. Last night they'd finished reading John Steinbeck's *Tortilla Flat*, and before that it had been *The Thin Man*. Spending the evenings in this fashion after the children were in bed had become a favorite part of his days.

"'A great joke, this growing old,'" he read, "'but a sad joke, too, in a way. And as Chips sat by his fire with autumn gales rattling the windows, the waves of humor and sadness swept over him very often until tears fell, so that when Mrs. Wickett came in with his cup of tea she did not know whether he had been laughing or crying. And neither did Chips himself.'" Andrew turned the book face down on the table.

Helen looked up from her knitting. "Why did you stop?"

"Do you suppose it will be like that for us?"

"When we get old? I imagine so."

He reached out to place his hand on her belly. "Old age is a long ways away for us."

"Mother says everyone our age believes that, but that old age isn't as far off as we think. It gets here in the blink of an eye." She placed her hand over his on her belly. "If that's true, why do nine months pass at a tortoise's pace?"

He laughed with her. But when he leaned back in his chair, he let himself imagine the two of them, sitting in this same kitchen, in another forty or fifty years.

Hair turned white.

> "Lord, make me to know mine end,
> And the measure of my days, what it is:
> That I may know how frail I am."

Faces lined with wrinkles.

> "Behold, thou hast made my days as an handbreadth;
> And mine age is as nothing before thee."

Fingers gnarled from many years of work.

"Seeing his days are determined,
The number of his months are with thee,
Thou hast appointed his bounds that he cannot pass."

Now he took Helen's hand in his, causing her to meet his gaze again. "'Grow old along with me! The best is yet to be.'"

"Robert Browning?"

He nodded.

"You've always been a romantic, Andrew Henning."

"Only with you."

She smiled as she resumed her knitting. "Read some more, dear."

Obediently, he picked up the book on the table. "Chapter Two."

Chapter 28

It amazed Jessica that, even as she grew as broad as a barn, Ridley had a way of making her feel lithe and beautiful. When he looked at her, her heart skittered. And when he kissed her . . . Oh, when he kissed her. Neither of them had declared their love in so many words, and Jessica had come to understand why it was so. They were waiting on the baby. Both of them, although in different ways, perhaps for different reasons.

All the same, she was happy in a way she'd never expected to be again. She was content to let the days of summer meld one into another. Ridley threw himself into the task of launching his retreat center while Jessica worked in her studio as much as possible, nested a little in preparation for the baby, and reveled in the hours she spent with Ridley. And when she wasn't with him, she daydreamed about him. Like she was doing right now.

"Jessica." Her mom's voice from upstairs interrupted her pleasant thoughts.

"What?"

"Do you care if I move things around in the bathroom?"

"Of course not." Drawing a breath, she climbed the stairs. "Do whatever you want, Mom." She stopped outside the guest bathroom, leaning her shoulder against the jamb. "Make yourself comfortable. It could be weeks before the baby comes."

Her mom stopped what she was doing and faced Jessica. "My place is with you. Although I do wish you would agree to come stay in Boise and have your baby in the hospital."

"The clinic was fine when Angela was born. It will be fine this time too. Besides, I like and trust Dr. Young. I want to have my baby in my hometown."

"But what if there's a problem? The clinic isn't set up for real emergencies."

Jessica sighed. "My plan was always to have the baby in Hope Springs. You knew that."

"Yes. That is what you said."

"And there is no reason to expect any problems. I'm healthy and strong."

Her mom nodded. "You're right, of course. I don't know why I'm anxious."

Jessica stepped into the bathroom and gave her mom a hug. "You don't need to worry, but I love you for it, all the same."

The doorbell rang.

"Do you want me to get it?" her mom asked.

"No. You settle in. I'll get it."

She descended the stairs slowly. That was her only option. After all, she couldn't see her feet or the next step. She wasn't quite to the door when the caller switched from the bell to a knock. When she opened the door, she found a stranger on her stoop. An attractive woman, about Jessica's age, with big brown eyes and ink-black hair, worn long and straight. She wore a white sundress with yellow trim, striking against her tan.

"Hi," the stranger said. "Sorry to bother you. I'm looking for Ridley Chesterfield. I think that's where he's staying." She pointed to the house next door. "But nobody's answering and his car's not around. Am I on the right road?"

"Yes. You are. That's his parents' home."

The woman smiled. "Oh, good. I was afraid I'd messed up the directions he gave me. I've never been up to Hope Springs before."

"He's probably out at the Pearson house."

"Of course. I totally forgot he'd mentioned that. I guess I'll have to wait for him to get back. Thanks." She took a step backward, starting to leave.

Jessica wondered if the woman was one of Ridley's potential counselors. She wouldn't want him to lose out because he'd forgotten to return home for an appointment. "It's awfully hot out. You're welcome to wait in here if you'd like."

"I wouldn't want to put you out."

"You're not. Please. Come in."

"If you're sure."

"I'm sure." She pulled the door fully open. "I'm Jessica Mason."

"Selena Wright." She stepped inside. "This is very nice of you."

Jessica motioned toward the sofa. "Would you like something to drink?"

"No. I'm good. I've got my water bottle here in my bag." She looked around the living room before taking a seat. "Your home is nice."

"Thank you." She sat opposite the woman. "Do you have an interview with Mr. Chesterfield?"

"An interview?" Selena waved a manicured hand dismissively. "No. He's my boyfriend."

An odd feeling shivered through Jessica.

"It's been a long summer without him, I'll tell you. I mean, I know why he came up here, what with all the newspapers and all that mess he was involved in. But I've missed him something fierce. Phone calls and an occasional visit aren't enough."

Jessica wanted to stand but a sudden pain kept her in the chair.

"Honey, I was wondering—" Her mom stepped into view. "Sorry. I didn't know you had company."

She isn't company. She's . . . Ridley's girlfriend.

She didn't believe it. Or maybe she didn't want to believe it.

Which was it?

As quickly as the question formed, she knew her answer. Knew it as surely as she'd ever known anything.

෨෧

Ridley could hardly wait to reach home. He had so much to tell Jessica. The last of his investors was on board. The bank had approved the business loan, and the sale of the Pearson place was scheduled to close in two more weeks. Another counselor had committed to working with them. New Hope Retreat Center was soon to become a reality. Even earlier than he'd hoped.

He was grinning as he drove past Jessica's house, but the smile disappeared when he recognized the car parked in his driveway. It was Selena's car, a bright-yellow Mustang convertible. He hadn't thought of her since Chad had told him she'd called again, wanting to be reunited. He'd assumed his message of disinterest had been passed along to her, although he'd failed to ask when Chad came to see the Pearson house.

He parked and got out of his car. He looked into the Mustang. She wasn't there. No surprise, given how hot it was. He went to the

270

back door, unlocked it, and let Kris out, then walked toward the trees that provided some shade to the backyard.

"Selena?"

No answer. No sign of her anywhere.

"Selena!"

Where could—A sick feeling twisted his gut as his gaze went to Jessica's house.

"Come on, Kris."

He started to walk across the field but soon broke into a trot. He wasn't sure what he feared about Selena's unexpected visit. All he knew was he'd experienced her nastier side and didn't like the idea of Jessica being exposed to it. At the back door, he rapped, feeling as if he'd jump out of his skin before his knock was answered. And when the door opened, it wasn't Jessica he saw but her mom.

"Hi, Pat." He'd forgotten until that moment that she was coming to stay with Jessica until after the baby was born.

"Hi, Ridley. Come on in. Jessica's in the living room. With a friend of yours."

He swallowed a groan as he went inside, and when he saw Jessica, he knew Selena had already been up to no good.

"Ridley!" Selena jumped up from the sofa. "You're back." She crossed the room almost too quickly for him to prepare. "I've missed you." She hugged him.

Over Selena's head, he met Jessica's gaze. He shook his head, praying she understood, fearing she didn't. Then he firmly but gently moved Selena away from him. "Come on. We've taken up enough of Jessica's time. Let's go back to my place." He didn't give her a chance to say anything to Jessica as he steered her, hand on the small of her back, out of the house.

They were halfway across the field before she stopped and jerked away from him. "What's the matter with you?" The artificially sweet smile she'd worn when she first saw him had disappeared.

Her expression couldn't be any more thunderous than his own. "What are you doing here, Selena?"

"I came to see you. I missed you."

"Didn't Chad tell you I wasn't interested in renewing a relationship?"

"Yes." She pouted, looking up at him through long lashes. "But I didn't believe it."

"Believe it, Selena."

"Oh, Ridley. Don't be stubborn. I made a mistake to break things off. So let's get over it. Come back to Boise. We always had fun together."

"How did you find out where I was?"

"It wasn't easy. I'll tell you that." She tipped her head to one side and smiled seductively. "But I have my ways."

He realized it didn't matter to him how she'd discovered his whereabouts. He simply wanted her gone. He turned on his heel and strode toward her car, not looking to see if she followed. He didn't believe she'd missed him. And it wouldn't have mattered to him if she had. She'd done him a favor, giving him his walking papers.

"Ridley."

He yanked open the door to her car. "Goodbye, Selena."

"Aren't you going to even give us a chance?"

"There is no us. There wasn't ever going to be an us. We're too different. We want different things, you and I. I knew it even before you told me to get lost."

"But we—"

"Go home, Selena."

Anger returned to her eyes. "I was right about you." She muttered the same foul name she'd called him the last time they spoke on the phone. Then she slid into the car behind the wheel.

He nodded as he closed the door. Moments later, the Mustang's tires threw up a spray of gravel as Selena sped away.

"Good riddance."

He took off for Jessica's house, only realizing as he reached her front door that his dog hadn't followed him and Selena. Good. Kris must still be inside with Jessica. That gave him an excuse—if he needed one—for his quick return.

His knock was answered by her mom's voice calling out. "Come in." He opened the door and looked in. Pat Alexander was leaning over Jessica. When she looked up, she said, "Ridley, we need to go to the clinic. Right now. Jessica's in labor. Help me get her into the car."

KUNA, IDAHO
Sunday, April 5, 1936

Andrew Michael Henning Jr. was baptized on the first Sunday in April. Little Andy, as he'd been called from the day of his birth, slept quietly through the entire service.

"Such a good baby," Helen cooed softly as they left the church after the final benediction.

The Hennings celebrated the day with a dinner of fried chicken and mashed potatoes with gravy plus two kinds of pie for dessert. They all crowded around the table, five adults, four children, and one babe in arms, all but the baby talking and laughing, often at the same time. Andrew observed the three generations of his family and felt contentment warm his chest.

Hard to believe that he'd once been in such a hurry to escape the life of a farmer. The same for Helen. And yet, the farm was where

273

they'd found real life. As individuals and as a couple and a family. It was a good life. Good for themselves. Good for their children. No, he didn't have the wealth he'd once hoped for. He couldn't lavish gifts on his kids the way he might like. But he could give them love. He could give them guidance. He could be an example to them. He could share his faith, and he could pray for them.

It would all be well. He felt it in his bones. They had come through the worst of times. God had brought them into a good land, like the Israelites of old, and now all would be well.

Chapter 29

Ridley hadn't been asked to drive Jessica to the clinic, but nothing would have stopped him from doing so. Not even her mother. He drove his car over to the front of Jessica's house and left it idling while he raced inside. Jessica was alone in the living room. Standing now, she was bent over at the waist, a soft groan escaping her lips.

"I'm here," he said. "I'm ready. Should I carry you to the car?"

She straightened slightly, and her look seemed to say he was a certified idiot. "No. I can walk." She inhaled as she straightened.

"Are you sure?"

Now she gave him a tight smile. "I'm sure."

Pat returned to the living room, carrying a couple of canvas bags on one arm. "I've got everything."

Ridley put one arm around Jessica's back and took her hand with his other. They'd only taken a few steps before she had to stop and wait out another pain.

"They're coming awfully close together," Pat said from behind them.

Ridley didn't know a lot about a woman giving birth, but he

knew enough for that information to make him nervous. When the pain had passed, he got her out of the house and into his car.

By the time he was in the driver's seat, Pat was in the back seat. "I called the clinic," she said, "and they're expecting us."

"Good."

He made the drive into Hope Springs in record time, making sure he balanced speed with safety. After all, there was precious cargo in the car.

There was a nurse waiting for them at the clinic entrance with a wheelchair. Before Ridley knew it, Jessica was in the wheelchair and being whisked away. He'd wanted to talk to her. He'd hoped to explain about Selena and make sure Jessica didn't have the wrong impression. Most important, he'd needed to tell her he loved her. He needed her to know that. He needed her to know she was as important in his life as the air he breathed. He needed her to know that he already loved her baby, because it was a part of her. He'd waited to tell her, wanting her to be sure about him, wanting to give her time to learn to love him without any lingering doubt. But he shouldn't have waited. He was crazy to have waited. He should have told her the moment he'd realized his own feelings.

He parked the car in the nearest space and hurried into the clinic. He asked for Jessica but was sent to the waiting room. Relatives only with the patient, he was told. What an insane rule!

He paced. He flipped through a magazine without reading a word or seeing a photograph. He paced. He bought a soda from the machine and forgot to open it. He paced some more. Every passing minute seemed an hour long.

It was the sound of running feet that drew his attention. Several people whisked down the hallway and disappeared through the same door. A muffled male voice barked orders, words he couldn't make out but that filled him with tension. He stepped to the entrance to the waiting room and waited, hardly daring to draw breath.

After what seemed an eternity, Pat Alexander came out of the room, a hand over her mouth. Her eyes found his, and he read fear in them, even at this distance. He strode toward her.

"What's wrong?"

"I . . . I'm not sure. Something about the baby's heartbeat. I don't know . . . They wouldn't tell me . . . They made me leave."

Ridley longed to break his way into the delivery room and demand answers. Instead, he put his arm around Pat's back and gently drew her to the waiting room. In silence they sat, side by side, and waited. He took her hand in his, offering comfort while needing some for himself.

Gaze still locked on the doorway down the hall, he began to pray silently. For Jessica. For the baby. For the doctors and nurses caring for them both. Five minutes passed. Then ten. Then twenty. Neither of them moved. Neither of them let loose of the other's hand.

Finally, Pat said, "I should have made her come stay with me. Why didn't I make her move down to Boise?"

"Can you *make* Jessica do anything she doesn't want to do?" He looked at her.

"No." She shook her head. "She has a mind of her own."

"I like that about her."

"So do I."

"Pat?"

"Hmm."

"In case you don't know, I'm in love with your daughter."

"I'm glad, Ridley. Because I believe she loves you too."

"If you're right"—everything in him wanted her to be right— "I'll never let her regret it. Not ever."

She offered a smile before touching his cheek with her fingertips. "I believe you, young man."

Footsteps alerted them to the presence of another. A woman in medical scrubs stepped into the waiting room. Ridley and Pat were both on their feet before the nurse could speak.

"Jessica?" Pat whispered.

"She's fine," the woman answered with a smile

"And the baby?" Ridley asked, chest tight.

"She's fine too."

"She?" He grinned, feeling indescribably, perhaps stupidly, happy. He looked at Pat. "She's fine. They're both fine."

"They're both fine." Pat hugged him.

The nurse motioned with her hand. "Follow me. I'll take you to them. Jessica's asking for you both."

Ridley hesitated. "They told me relatives only."

"That's during the delivery. Not after."

They followed the nurse down the hall, but Ridley hesitated before entering the room. "Maybe you'd better go in first."

"She asked for you, Ridley."

"But—"

"Come on." She led the way into the room.

Drawing a deep breath, he followed. His gaze went straight to the hospital bed where Jessica lay, a small bundle cradled in her left arm.

She looked up and smiled, first at her mother, then at Ridley. "Come see her."

Ridley had never felt as uncertain as he did at that moment. Uncertain. Half afraid. Still, he moved to the left side of the bed while Pat moved to the right.

"Meet Hope," Jessica whispered.

"Hope." He lowered his gaze to the infant in her arms. "What a perfect name. But she's so little."

"Six pounds, nine ounces."

"She's got your hair color."

"It may not stay blond." She ran a fingertip over the peach fuzz on the baby's head. "And she'll probably lose what's there."

"Really?" He didn't know that about babies.

"May I hold her?" Pat asked.

"Of course."

Ridley watched as Jessica passed the baby into her mother's waiting arms. Pat cooed to Hope. Nonsensical words. Then, after a quick but meaningful look sent in his direction, she moved away from the bed and went to stand near the window.

Ridley drew a nearby chair closer to the bed, sat on it, and took hold of Jessica's hand. "I've never been so scared as I was when your mom came out of the delivery room. I don't think I've ever prayed as hard either."

Her smile was tender. "I knew you were praying. It kept me from being afraid."

"Thank God. Because I can't imagine my life without you in it. If anything were to take you away . . ." His words drifted into silence, the thought of losing her unbearable.

❧

Tears welled in Jessica's eyes. Although he hadn't yet said the words, she felt his love.

"I wanted to give you plenty of time to be sure about me. To know that I'd never make a promise and not keep it. I will never lie to you, Jessica. Not ever."

"Oh, Ridley, I've known that about you for a long time." Then, as tired as she was, she saw the worry in his eyes and understood that there was more behind it than her sudden and complicated delivery. "Are you concerned about what that woman said when she came to my house?"

"It was over between me and Selena before I ever came to Hope Springs. I need you to—"

She reached out and laid the flat of her hand on his cheek, stopping his explanation. "I know you, Ridley. I trust you."

"Thank you," he said softly. "But what I really need you to know is I love you."

She nodded and let the tears she'd been holding back fall.

"I love you and want to marry you, if you'll have me. When you're ready." He leaned in and kissed her lightly. "You and Hope, of course."

"And Hope?"

"I'm not just asking you to be my wife, Jessica. I'm asking for us to be a family. You and Hope and me. Will you let me be your husband and her father?"

The lump in her throat kept her from answering.

Softly, he asked again, "Will you?"

She swallowed the lump. "Yes."

"Yes?"

"Yes." She smiled and swiped away tears.

"You're sure?"

"I've never been more sure of anything, Ridley Chesterfield."

KUNA, IDAHO
Monday, May 25, 1936

The farmhouse across the road had stood empty for almost four years before it was purchased by Hirsch and Ida Finkel, recent German immigrants to the States. A couple in their early forties with no children, the Finkels were well educated and both able to speak English, although their thick accents sometimes took deciphering on the listener's part.

Hirsch hadn't been a farmer in his native land—trained as a teacher, he'd lost his position because he was Jewish—but he was determined to learn to farm in his new country. Andrew took an immediate liking to his neighbors and tried to advise Hirsch about crops and equipment and livestock. And when Andrew wasn't talking about farming, he listened as Hirsch Finkel explained what had happened in Germany since the Nazis came to power. The information disturbed Andrew deep in his soul.

He remembered thinking, on the day of Andy's baptism, that all would be well, that they had been through the worst. But listening to Hirsch, he began to wonder. He had been a boy when the war to end all wars was fought, and he'd believed others who'd told him that such a thing could never happen again. Germany had learned its lesson, some said. No matter what happened across the oceans, others said, America would never participate in another European war.

God help them, he wanted all of that to be true, but he had a hard time believing it, thanks to Hirsch Finkel's personal insights.

That was when Andrew began to pray in a different way. He broadened his prayers beyond himself and his loved ones, beyond his immediate needs, beyond weather and crops, clothes and shoes, health and happiness. Now, after he prayed for his family and friends, he went on to pray for his nation and for the world, praying for peace for all mankind, all the while knowing that true peace would never reign on the earth apart from the presence of Christ.

And so each night, he ended those prayers with the same five words. "Even so, come, Lord Jesus."

It was a prayer that would carry him through a lifetime.

Epilogue

Jessica married Ridley in the morning on Thanksgiving Day. While there were some people in Hope Springs who wondered if Jessica had married too soon after the death of her first husband, none of them were among those who actually knew the couple. Their friends and family had watched their love blossom and then deepen, and they rejoiced in it.

For the wedding, Jessica wore a pale peach-colored dress of satin and lace, and the spacious living room of the New Hope Retreat Center—one week away from opening its doors to clients—was filled with flowers in all the colors of autumn. Her sister stood on her left while Ridley's best friend stood on his right. Instead of a bouquet of flowers, Jessica held Hope in her arms as she exchanged vows with Ridley. Behind them, family and friends stood witness to the entwining of their three lives.

Tears filled her eyes as she remembered the bitterness that had sought to separate her from faith, from friends and neighbors, seemingly from life. Only God Himself could have brought her from that place of unhappiness to this moment of joy. Straight into Ridley's love.

"Happy?" he asked her a short while after the ceremony concluded with a kiss. Now, as they watched their guests mingling throughout the old Pearson mansion, he was the one who cradled the still sleeping infant.

"Unimaginably so." Standing on tiptoe, she brushed her lips against his. "And you?"

"The same. Only it's more than that. I like who I am with you. I like the man I am because you're a part of me." His gaze lowered. "And because Hope's a part of me. Does that make sense, Mrs. Chesterfield?"

"Mmm." She pressed her head against his shoulder. "Perfect sense, Mr. Chesterfield. Absolutely perfect sense."

She knew, of course, that there would be moments when they weren't unimaginably happy. She knew there would be times when they would disagree and even speak words they shouldn't out of anger. But she also knew God had brought them together, for better or worse, and that they would make it through both the highs and the lows in their lives.

It was good to believe in tomorrow again. Ridley had given her that. Ridley and the words of life and faith she'd found in her great-grandfather's beloved Bible.

A Note from the Author

Dear Friend:

I hope you enjoyed your visit to Hope Springs, as well as your introduction to Andrew Henning and members of his family, both past and present.

As an author, I am often asked where the ideas for my books come from. Many times I can't answer that question with specifics because so much of my creativity and storytelling happens in my subconscious first and then seems to bubble up in just-when-needed moments without me hardly being aware of why or how.

However, the same can't be said for the Legacy of Faith series. I know exactly how it came to be. In 2017, after turning in the manuscript for *You're Gonna Love Me*, I was reading my long-used (over twenty years), well-loved Bible, which is full of highlights, dates, and notes in the margins. Suddenly, I wondered what this Bible might mean to members of my family after I am gone. Will one of my daughters or grandchildren or as-yet-to-come great-grandchildren one day leaf through this book and hear God speak to them because of something I wrote or marked within those leather covers? This led me to the idea for this new series, where an ancestor's Bible touches the lives of those who never knew him.

As I write this note, I am hard at work on the second book in the series, *Cross My Heart*, and I have loved returning to the Henning farm in Kuna, Idaho, this time in both the present and the past. An excerpt is included, just to whet your appetite.

Thank you, as always, for reading my books. It is a joy to share my storytelling adventures with you.

Warm regards,

Robin

Acknowledgments

Many, many thanks to the fiction team at HarperCollins Christian Fiction for helping to birth another of my stories, from conception through editing and cover design through marketing and publicity and sales. I appreciate you all more than you know.

Special thanks to my editor Jocelyn. You are such a delight to work with, and I love that you caught the vision for this story and the series from the get-go.

I can't imagine my writing career without my terrific agent of 29+ years, Natasha Kern. Natasha, you are a friend, confidante, sounding board, brainstormer, and so very much more. Thanks!

Of course, my husband, Jerry, deserves a boatload of thanks for holding down the fort when my writing keeps me tied to the chair in my office. I love you, honey.

Finally, to the Author of life, who created me to create, who gave me a passion for storytelling and put a love for His word in my heart. May my story always be for Your glory.

Discussion Questions

1. Which character did you most relate to and why?
2. Both Ridley and Jessica are trying to hide something about their personal lives from others. Have you ever tried to hide the truth from friends or family?
3. Jessica's grief was mixed with anger because of her husband's betrayal. What has been your experience with grief? Is anger always a part of the process?
4. Have you ever wondered why God has allowed difficult trials to enter your life? Have you blamed Him or turned to Him for comfort and guidance?
5. Ridley was falsely accused of bringing down the candidate he worked for. Have you ever been falsely accused of something in public (the press, the internet) and been unable to clear your name because no one seemed to listen? How did you deal with it?
6. A lost sheltie named Kris helps bring Ridley and Jessica together. How have you seen pets bring people together?
7. Jessica's friends, Billie and Carol, tried to keep her from

withdrawing from life. How have you been a friend to someone who is/was struggling? Also, they seem to have known the truth about Ellery, long before Jessica discovered it. Were they wrong to keep it from her?

8. Andrew's Bible becomes a source of comfort for Jessica. Do you write in your Bible? What will your descendants find therein to encourage them even after you're gone?

Enjoy this excerpt from the next
book in the Legacy of Faith series
by Robin Lee Hatcher.

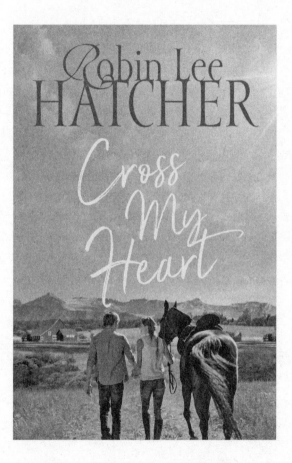

COMING IN JUNE 2019!

Prologue

April

Ben Henning showed his cousin Jessica into the kitchen of the old farmhouse. "I'm not really ready for company," he told her as he motioned to one of the chairs.

"I can see that." She smiled as her gaze took in the stacks of boxes in the kitchen, in the living room, and down the hallway.

"Want some coffee? It's fresh made."

"No thanks. I don't plan to stay long. I know you're busy with moving and all. Besides, I need to get back to Mom's house before it's time to feed Hope again. She's growing so fast, and she's always hungry."

Ben settled onto a chair opposite Jessica. "How old is she now?"

"Almost eight months."

"Can't hardly believe that."

"Me either." Jessica leaned toward the tote she'd set on the floor next to her chair. A moment later, she drew out a large book.

"Is that—" he began.

"Andrew Henning's Bible," she finished before sliding it across the table to him. "I brought it for you."

"For me?" The leather cover was worn and cracked, the outside edges curled. He ran a hand gently over the Bible that had once belonged to his great-great-grandfather.

"Great-grandpa Andrew . . . Well, I guess he was your great-great-grandfather, wasn't he? Confusing since you and I are close to the same age. Anyway, he gave it to my Grandma Frani before he died with the instructions that she was to keep it until she felt God tell her to pass it along to another family member. Then they were to do the same whenever the time came. Grandma Frani left it to me, and now I want you to have it."

Ben opened the front cover and saw that the first page had been torn, then mended with tape. Several pages stuck together when he turned again, revealing the Henning family tree. His namesake, Benjamin Tandy Henning, was the first child listed beneath Andrew's and Helen's names. He ran his finger down the list. The change in penmanship told him when someone else had taken over the task of filling in the names of great-grandchildren and great-great-grandchildren.

"Are you sure you're ready to give it up?" he asked. "You haven't had it very long. Not even a year."

"I'm sure."

He heard the smile in her answer before he looked up to meet her gaze.

"When I heard you were moving to the farm to live, I knew God wanted you to have it. I don't know why, but I believe He's got something special in mind for both you and this farm." She leaned toward him. "When my mom gave me this Bible after Grandma Frani's funeral, she told me to let what I found inside bless me. And it did, Ben. What I found inside gave me back my faith and restored my hope, and those two things allowed me to open my heart again to love. I don't know what is in store for you, but I believe God wants to encourage you through His Word and the notes Andrew Henning made inside that old Bible. I think God wants you to be blessed by it next."

Ben felt a quickening in his heart as his cousin spoke. He hadn't shared his ideas for this property with anyone but God as of yet. He knew the Lord had listened to him. He was sure He'd led him to this place at this time for a purpose. Now his cousin's words seemed to confirm what his heart had told him was true.

"Thanks, Jessica." He closed the leather cover. "This means a lot to me. More than I can tell you."

She nodded, and he had the feeling she understood even if he couldn't put it into words.

Monday, Sept 4, 1939

Andrew Henning was in the Kuna Feed and Seed when he learned Britain and France had declared war on Germany. He'd expected other nations to declare war ever since the Nazi invasion of Poland three days earlier, but when it happened, it still caught him by surprise.

"Mr. Finkel warned us this'd happen," Andrew's oldest son said. Sixteen and several inches taller than his father, Ben wore a conflicted expression, a cross between righteous anger and anticipation. "When the Nazis marched into Austria, he said this would happen. And then they took Czechoslovakia, and nobody did anything to stop them. Mr. Finkel told us they wouldn't stop there."

"You're right. He did."

The Finkels had purchased the property across from the

Henning farm three years earlier. Jewish immigrants from Germany, Hirsch and Ira Finkel had often expressed their concerns for what Hitler meant to do in Europe. It had been happening as the Finkels predicted, step by step.

Ben lowered his voice. "Will America join them? Will we go to war, too, Dad?"

"I don't know. I don't know. I hope not." He reached out, intending to ruffle Ben's hair, the same as he'd done for years. Then he thought better of it and placed his hand on the boy's shoulder instead.

Ben was approaching manhood at a rapid rate. If America went to war, Ben would soon be of age to serve in the military, and given his personality, he would be among the first to volunteer. Ben's brother Oscar was twelve. Surely a war, if America was drawn into it, wouldn't last long enough for Oscar to be in danger. Would it? But Oscar would want to be wherever his older brother was, and that worried Andrew. At least little Andy, the youngest of the Henning sons, was only three. He should be safe.

All the same, war was war, and Andrew wondered what it might mean for his family—and country—in the months and years to come.

Chapter 1

Sweat trickled along Ashley Showalter's spine and down the sides of her face as she carried a board up the ladder. She would rather be inside sipping a cold beverage than be outside in this intense August heat. But she was expecting another horse to arrive today and wanted the new shelter finished before the truck and trailer pulled down her driveway.

The crunch of gravel warned her it might be too late to finish. She looked up, but the silver truck coming slowly toward the shed wasn't pulling a trailer. Great. The last thing she wanted was an interruption right now.

The truck stopped, the door opened, and a man got out, followed by a yellow lab. Ashley was about to shout a warning about her own dogs, but the driver moved to the back of the truck and lowered the tailgate. An instant later, the lab jumped into the bed and lay down in the shade cast by the nearest tree.

She watched as the man—thirty-ish, tall, blond, and impossibly good-looking—headed for the door of her house. Before he reached it, she called to him, "Nobody's in there." Not waiting for him to answer, she went down the ladder. By the time she reached the ground, he was approaching her.

"Are you Miss Showalter?"

"I am."

"I'm Ben Henning."

She acknowledged his introduction with a nod while raising her right hand to shade her eyes from the bright sun.

"I was told you might be able to help me."

"Are you looking to buy a horse?"

"Yes and no."

Ashley raised her eyebrows, waiting for a better explanation.

"I can probably afford to buy one horse now, maybe two. But I'm in need of more. It would serve my purpose best to have half a dozen or so."

She didn't like the sound of that. Serve his purpose? What exactly did that mean? Sounded fishy.

"I own forty acres outside of Kuna." Ben Henning stuck his fingers in the back pockets of his jeans. "I leased the land to a farmer last summer and this one, but now I'd like to put the barn and some of the land to use in a different way. I'd like it to be an equine therapy barn, to help kids recovering from trauma."

Ashley felt a quickening in her chest. She couldn't help it. She believed in equine therapy. Being around horses healed a person's spirit. She knew that firsthand. All the same, she wasn't convinced about this guy. "Do you know anything about horses, Mr. Henning?"

"Call me Ben, please. As for horses, I'm no rodeo cowboy—" He grinned, showing he wasn't offended by the tone of her question. "But I know the front end of a horse from the back end, and I can saddle and ride one without help."

She relaxed slightly. "Let's go sit in the shade."

"I'd like that, Miss Showalter."

"Ashley."

"Ashley," he echoed.

The way he said her name made her feel funny on the inside. The timbre of his voice was like warm honey.

Once they were seated on chairs under the covered patio, Ben told her more about his aspirations for a therapy barn. He had a friend whose kid brother, after suffering a traumatic injury, struggled to find his way back to any sort of normalcy. Eventually he'd taken his own life. Sometime after that boy's funeral, Ben had seen a clip on the news about horse therapy that caught his interest.

"A few months later, I went to my cousin's wedding, and her new husband was about to open a retreat center for people who've suffered from bullying or bad press. Stuff like that. And it made me think, if Ridley—that's my cousin's husband—can do something like that, maybe I could make a go of a horse therapy barn. I don't expect to make a living from it. But if a few hours in the evening or on a weekend could help a kid who's struggling . . ." He let the words drift into silence. After a moment, he said, "Sorry. Didn't mean to go on like that."

"No. You shouldn't apologize for having a passion for something. Especially something that could help others."

"Thanks." He leaned back in his chair.

"But I'm not sure what you want from me. You said you can buy one or two horses but need more."

Ben Henning's slightly crooked grin made him look mischievous. "I guess I didn't explain that part well, did I? I was told that you rescue abused horses, and that you know people all around the valley who own horses. It seems to me, maybe we could help each other. You could find horses that could help my kids. Well, not *my* kids, but the kids I hope will be coming to the barn for therapy. And at the same time, we could help horses who need a new home, whether permanent or temporary. Not mustangs or wild horses, of course. They have to be saddle horses, well-trained and gentle." He leaned forward again, and his gaze was intense. "Would you be willing to help me find the right kind of horses for a therapy barn? Whether we could buy them or lease them for a year at a time?"

Ashley frowned. "I don't know. I'd have to see your setup. Talk to whatever vet you plan to work with. Get an exact idea of what you plan to do, what your needs are."

"Fair enough." His gaze shifted to the shelter. "I interrupted your work. Would you like a hand with that?"

"No thanks. I'm good." She answered more out of habit than because she wouldn't like help. She was simply used to doing things on her own. She had a serious independent streak.

Ben got to his feet. "Well then, I'll leave you to it." He took a card from his wallet and laid it on the table next to her chair. "Call me when you'd like to go have a look at the barn and property."

"I'll do it." Picking up the card, she rose too.

"Thanks for listening."

"Glad to," she answered, realizing it was true.

❧

Ben smiled to himself as he drove toward the farm. He'd seen the spark of interest in Ashley Showalter's eyes, and his gut told him he would hear from her before the week was out. But then he heard his mom's voice in his head, calling him stupid, and the smile vanished.

I'm tired of trying with her. Guilt followed. Such thoughts weren't the best way to honor his mother, as the Bible told him to do.

Ben couldn't remember a time when things had been good between him and his mom. Not even when he was a little kid. She'd resented him too much. He'd ruined her plans, she'd told him more than once. Pregnant at sixteen and a mom at seventeen, Wendy Henning hadn't married the boy who fathered Ben. Had she even known who the father was? Not that she'd ever told Ben. He only knew she blamed having a kid for every problem she'd ever had.

Any stability experienced during Ben's childhood had been because of his grandfather, Grant Henning. The two of them remained close to this day, and when Grandpa Grant decided it was time for him to settle into a retirement community, he'd deeded the Henning family farm to Ben. Which had ignited his mom's fury.

"*Sell it*," she'd shouted at Ben over the phone just that morning. "*Do you know what that land is worth?*" When he repeated the same thing he'd said for the past year, that he wasn't going to sell, she'd called him stupid—for the umpteenth time—and hung up.

Ben had done plenty of dumb things in his life. Keeping the farm wasn't one of them.

He slowed the truck and turned onto his property, seeing it through the haze of happy memories. He'd spent countless weekends here in his boyhood. And ten years ago, after a stint in rehab, Ben had lived with his grandparents for a year. When he thought about it now, that year had changed him more than any other.

The house was small by today's standards. A small kitchen, small living room, small bath, and three small bedrooms on the ground level with an attic room above. His great-grandfather, for whom Ben was named, along with his two brothers, Oscar and Andy, had used that attic bedroom during the thirties and forties. In the decades since, the kitchen had been modernized, and the house was now heated by natural gas rather than wood or coal. And yet whenever Ben stepped through the door, he felt transported back in time. It seemed to him he could hear the voices of all of his ancestors who had lived there, even those he'd never known.

He parked his truck beneath the carport, but instead of going into the house, he strode toward the barn. Dusty, his yellow lab, followed close at his heels. There were no horses or cows in the barn or nearby pens, no chickens in the coop. There hadn't been any livestock since before his grandfather gave him the place. Ben hadn't moved into the house until last April. But now that he was here, he looked forward to watching the barnyard come to life again. Horses for the therapy sessions. Maybe a cat or two for the barn and even some chickens in the coop. After all, fresh eggs wouldn't be unwelcome.

Dusty trotted off, exploring, and when he returned, there was a large stick in his mouth. Ben took the stick and gave it a good throw. The dog raced after it, mindless of the heat of the day. Ben, on the other hand, was ready for a cold drink in the air-conditioned living room.

"Come on, boy. It's too hot to play fetch."

Fifteen minutes later, Ben sat on the sofa, a glass of diet soda with ice in his hand. As he sipped the drink, his thoughts returned to Ashley Showalter. He didn't know what he'd expected, but it hadn't been the woman who stepped down from that ladder upon his arrival. Her light brown hair had been caught in a ponytail but enough strands had pulled loose to give her a delightfully disheveled appearance. Her face had glistened with perspiration. Slender as a reed, she hadn't looked strong enough to carry boards up a ladder or to hammer those same boards together into a shelter. Apparently looks were deceiving.

He sure hoped she would call him soon.

About the horses, of course. His interest in her phone call was all about the horses.

Wednesday, Jan 17, 1940

"Dad?"

Andrew looked up from the workbench in the barn and watched as Ben approached him.

"Is there any chance I could go to college?"

It was a question Andrew had never expected to hear from his eldest child. From the time Ben had come to live with them at age nine, he had struggled with his schooling. The primary cause was disinterest, not because he wasn't smart enough to excel.

"I want to become a pilot, and I found out today that the Army Air Corps Training Center requires a couple of years of college or three years of technical education before a guy can join."

There was a lot of information in Ben's sentence, but what Andrew heard the loudest were the words "Army Air Corps." His son wanted to be a pilot in the military. A chill went through him that had nothing to do with the winter wind whistling outside of the barn.

The president and many other US politicians preached isolationism. They promised to keep America out of the war that was raging in Europe. But Andrew wasn't sure the politicians and diplomats could keep that promise. Spending time with Hirsch Finkel had changed his faith in their abilities. Thanks to his neighbor, Andrew knew more than he wished to know about what had happened in Germany after Hitler's party came to power.

Andrew had read a quote by an Irish statesman that said, "The only thing necessary for the triumph of evil is that good men should do nothing." It was a phrase that ran through his mind a lot lately. Could Americans do nothing for long?

"Dad."

He gave his head a shake. "Sorry, Ben. I got distracted. Army Air Corps. Becoming a pilot. You caught me by surprise." He cleared his throat. "College is expensive, and you know we don't have much extra cash, even with the economy improving a little. You'd have to bring up your grades if you want to go to college, and you'll have to get a job to pay some of your expenses while you're in school. That means going to classes, doing your studies, and holding down work at the same time. It'll be tough. You'll have to want it bad."

"I do want it bad."

"You'll have to be willing to stick with it, no matter what."

"I will."

Andrew released a breath. "Then we'll try to figure out how to make it happen. No promises, son, but we'll do our level best."

"Thanks, Dad. I'll do my part too. I promise."

DISCOVER MORE FROM ROBIN LEE HATCHER!

About the Author

Bestselling novelist Robin Lee Hatcher, author of more than seventy-five books, is known for her heartwarming and emotionally charged stories of faith, courage, and love. Robin is an eleven-time finalist and two-time winner of the prestigious RITA Award. In addition to many other awards, she is the recipient of lifetime achievement awards from both Romance Writers of America and American Christian Fiction Writers. When not writing, she enjoys being with her family, spending time in the beautiful Idaho outdoors, Bible art journaling, reading books that make her cry, watching romantic movies, and decorative planning. A mother and grandmother, Robin makes her home with her husband on the outskirts of Boise, sharing it with demanding Papillion puppy named Boo and a persnickety tuxe cat named Pinky.

For more information, visit www.robinleehatcher.com
Facebook: robinleehatcher
Twitter: @robinleehatcher